ALSO BY TRACEY BAPTISTE

ALSO BY TRACEY BAPTISTE

The Jumbies
Rise of the Jumbies

MOJANG
MINECRAFT™
THE CRASH

MOJANG

MINECRAFT™
THE CRASH

TRACEY
BAPTISTE

DEL
REY

NEW YORK

2021 Del Rey Trade Paperback Edition

Copyright © 2018 by Mojang AB and Mojang Synergies AB. MINECRAFT and the Minecraft logo are trademarks of the Microsoft group of companies.
All rights reserved.

Published in the United States by Del Rey, an imprint of Random House, a division of Penguin Random House LLC, New York.

DEL REY is a registered trademark and the CIRCLE colophon is a trademark of Penguin Random House LLC.

Originally published in hardcover in the United States by Del Rey, an imprint of Random House, a division of Penguin Random House LLC, in 2018.

LIBRARY OF CONGRESS CATALOGING-IN-PUBLICATION DATA
Names: Baptiste, Tracey, author.
Title: Minecraft : the crash / Tracey Baptiste.
Description: New York : Del Rey, [2018] | Series: Minecraft |
"An official Minecraft novel"
Identifiers: LCCN 2018014908 | ISBN 9780399180682 (trade paperback : acid-free paper) | ISBN 9780399180675 (ebook)
Subjects: | CYAC: Minecraft (Game)—Fiction. | Video games—Fiction. | Virtual reality—Fiction. | Adventure and adventurers—Fiction. | BISAC: JUVENILE FICTION / Action & Adventure / Survival Stories. | JUVENILE FICTION / Media Tie-In. | JUVENILE FICTION / Fantasy & Magic.
Classification: LCC PZ7.B229515 Mi 2018 | DDC [Fic]—dc23
LC record available at https://lccn.loc.gov/2018014908

Printed in the United States of America on acid-free paper

randomhousebooks.com

3rd Printing

Book design by Elizabeth A. D. Eno

Consultant: Adam Baptiste

For Adam, Elliot, Avery, and Lindsay

⬛MOJANG

MINECRAFT™
THE CRASH

CHAPTER 1

I'd like to find whoever came up with the phrase "everything happens for a reason" and give them a piece of my mind. Because the exact last thing anybody needs to hear when their world is completely screwed up is that it's actually a good thing. Like, even if you had a magical time machine that could go back and fix your mistakes, you totally shouldn't use it? Yeah, right. *Nobody* really believes that.

Of course, there's really no good thing to say after everything's turned into a complete and utter mess. Better to keep moving forward, try to fix your mistakes, and hope everything eventually works out. I feel like I should have something wiser to say here, but nope. That's all I've got. Oh, that and the time machine thing. There's always that.

Anyway, the mistake I wish I could go back and fix happened days ago. How many days, I couldn't tell you. Time is sort of . . . a mess right now. But one Friday, some time ago, my best friend and I were headed to participate in the social event kickoff of the school year, also known as the homecoming game.

I'd convinced Lonnie to go with me, even though neither of us were sports fans. We were gamers, really. Sports—outside of a video game—was not high on our list of priorities. But I figured homecoming was one of those hallmark high school experiences they make a big fuss about in the movies, why not check it out? As a newly minted freshman, I was secretly excited about high school. It was like unlocking a new level in the video game of life—full-sized lockers for larger inventory, bigger bosses like the SATs, you get my drift. Lonnie, on the other hand, was not so convinced about homecoming. So I sweetened the deal, literally. I told him that I'd make my famous brownies and bring a blanket so we could huddle up together with chocolate in our teeth. I'd like to think it was the brownies and the blanket that appealed to him, but I'm not sure. I mean, there aren't a lot of high school juniors that would want to be seen hanging out with a freshman, but we had been friends since I was six and he was eight. So we kind of went beyond the usual high school friendship parameters. Still, the point of all this is, it was all my fault. Everything that happened is on me.

Lonnie showed up around five. I bounded out with brownies and the blanket, got in the car, let him drive off, and we started talking about Minecraft. Our usual convo.

"Did you build all the traps?" he asked.

I scrunched up my nose. I hadn't. Mainly because I forgot.

"Actually, I thought it would be better to build up on the base instead. I decided to make the floor of the greenhouse glass, so you can look down on everything."

"You mean you didn't finish what you said you were going to. Again." Lonnie sounded more like a disappointed dad than my friend, putting me on the defensive.

"I'll get back to it after I finish the new greenhouse," I said. "I don't know why you have to get on my case about it."

"Bianca."

"Lonnie."

"You need to stick to the plan. This whole world is going off the rails. If we want to have something that works really well, we have to do what we set out to make. Isn't that the whole point of the test world? Perfect it there, and then move it to the real game?"

"I thought the point of the test world was to do crazy stuff so we could see what works and what doesn't. To go as bonkers as we can go, blow stuff up, make a mess, and never have to fix it."

Lonnie sighed. He passed his hand over his close-shaven head, and squeezed his eyelids down for a second as if he was in pain. When he opened his eyes again, they were a cloudy gray, like the sky, not the sharp steel gray that meant he was in a good mood.

"I thought you wanted to do this project," he said. "You said you wanted to craft a whole world. New landscapes. Entire villages. A whole set of society rules, and then mess around with it."

"Yes, but—"

"But first we have to make it. And to make it, we need to have a plan, Bianca."

I didn't mean for us to fight. I wasn't sure what to say to get him to stop breathing heavily like he was an angry dragon cooking up a fire to blow in my direction.

"You never follow the plan. First you say you want to do something, and I say, 'Okay, here's the plan.' Then you say, 'Great plan!' And then you don't even pretend to do what I outlined."

Oh, so this was going to be a full-on fight.

"But here I am being your chauffeur," he added.

"You just got your license. You need the practice," I said. "Plus, think of all that horizon-expanding you'll be doing by finally going to an actual sporting event!"

"Since when do you like sports?" he asked.

I shrugged. "Since it's my first time ever going to a big school thing, and I just want to see what it's like to be out with the masses."

"'Masses' is just another word for mobs. Trust me, high school's not all that it's cracked up to be." He turned, screeching down West Elm Road. "Where is the stupid field again?"

"Two streets down and then a right," I said smugly.

He pulled up at the light and revved the engine. Even his body movements seemed annoyed. I sucked in my top lip and chewed on it as I pulled at one of my cornrows and wrapped and unwrapped it around my finger.

"You know, they're bulldozing the playground," I said suddenly.

The light changed and he lurched forward.

"So?"

"Do you want to see it before everything's gone?"

"What for?"

"Uh, because it was the scene of our greatest adventures?" I asked. "Because it'll never look like that again? Because it was *our* place first?"

"Yeah, sure."

"Do you remember how to get there?" I teased. He turned his steely gray eyes on me, and I grinned. I knew that look. It meant that our little fight was over.

Instead of turning right on Grandview, he turned left.

The playground already looked like a ghost town. The swing seats were gone. All that was left was the A-frame, mottled blue from the faded and peeling paint. The rope bridge was lying half in the black rubber mulch, one end still attached to what used to be the climbing wall when all the foot- and hand-rests were still attached.

I climbed up the ladder, which wobbled now that it wasn't attached properly, and I went down the tube slide, coming out at Lonnie's sneakered feet.

"Have a go?" I asked.

He shook his head. "I'm surprised this is the first renovation they're doing since we were little," he said. "They probably should have condemned it a long time ago."

"But it's our place!" I said.

"It *was*," Lonnie replied, not unkindly. This playground was where we'd met, and where we'd become friends and imagined our first worlds together. We would pretend to be swashbuckling pirates on the rope bridge, launch ourselves like trapeze artists off the swings, and defend our fortress from invading imaginary zombies. In fact, one of our first projects in Minecraft was to create a better version of the playground. The ground was always lava, naturally.

After all this time, we always stuck together, even as the playground itself fell apart.

"Remember the time I tried to flip off the monkey bars and you broke my fall?" I asked, looking to stoke some nostalgia.

"Yeah, I got a broken wrist for my troubles," Lonnie said, shaking his head. "You never were a great planner even then, always wanting to push the limits but never thinking about the follow-through."

"You know, if I wanted a lecture, I could just go to class." I crossed my arms.

Lonnie shrugged and kicked the faded yellow plastic cap from something and walked off to what used to be a dome of monkey bars. Most of the bars were in a pile on the ground. I followed him. He stared down at the pile quietly. The sun was just going down, casting an orange glow over the playground. Silence settled around us.

He was right. This place wasn't ours, not any longer.

"Let's just go," I said.

"Homecoming rally, yeah!" he mocked.

I reached my hand out to him and felt a jolt of electricity when he caught my fingers, swinging them as we walked back to the car. Most people thought it was really weird, the two of us hanging out the way we did. A two-year difference in high school is a chasm. Especially when you're going to two different high schools. It's like trying to have a conversation with someone on the other side of the Grand Canyon with nothing but your cupped hands around your mouth. He turned over the engine, and made a U-turn on the tiny street, then peeled off.

I pulled out my phone and loaded the Minecraft app.

"If you're going to give me grief all night over not building your dumb traps, you should at least appreciate this sick glass floor I put into the greenhouse."

I waved my phone screen in his face.

"Look!"

"Bianca, quit it. I'm driving." Lonnie batted the phone away with an arm.

He turned sharply to the left, tires screeching. The orange glow from the setting sun blinded us momentarily and we skidded a little, and Lonnie turned the wheel to right us. Then we realized, too late, that something was coming toward us, that we must have run the red light, but we still weren't able to make out whatever the object was with the sun in our eyes, but we knew it wasn't a small thing. It all felt like it was in slow motion, a few seconds strung out into years, until a robotic female voice suddenly blasted over the car's speakers.

"Proximity alert! Evasive action recommended!"

The air in the car went from electric excitement to sharp fear in an instant, as an oncoming car came straight for us too fast to do anything about it.

Once the car was close enough and blocked out the sun, I

could see the other driver's face, though not clearly. He had dark eyes and straight hair that spiked in every direction. His head lurched back as his green car collided with our blue one. I remember how the metal crunched as we crushed into each other, folding blue on green on blue on green, how pieces of things began to fly around. Glass, metal. At one point, even the light seemed to fracture and splinter off, bursting into fractals of beams, searing my eyes and my skin. And then there was the smell of smoke. And the taste of blood. And the scrape of something against my body that felt like it had gutted me open somewhere in the middle. I wondered if I'd been halved. I turned, trying to see if I could figure out what was happening, if I could see Lonnie's face to know from his eyes just how bad it all was. But I couldn't see him. It was like he'd disappeared and all that was left was me, and the blue car and the green car that now looked like one wrapped-up thing with glass tinkling as it fell like rain all around me, and the shocking realization that the man from the other car was right up on me, like we had been riding together. He was right there. I could reach out and touch him. And I tried. Only my hands didn't move. Nothing moved but the cars still rippling toward and away from each other. So, I tried to scream for Lonnie, but nothing came out of my mouth.

And then everything went black.

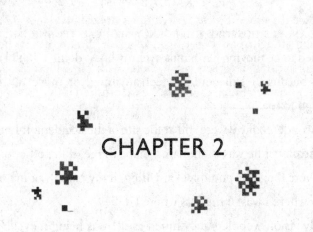

CHAPTER 2

There was a halo of light over me. I panicked for a moment until I realized it was just a streetlamp. I must have been lying on the ground. Only, I couldn't feel anything. Not the ground, not my body. I couldn't even move. I tried to say something, but my mouth didn't work either. A woman with a blond ponytail leaned over me, frowning. She looked up and mouthed something to someone I couldn't see. No, she was talking. But I couldn't hear her. I couldn't hear anything. Only my eyes seemed to be working, and even that . . . Everything was dim, and restricted, as if I could only look up.

I tried to move something. Anything. A finger. My tongue. Nothing worked. I wondered if I was dead, and my spirit was just hanging out for a bit before it went to . . . wherever spirits go. Maybe it was stuck, too, and couldn't move. Maybe we were both paralyzed.

The blond lady was wearing a shirt that had a patch that read

HOLY ANGELS HOSPITAL EMERGENCY MEDICAL TECHNICIAN. She seemed to be moving her hands over my body, doing I don't know what because I still couldn't feel anything, or move my eyes enough to see.

I wondered if we were still at the site of the accident, if Lonnie was nearby, if he was in the same shape as me, if the other driver was there too, if he could feel anything, if my parents or my sister knew where I was, if this was where I'd die.

My vision wobbled and shifted as if I was being moved. The halo of light from the streetlamp was gone. Above me the sky was dark, much darker than it was when Lonnie and I left the park. I tried to think of how long it takes for the sky to get so dark. A few minutes? Hours? How long had I been there?

Then my other senses started to come back.

First, the EMT's voice rang out over me. "Get her in the rig!"

Behind that was the sound of sirens, people shuffling about, shouting things I couldn't make out, and the unmistakable sound of metal warping. I heard the crunch of gravel underfoot, and the click of something snapping into place beneath me. I was being moved, slowly and smoothly. The stars twirled.

Smell came next. A burst of pungent smoke and acrid rubber. Sweat, and something earthy.

Then I tasted blood in my mouth. I moved my tongue and tried to feel around. Everything was tender, and I felt jagged pieces against the tip, and bare spaces of swollen gums.

More sounds. Screaming. Crying. Moaning. The car's alarm was going off, as the robo-voice calmly intoned that help was on the way.

Lights flashing red against the shiny white paint of the ambulance.

The inside of the ambulance. Smooth white roof. Metal latches on supply bins overhead. The face of the EMT lady and another guy leaning over me. One smiling, the other frowning, only I kept mixing up which was which because my eyes couldn't focus on one or the other, and I kept being bumped, and the siren was going, so we must have been on our way to Holy Angels.

We hit a smooth, straight patch of road and my vision became less jangly.

It was the man. The man was smiling.

Next, I was lifted out and the smell of antiseptic immediately washed over me. The hospital lights were a bright white. Someone should tell them it wasn't soothing. They should get halo lights like the ones out on the street. I closed my eyes and heard squeaky, sneakered feet running beside me as the wheels on the gurney swiveled and bumped over the hospital floor. I saw the light still beaming down through my eyelids, and I could tell every time someone leaned over me because they cast my face in shadow.

Suddenly, I started to feel again. It began like a wave at my extremities. My feet and hands felt like the skin had been peeled back. I could feel everything and it was all pain. I screamed out and the running picked up speed. The pain moved inward to my stomach and then radiated out to the top of my head. There was nothing that didn't hurt. My legs, my arms, my torso, my neck, my head, my mouth, my eyes. I felt like I'd been through a grinder. I couldn't stop screaming even though it hurt my throat even more.

I couldn't stop. I think they were trying to make it stop. I could feel them moving me, jostling me, and I could hear them trying to tell me something, but I couldn't make anything out over the sound of my own screaming. I could only make out the way I felt, and the way everything hurt, and I thought, *Is this dying?* I tried to tell them, *Make it stop!*

Then everything did.

I woke up in a small beige room with vertical vinyl blinds, and equipment beeping around me. There were two upholstered chairs with wooden arms sitting on either side of a beige plastic table with attached wheels. A blue blanket covered my body. I couldn't see what condition I was in other than my legs appeared to be much larger than usual, so I figured they were both in casts. Awesome. I couldn't see my arms either. I tried to move them and couldn't. Either I was armless, or whatever anesthesia they had me on hadn't dissipated yet. I felt groggy with a side order of dull pain all over. At least I could move my eyes to look around. I was alone. It was just me and the beeping monitors, and a pink plastic jug that was sweating on the wheeled table. But no cups. I stuck my tongue out of my mouth. My lips were dry. I could have used some water, but my voice didn't seem to be working, so I couldn't ask even if I wasn't alone. I tried to move my fingers to see if there was a call button or something nearby to let someone—anyone—know that I was awake and they could start tending to me, or telling me what happened, or anything, but I still couldn't feel my fingers or tell whether or not I still had any.

I wondered what I looked like.

I wondered where everyone was.

I wondered what happened to Lonnie.

When I woke up again, I got an eyeful of hospital ceiling tile. The really generic kind that's a hybrid of gray and beige—my foggy mind thought, *Greige?*—laid out in a grid that makes you want to count it, especially if it's the only thing you can see. The lights were dim and I couldn't tell if this was the same room I was in before, or if I'd been moved. It was smaller than I remembered, and there seemed to be less humming and beeping than the last time I was conscious. That was progress, I guessed. I tried to move, was unsuccessful again, and this time I couldn't see my body at all because I was lying flat. Maybe my legs had disappeared. Or my entire body. I wondered if a person could technically survive as just a head.

I also considered that the drugs were making me loopy. It seemed a wise assessment of my mental faculties.

The door opened and closed, and I heard my mother whispering, "How much longer, do you think?"

"It's going to be a difficult recovery, Mrs. Marshall. Her injuries are extensive. We're going to have to take it one day at a time."

I heard something like a muffled cry and then my father's voice. "Carrie would like to see her. I'll bring her by after school."

Carrie didn't have school on Saturday. I wanted to ask what they were talking about. But then it occurred to me that it probably wasn't Friday anymore, or even the weekend. I tried to say,

Hey guys, but what came out was a rather elegant "Unghh." I'd been reduced to the vocabulary of a Minecraft villager.

My parents ran over to the side of the bed, excited that I seemed able to vocalize at all.

Hey, I tried again. "Uhh" came out.

"Bianca!" my mother said softly. Tears rolled down her face, tracing light-brown tracks in her makeup.

"How are you feeling?" my father asked.

I tried to nod. It hurt.

Next, a woman in a white coat came up and my parents moved away. She had large dark brown eyes and a black braid that came down over one shoulder. When she leaned in closer, her hair moved away from her name tag. It read DR. NAY.

"Hello, Bianca," she said. "Glad to see you awake."

"How long have I been out?" I tried to ask. But there was more moaning. And some drooling, I'm sorry to say. My mother leaned in with a paper towel to catch the dribble, wearing her worried face.

"It's been almost a week since your accident," Dr. Nay said, as if I were perfectly coherent. "You're finally stabilized enough for us to wake you."

"What's the damage, Doctor?"

Dr. Nay tapped a few buttons on her tablet and a hologram projected from a camera attached to the tablet's edge. A miniature version of me displayed before my eyes. It was eerie, like looking at a blueprint version of myself.

"You're very lucky, Bianca. If you'd had this same accident a few years ago, I'm not sure we would have had the right technology to help you through it."

I certainly didn't feel very lucky, being in a full-body cast and all, but I took her word for it. Dr. Nay tapped a few more buttons and the hologram of my body glowed red in nearly ten different spots. The news was abysmal: two broken arms, a broken thigh bone, three broken bones in my right foot, two broken ribs, a collapsed lung, and a concussion. I looked like a game of Operation gone horribly wrong.

"Good thing you're a fighter," Dr. Nay said.

I didn't recall being aware enough to fight, or know who was around me, or even how I managed to get to this hideous little room that smelled of pine cleaner, medicine, and pee—which I hoped was not my own, but I knew probably was.

Dr. Nay leaned over me and adjusted the flow rate on a bag that fed into an IV. I suddenly felt something on my right go colder, and I smiled again, able to feel my arm at last. The coldness spread and washed over me, then more dullness descended like a fog. Dr. Nay continued talking over me to my parents. There seemed to be a lot to tell. I tried to follow along, but I was struggling to hear. I was struggling to feel. I was just struggling. Like swimming upstream against a strong tide. And then it was lights out again.

Third time's the charm, I thought when I woke up again. This time, the light was brighter, my body was propped up, and I could see around the beige room, with the covered chairs, the plastic table with the wheels, and the sweating pink jug again. Déjà vu. Except for my father, who was sitting in one of the chairs, reading *InfoTech* magazine. For an old guy, he's always on the cutting edge of all the newest tech stuff. Well, I guess it's his job.

"Hey," I said. This time it actually came out as a recognizable word, which surprised me, so I made a little sound that was half hiccup and half moan. Yeah. It was as weird as you imagine. Trust me.

My father practically jumped out of the chair. "Hey," he said. "How are you feeling?"

I shrugged, or at least I thought I did. I don't think any part of me actually moved.

"What happened?" I asked, knowing full well what happened, but unable to come up with a better question.

"You got banged up pretty badly," he said in a low voice, as if saying it any louder might make things worse. He reached over to one beeping machine and touched the screen. It made me nervous, but nothing happened. "You're going to be here a while." He sighed. "You had a couple of surgeries, and there are some casts." He put his warm hand on my forehead. "We had to get you a plastic surgeon, too. So the scarring won't be so bad."

I must have flinched or something, and his face blanched.

"It's not so bad. And you'll be fine. You're out of the woods, as they say." He chuckled, rapped his magazine on the plastic bed rail, and took a step back. He clearly didn't want to say any more.

"Lonnie?" I asked.

"What?" he asked. His face looked totally pained. Then he blinked a couple of times, and looked ill. "Bianca—"

The door opened and Dr. Nay strode in. "Good morning, Bianca! How are you feeling?"

Like I've been hit by a car, I wanted to joke, but thought better of it.

My father stepped aside so she could get closer. She took the stethoscope from around her neck and listened to my chest. "Breathing's good, finally."

Wasn't I breathing? When wasn't my breathing good? I wondered.

She looked over at my father and nodded. "She's a champ, this one." Then she turned to a tablet that she had placed on the table, tapped the screen a couple of times. Smurf me, blue and floating above the device, reappeared as Dr. Nay walked me through all the surgeries that had happened while I had been out.

"All the tests are coming back better," she said. "Now it's just a matter of recovery, which means you may be here at the hospital a while."

My father looked at me with his sad eyes, and I felt my heart sink. How much was this going to cost us in bills? How much school was I going to miss?

"We've administered the strongest painkillers we can under the circumstances," the doctor continued, looking at my father, "but the nurses say she's still waking up every few hours, trying to move. She's at the most we can safely give her right now, which is probably why she's awake and comfortable enough. But we have to make sure she stays still."

I didn't remember waking up. I didn't remember pain, but the look of horror my father gave me said that he'd probably seen this waking-up live and in person.

"What I'm saying is that we're not going to be able to give her any more for a while, and she's awake, so it might be . . . a difficult evening."

My father nodded. The muscles around his jaw tightened, and his fists gripped the bed rail hard enough that I thought it might snap.

"I'll be with her all night," he said. "Her mother will be here in the morning. We'll get through it."

With that, Dr. Nay left, and my father adjusted the blankets that were covering me. Slowly, the sensations in my body started coming back, and I began to understand what Dr. Nay was talking about, and why my father had looked so worried. It was like being dipped slowly into molten lava. You maybe think, *Oh sure, I can have a toe seared off, or even my foot, no prob!* But it just kept on consuming more and more and more of my body. I felt weak with pain. Even looking at my father's face hurt. Because he couldn't do anything, and I was mad at him for not being able to do anything, and then mad at myself because I knew he was helpless and this was torture for him, too.

But also? It was all my own fault.

It was the middle of the night when I woke up again. My father was asleep on the chair with the magazine draped over his chest.

His shoes were off and he was snoring lightly. The door to my room was open, and a shard of light hit my face from what I guessed was the nurses' station. I still couldn't find a call button, but I figured that the time had passed for more medicine, because everything felt dull again. The pain was down to a smolder. I would have liked some water, but I didn't want to wake my dad. I had no idea how long he'd been up. His clothes were a mess. His usually neat hair was a tangled mat. He might have been here for hours, if not days, without a break. Someone had to be home with Carrie. I remember he said something about him and Mom switching out, so maybe he was due for a break soon.

But there was a huge part of me that was glad that my father was asleep and there was no one I could call. Because I knew the moment they thought I was well enough, the moment they figured I could handle a real conversation, there were going to be questions. A lot of them. And then they'd all know what I'd done, that everything was my own fault.

A shadow crossed my door, and someone with a small voice whispered, "Hey."

"Hey," I managed.

And then a boy about eleven years old walked in, wearing pajamas that said GAMER 4 LIFE, and a robe with glow-in-the-dark planets all over it.

"Who . . . ?" I asked. It was all I could manage. My throat hurt to talk.

"I'm A.J. I'm in the next room," he said. He came a little closer, but stopped when my dad snorted a really loud snore, and the kid seemed surprised anyone else was in here. A.J. came up to the machine with the IV and tapped the screen. This seemed to be an established way of communing with patients. I made a note of it for if I ever went into another patient's room. Assuming I was ever able to walk again.

"I'm—"

"Bianca Marshall. I know. I saw your chart when Dr. Nay came in."

"Oh," I said.

He grinned.

"Lonnie," I said. "Elon Lawrence." It took a lot out of me to manage that much.

A.J. looked confused. He shook his head. His tight dark curls wobbled on his head. "No, you're Bianca," he said, stressing every syllable in my name.

"My friend," I said. "We were in a car. He might be worse."

A.J.'s eyebrows shot up. "Worse than you?" he asked. "You're pretty bad. Anybody worse off than you would probably be dead."

I waited for him to laugh, or grin, or say that he was just joking. But this kid was straight-up telling the truth as he saw it, and there was a stabbing pain across the top of my head that told me that he was right, that worse off than me was not survivable. And that if anyone had something good to tell me about Lonnie, they would have already.

"I could sneak into the nurses' station and see if I can find his chart, though," A.J. offered.

This had the immediate effect of dulling the pounding anxiety that was rising through my chest. Or maybe it was the medication. There was a series of beeps, and then the machines around me whirred a bit. Seconds later, I started feeling a little better. "Thanks, A.J.," I said. When he turned to leave, I saw something in his hand. "What's that?"

He turned back. "These?" He held up something that looked like a white plastic headband. "They're VR goggles," he said. He moved closer to show them off. "You can watch movies and stuff, but I've been playing Minecraft."

"I like Minecraft."

"Yeah?" A.J.'s eyes really lit up at that.

"My friend and I have been building a world together," I said, a little surprised at how much I could talk. I glanced at the nearest machine. Yep. It was definitely painkiller time.

The kid blinked and nodded, I guess waiting for me to add some details.

"It has lots of villages with different configurations and rules and stuff."

That brightened the kid right up. "Oh yeah? I just like to play survival mode. I use mods, though, and I even made some of them myself!"

"That's cool," I said.

"You should check these goggles out then," he said. "They'll blow your mind."

Before I could respond, A.J. had come up to the side of the bed and placed the goggles on my head. The two ends pinched the sides of my temple. Though compared to what the rest of my body was feeling at the moment, it was nothing. I felt a tickling sensation on either side of my face, and it spread across my forehead. Suddenly the pain across my head rose like a tidal wave, but I tried not to moan or wince because I didn't want to upset a kid who probably figured he was doing me a solid.

I opened my eyes and was surprised to see that the hospital room had completely disappeared. The game was already queued up, paused in the middle of whatever A.J. had been doing before.

"It's a little weird at first," he warned me. "But you get used to it after a while."

He wasn't kidding. Being thrust into a fully realized world that was mid-play was disorienting. It was brighter than my hospital room, that's for sure. And the unrealistic cartoon shades of green and brown and blue felt a little like a smack in the face. I started looking around at the forest biome I'd been shoved into, and realized that if I looked somewhere for a while, I'd start moving in that direction. The movements were sudden, and made me want to hurl immediately. I closed my eyes and tried to breathe deeply, not wanting to say that I wanted out. I had a small child to impress, after all. Plus, there was a feeling of just being a head with no body. I tried to move again, and felt a lurch in my stomach.

"Are you gonna throw up?" A.J. asked.

"No . . . I . . . um . . ."

"Maybe you should stop," he said. Without warning, he pulled the goggles off and, to tell you the truth, I don't think that was any better. Returning to the real, dull world made me feel extra sick, and I turned to the other side of the bed, away from the kid, and threw up.

As I tried to wipe my mouth on the edge of my blanket, A.J. backed away to the door. My father stirred but didn't wake up. A nurse came running in, looked at the kid, at me, back at him, and then walked slowly over to clean me up. There was hurl in my braids. I wasn't really thinking about my aim when I spewed.

"Groooss," A.J. said.

"Get back to your room," said the nurse. "I'll come check on you later. You know you're not supposed to be out walking around. And you're definitely not supposed to be in other people's rooms."

My dad woke up then, straightened, and tried to make sense of what was going on.

A.J. made a face, but backed all the way up to the door. "Getting in and out is tricky," he said. "Not everybody can do it. There's a different way out you can use that I can show you." He shrugged. "It's mostly for noobs."

"Get out of what?" my father asked.

"Just the game," A.J. said, showing him the goggles.

I took offense at the noob comment and wanted to tell him that I could do it, but obviously I was not at my best in this moment, lying in a hospital bed mashed to a pulp with a nurse wiping vomit off me. I watched him back off into the hall and disappear.

But I was going to show him that I could. I was no noob.

What kind of gamer would I be if I couldn't do it?

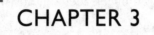

CHAPTER 3

My mother was talking to someone in the room when I blinked my eyes open. The room was brighter. And for a moment, it felt almost like being inside the game again. Things felt somehow less real, and images appeared blocky and undefined for a couple of seconds until the sleep faded from my eyes. Maybe I was still traumatized by being put in the kid's Minecraft VR world, and then being kicked out without a chance to get used to it all.

"Hey," my mother said. She came over to the side of the bed and twisted a couple of my braids in her fingers, arranging them on top of my head. "I heard you had kind of a rough night."

I shrugged. Or at least I tried to. I still wasn't sure if my shoulders actually moved or not.

Dr. Nay stepped closer. Today her hair was piled in a bun. "I heard you met A.J." She took a sharp breath. "He knows he's not supposed to be in other people's rooms. He's a little overenthusiastic and gets underfoot sometimes, especially during shift changes."

I looked past Dr. Nay to a uniformed police officer who was hovering near the door. Immediately my body stiffened. One of the machines beeped oddly, and Dr. Nay frowned as she looked at it. Then she looked at the officer and shook her head. He nodded once, and left. A few seconds later, the machine stopped beeping.

"Don't get mad at A.J.," I said. "I think he was just trying to be friendly."

"I understand, Bianca. But your recovery is the most important thing right now," Dr. Nay said. She projected another hologram from her tablet into the space between us. This one was a line graph showing various peaks and valleys. "You see, A.J. came in around two a.m., and you had quite a spike in adrenaline and heart rate."

Dr. Nay paused for a second as she stepped closer to the hologram. She pointed at a spot on the graph with the highest peak, and then squinted at one of the machines near my head.

"Do you remember what happened?"

"I got sick," I admitted. "From the game."

Dr. Nay looked confused. "What game?"

"Minecraft," I said. "A.J. showed me his VR goggles and I got too dizzy."

"What does that mean?" my mother asked.

"We have a number of VR machines here in the children's ward. They're good for entertaining some of the kids who have to stay here awhile. I wasn't sure that Bianca was stable enough to be offered one."

Considering my initial reaction to A.J.'s goggles, I wasn't sure if I was stable enough either. But I wanted badly to no longer have to stare at the ceiling or another darn hologram image.

"Could I get a set of my own? Please?"

Dr. Nay shook her head. The bun on her head wobbled.

"Not until I've run a few more tests to make sure it's okay. You had a concussion after all, I'm not sure of the effects of VR on that."

"Okay, but what about Lonnie. Nobody's telling me what happened to Lonnie."

Dr. Nay looked at my mother, who had gone immediately stiff at the mention of Lonnie's name. "You need to focus on your own recovery," the doctor said.

I looked at my mother's face. It was not a *Your friend is fine* face. It was a *We don't want to tell you how bad it is* face. She never looked at me. She looked at the floor, and at Dr. Nay, and then at the floor again.

I felt a weight pressing down on my chest, and cold sweat sprung up on my body. The machines began to beep in sharp tones. That same piercing pain darted through the top of my head, and I squeezed my eyes shut. I could hear bustling footsteps around me, and the feeling of people pressing in close, but everything they said was garbled and muffled somehow, as if my head was somewhere else, but my body was inside the room getting worked over by the nursing staff. I thought I would throw up again, but didn't. When I was able to open my eyes, Dr. Nay was pressing the plunger of a needle into my IV drip.

"No," I heard myself saying, but it was too late. I woke up what felt like hours later in the dark. And the kid was back, staring at me.

"Do you want to try playing again?" he asked. A pair of VR goggles dangled in his hand. I looked around. It felt like a repeat of the night before, including my father sleeping in the chair. It was almost as if the entire day had never happened.

"What day is it?" I asked.

"Wednesday," he said.

I chuckled, realizing I didn't know what day it was previously, so I had nothing to compare it to.

"Were you here last night?" I asked.

"I've been here for three weeks," he said.

"No, I mean—" My head was fuzzy, so I stopped. I wasn't getting anywhere.

He stepped closer. "The goggles take getting used to. It almost never goes right the first time, but the second time it's usually better."

I nodded.

"You should close your eyes while the VR adjusts to a new user," A.J. said. "Sorry, I forgot to tell you that last time. That's probably why you puked."

"Yeah, I'm not interested in a repeat performance."

"Me neither."

I closed my eyes as A.J. put the goggles on me, gentler than the last time. This time, the strange tickling sensation that started on the sides of my temples expanded to cover my face. A wave of vertigo hit me, like I was falling but without my actual body. I gritted my teeth together. Finally, the motion stilled. When I opened my eyes, I was standing in a strange lobby-like environment, with a giant menu display floating before me like a jumbotron. Whenever I looked at or thought about looking at something, the screen responded—flipping through movies, music, and games.

Creepy, I thought. It was like the goggles could almost read my mind. Using this interface, I navigated to the games tab and chose Minecraft. The display opened to the beginning of the game, which allowed me to choose a world, an avatar, all the settings.

"By the way, there are a few new rules to this version of Minecraft," A.J. said. "The goggles aren't like most video games. It syncs with your brainwaves or something, and reacts to your thinking."

I quickly punched the log-in info for the world I had started with Lonnie. It was fast; all I had to do was think about the letters. But it didn't give me access.

"Hey, why won't it let me log in?"

"You'll have to use the realm we share with the rest of the kids at the hospital," A.J. said. "Don't worry, though, I've coded some super-slick mods in that version, since you're new and all. For example, in survival mode, I've included some verbal commands that will respond if you're stuck or in trouble. All you have to say is—"

"I'm *not* going to having trouble," I said, irritated. "I'm not a total noob."

"You threw up in your own hair," A.J. said. "I saw you."

I breathed heavily, not willing to concede the point.

"I mean, if you just pull the goggles off, it messes with you in the head. So you really need to, like, ease out of it. Like I said, I can just come out and be fine, but not everybody is like me."

What a little snot.

"Okay, fine," I snapped. "I'll ease out of it. How do I do that?"

"You'll need to construct an exit portal. Any kind of portal shape will do, you just have to think about leaving the game for like thirty seconds."

"Are you kidding me? You made that up, didn't you," I said with a huff.

"I'm not! It's so your brain can prepare itself for exiting the game, kind of like when games don't let you log out in the middle of a fight. There's a cool-down period. Building a portal helps you concentrate on leaving." He paused a moment, probably looking at my *I don't believe you* face, and added, "I promise. It's like visualization or something. You don't want to exit the other way again, unless you want more throw-up in your hair."

"I'm not going to have materials to make an exit portal when I just get inside the game," I said.

A.J. sighed. "Oh, all the stuff is in the inventory already. It's all part of the mods I put in." I heard him move a little closer, and I cringed, thinking he might yank the goggles off again, but he didn't. Instead he whispered the log-in passwords for the shared realm.

I looked at the start button, and the screen went black. There were a couple of lines of code in the upper left-hand corner of my sight line that I didn't get a good look at, but a moment later the world of Minecraft spawned at my feet, spreading out in all directions, a pixilated world of bright colors, sunshine, and the gentle tinkling music of the game. I took a few hesitant steps forward, worried that the nausea would come back. This time, I felt fine.

Progress!

I had spawned in a forest biome. There were hills ahead of me covered with blocky trees, and flowers and grass in the valley where I was standing. To my left, a river trickled down in squares of blue. Above me, clouds with right angles floated in the sky. And on the other shore, more grass, and a small pre-built village.

I moved toward the trees, and spotted a couple of pigs. I got close enough to one, and tried to see if I could lean in. The goggles did exactly what I had hoped, bending over the animal so that I could look down on it. It was bigger than I expected. I mean, it was pig-sized; it's just that when you're looking at it on a screen it seems pretty tiny, so I wasn't expecting it to actually approximate the size and shape of a pig. But the entire world did approximate real sizes. It actually felt like I was inside a world that fit me, and that I belonged to. It was a surprise. I thought about reaching out to my new pig pal, and a pair of block hands came into view. Nice! Of course, I didn't feel anything when my hand hit the pig and it ran away squealing.

After being stuck in a full-body cast for who knows how long, it felt incredible to be in control of a body again, even if it was blocky. I moved my head this way and that. Did a few jumps. The connection from my brain to the avatar was seamless. I tried to recall what my real body felt like, thinking it might help me reconnect to it outside of the game, but nothing happened. I was a disembodied head inside the game, and my body was someplace else. Spooky.

"This is an unexpected bonus," I said, expecting A.J. to respond, but he didn't. I wondered if I really had said it aloud, or if I had only imagined saying it. I heard it. In my head, at least. Did that count? I wondered how much I was still in the real world, so I tried to think about my hands and my legs, in casts on the bed, to see if I could wiggle some fingers or toes. My hands and my feet made jerky movements in the game but I didn't sense anything else. Maybe I couldn't be in two places at once. Maybe I was really moving in the real world too, but I didn't know. I decided not to dwell on it, and started to explore instead.

I walked up the closest hill, past some grazing sheep, and looked around. The world was still spawning in the distance. Now, across the river, the village looked a little bigger. There were a few villagers walking around, interacting with each other. I'd check that out later. First, I wanted to get to the other side of the hill, and see how much of the world had spawned, and what kind of terrain I had to work with.

Maybe I could finish the world that Lonnie and I had been working on. It would be a good surprise for him, once we both got out of the hospital. I couldn't wait for the future when we could look back on this accident and maybe laugh about it like we did the monkey bars fall. And this time around, I would follow his plan. *Gotta follow the plan from now on*, I told myself. I was thrilled just to be somewhere other than the tiny hospital room, looking at old chairs, beeping machines, and vertical blinds.

I wanted to high-five someone. Or tell someone. I looked around, half expecting to see Lonnie on some other part of the hill, carefully constructing something sensible. Whenever I got inside the game, he was always somewhere nearby. But the land-scape was empty of everything but a few programmed animals munching blocky stalks of grass.

"Wish you were here, Lonnie," I said under my breath. The animals didn't change their movements, and nothing else seemed to react to my being there and talking. I looked in the upper right-hand corner and opened my inventory. The first thing I did was scroll through to make sure everything was there that was sup-posed to be. It's not that I didn't trust this kid, but better safe than sorry, you know? Once I was sure everything was in place, I se-lected spruce wood and constructed a small one-room house nestled against the side of the hill, with some openings for win-dows that I'd get glass into later. I put a door on the front, and then went out again looking for something to do. But there were no Lonnie creations for me to mess with, no other players for me to talk to. It was too quiet. I needed something to happen.

The light began to dim, so I went back inside the house, closed the door, and watched night descend on the world around me. In the darkness, there were still sounds. Two zombies made their way up the hill, but didn't come anywhere near the house. I waited out the night, watching the mobs wander by, and as soon as it was light again, I struck out for the village. I wanted to see what the kid had available, figure out what kind of mods he had in here, or if this really was a brand-new, empty world. I actually hoped it was the latter. Even though I didn't have Lonnie's and my test world, or the plans he'd drawn up, I still wanted to try making it. I'd be going purely on memory and guesswork.

I felt a little bit gleeful, to be honest.

For the first time in a long while, I felt good about where I was headed.

I could make this world into anything I wanted. And I wanted to make sure it was a world Lonnie would be proud of.

CHAPTER 4

I was getting used to moving around in the game. There was one thing that I really wanted to try. Flying. From the top of the hill, I jumped twice, expecting my avatar to soar into the sky. Instead, I tumbled down a few blocks. *Must be survival mode and not creative*, I thought. I climbed back up and looked around. On the other side of the hill, in the distance, was a field of brown. A desert biome, I guessed. There didn't seem to be any villagers or buildings, so I turned and went north, following the curve of the river. I ran past mobs of pigs and sheep, clumps of trees, and fields of flowers. Much farther away, things turned green. Swampy. I'd have time to explore all of that later. What I wanted was to check out the village on the other side of the river. So I turned my gaze, and the entire world turned beneath me, pointing me in the direction of the village near my home base.

Running in the game felt amazing. The world whizzed by me, and the exhilaration of being able to sprint around was intoxicating. I could almost pretend that they were really my legs pumping beneath me, sending me flying through the Technicolor scenery.

"Optical illusion," I said out loud. I knew I was really lying in bed in a hospital room, and the entire world around me was a projection of light that extended only as far as the goggles did. It wasn't real. None of it.

It reminded me of a unit we did on optical illusions with my eighth-grade art teacher, Mrs. Franklin. I loved it. There was the Necker cube—a cube drawn in two dimensions—that you could see two different ways depending on which plane you decided was "front" or "top," and also the Hering illusion, which showed how a flat illustration could appear to curve or even move with a series of strategically placed straight lines. But my favorite was the snake illusion, a circle of colors that only seemed to move when you weren't looking directly at it. It seemed like magic, like the colors themselves had a mind that could read me, and know when I wasn't looking, and prank me for its own pleasure. Even when we'd moved past the optical illusions unit, I was still making snake illusions, pretending that they were actively trying to interact with me, but only on their own terms.

"Vision is one of the primary ways we process the world around us," Mrs. Franklin had said. "But always remember, eyes can be tricked, which in turn can trick your brain."

I stopped near the edge of the river and batted a nearby flower, but nothing happened, so I went on my way. "Everything really is an illusion here."

At the water's edge, cubes of blue indicated a narrow river, and cubes of brown and green on the other side told me there was land. If I wanted to, I could count up the squares and know exactly how many cubes made up my vision, but why spoil the fun? That would be like going to a magic show and calling out all the ways the magician was making the tricks happen. First of all, it's rude, and second of all, it ruins everything. Despite it being an optical illusion, I was happy to be where I was, standing by a river, instead of lying down in my own dull reality.

From this side of the river, the village looked enticing. I opened up the crafting table, silently thanking A.J. again for giving me a full inventory at the start, and made planks of wood. Then I constructed what I thought was a pretty solid, sturdy boat. A sheep wandered over as I finished. It looked up. Not at me, just up, as I pushed off across the river.

"This is pretty cool. I gotta hand it to you, kid," I said to A.J. out in the real world.

The sheep lumbered off, and A.J. didn't say anything.

I looked at the water as the boat crossed the river. I wished I could dip my hand into the water and feel it, but I knew that wouldn't happen.

"Illusion, illusion, illusion," I said aloud. I laughed for the first time in . . . I didn't know how long.

The boat slowed as it got to the other shore, and I hopped out. Ahead was the little village, which looked much bigger now that I was so close up. Immediately a few of the villagers turned to look at me, and in a few moments I was surrounded by villagers muttering at me in several slightly different tones.

So, a couple of things. First, we were all the same size. I'm used to being short and having to look up at people, so that was weird. And second, all of them were looking at me with these blank, unfeeling eyes that I thought I'd be used to from playing the game, but something about the way their glances seemed to bounce right off me made me feel cold. I muscled my way through the throng of villagers and walked toward the first building—a butcher's shop. There was a bench outside and a pen around the back. This was all usual stuff, but I didn't expect that walking up to the building would feel so impressive and realistic. The door even squeaked a little as I went in. The butcher looked up and muttered in my direction, but when I didn't engage, it went back to working on something behind the counter. I thought about the meat I could get from the butcher, and that alone was effective enough that I thought my stomach actually rumbled. I wondered when the last time was that I'd had a solid meal. I didn't remember eating anything since before the accident. I wondered what had happened to my brownies. There was the IV drip, which I guessed was keeping me packed with nutrients, but what I was suddenly craving was a ham sandwich.

I picked up some pork, and the butcher came over. The trade popped up just over the villager's head, so I made it and walked out. The butcher muttered again at my exit.

With my VR hunger satisfied, I went back over to the water right outside the village and began to work on phase one of Lonnie's master plan—making obsidian for the nether portal. Everyone knows that if water hits a lava source block, it becomes obsidian. Most players would just carry some buckets of water into an underground cave, but Lonnie always had a flair for the dramatic. It was his idea to dig down until we hit a lava pool, then divert an entire river into it.

"Just imagine it!" he'd said as he showed me his schematics. "A waterfall into lava and *boom*, obsidian for days!"

"Man, now I *really* wish you were here, Lonnie," I whispered. He would make the work go by much faster. If I could have rolled up my sleeves in Minecraft, I would have. "Let's do this," I said to no one, dusting my palms together. Well, my limbs didn't really touch. My block hands moved near each other in a way that looked more like I was about to play rock, paper, scissors, with only the obvious draw as the outcome. Not having actual hands was a minor drawback, but there were many advantages in my new pixilated existence, too. Using the pickaxe in my inventory, I started digging out a new flow from the main river.

After a few minutes of working, I felt the weight of someone looking at me. I knew that I was inside a game. I knew that this was all an illusion. But that look felt real somehow. It was like those intense looks you feel when you can tell someone is staring at you from across the room, even if your back is turned.

"This is ridiculous," I said. "It's just a game."

Still, I turned to look. A villager in a dark blue shirt with a large X crisscrossing it stared at me from across the river near where the boat was docked. I blinked a few times, wondering if I was just being weird, or maybe I was getting disoriented again. But the villager simply stared back.

A spark of recognition ignited in my brain. The back of my neck prickled. I knew someone with that exact T-shirt.

"L-Lonnie?"

I could almost feel my pores constrict. How was this possible? It wasn't Lonnie's avatar, by any means. It lacked his skin mods and cape. But no doubt about it, the villager was somehow Lonnie.

The strangely dressed villager suddenly disappeared back into the village.

"Hey, wait! Come back!"

I took off after it. My mind was racing. Was there a glitch when Lonnie tried to log on, and he somehow got zapped into a villager?

I was running past the shops and houses, down a cobblestone street that turned away from the river and toward that villager. At every turn, the Lonnie villager eluded me, and ran down another path. I chased until I couldn't orient myself anymore, and I had to look around for the hills to know which way the river was, and therefore home base. I turned down what seemed to be an abandoned alleyway that was more crudely constructed than the rest of the village, and found myself staring down a villager in the shadow of one of the buildings. I moved forward, and it moved forward too, matching me step for step. I moved to the side. So did it. Now it was in the light and I could see that it was the same villager again. Blue shirt. Big X across the front. I could feel adrenaline start to pump through me. My head hurt for a couple of seconds, but then it stopped.

Until this villager showed up, I'd felt perfectly fine inside the game. But now? I could feel my heart beat in my ears. I gulped down some air and swallowed hard enough to settle the rising gall inside myself.

"What happened to you, Lonnie? What room did they put you in?"

The villager moved toward me in slightly jerky steps, like it was hesitating to see what I would do first. He made no sound and turned down a different path away from me. His avatar was really Lonnie-like, with dark skin and gray eyes. I tried to search his movements for some sign of the Lonnie I knew on the outside, something that could help me be sure this was really him. Just as I got closer, he looked up, directly at me, and I jumped back.

"Hello, Earth to Elon," I yelled, using Lonnie's real name. "You're on mute or something." I waited and strained my ears for any sound other than the music and sounds of general movement inside the game, but there was nothing. I looked around the interface. The only other villager I'd gotten up close and personal with was the butcher, and when it was close enough, the health bar and the trade bar came up right over it. But not with this one. I wondered if it was some kind of glitch or a new type of character that didn't interact the way others did. Maybe it was a VR feature and that's why I didn't get it.

"You're being super weird," I said. I tried to touch Lonnie's head but he just backed away. His eyes were dull, just like all the other villagers. It was unsettling, but I pushed that feeling down.

"Well, as long as you're here. I need your help by the river."

I took off in the direction of my ongoing project of diverting the water flow to a new pond. Surprisingly, Lonnie followed, still not speaking. Ahead were the hills where I'd built my one-room cabin, which meant the river was a little to the right. I moved down the street, knocking villagers out of the way as I went. Each of them turned to look in my direction, but not really at me. Like how villagers were supposed to do.

I got to the riverbank and quickly crafted Lonnie a second boat, saying, "Come on!" before jumping into my own. As we rowed to the other shore, I looked back at the village. It looked the same. Bright, bustling.

When I got out of the game world, I was going to make the nurses tell me where real-life Lonnie was. But for now I was content to have some help for once. There'd be plenty of time to figure out real life. What I wanted to do was explore and build with my best friend.

Now, it was time to play.

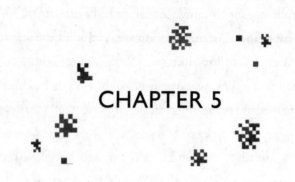

CHAPTER 5

"Be careful where you stab that shovel! We're probably getting close!" I shouted down to Lonnie. I stood overlooking the ridge of a very large hole we'd dug beside the new pond, waiting to unleash the water. It was Lonnie's job to hit the first level of lava, and hightail it out of there using the stone steps we'd built leading out of the massive ditch.

I had instructed Lonnie to start digging down, which he did. However, he didn't really seem to understand my directions, digging straight down rather than creating more of a downward slope to use as an escape if necessary. Avatar or not, the last thing I wanted to deal with was a roasted Lonnie.

"Slow down!" I yelled again.

There was a sudden hiss and pop, and red-hot lava started bubbling up from the hole Lonnie had made in the ground. Lonnie just stood there, blank-eyed, as flames licked at his clothes.

"What are you doing, you dummy? Get out!"

Lonnie jumped up as if my command, and not the heat, had alerted him to the imminent danger. He began to run up the stone steps with the lava flow right on his heels.

I shook my head. Something was off about Lonnie's avatar. He didn't act like the Lonnie I knew. Maybe it was the lag time, or maybe something was wrong with his goggles.

"Have you tried logging out and rebooting your goggles?" I asked. No response. Lonnie just sat on the edge of the hole, staring across the gulf.

Striking my axe on the remaining dirt blocks, I watched the water pour into a giant fall, straight into the pool of lava. Peering below, I could see some of the lava blocks turn inky black. Soon we would have more than enough obsidian to create twenty nether portals if we wanted. And Lonnie was right, it did look pretty awesome. Okay, I had to admit following the plan worked out great.

"These traps are so annoying to build," I complained, tapping away at the keyboard and squinting down at Lonnie's graph paper schematics. "Why can't we go out and hunt down the endermen like everyone else does?"

"These are more efficient," Lonnie said.

"What about *fish*?" I asked.

"Eee-fish-ent," Lonnie retorted. "It means more bang for our buck. Not every enderman drops a pearl. We could be running around for hours, or we could build these traps and get started on phase three."

I rolled my eyes. "Okay, excuse me, Mr. Vocabulary. I happen to like running around and hitting things. I thought that was the point of playing survival mode."

"Only if you want to play like a two-day noob in the Overworld forever. I, on the other hand, have bigger ambitions." Lonnie passed over another stack of graph paper, one that he'd been doodling on for hours. I took it and read aloud his chicken-scratch handwriting on the top page: *How to Get to the End in 5 Steps*.

"The End?" I asked. "Why would we want to get to the end of Minecraft?"

"Because that's where the *real* bosses are," Lonnie said, his voice cracking a little from excitement. "Check this out." He opened up a Minecraft guidebook he'd borrowed from the library. There was a bookmarked page with an illustration of a black dragon with purple eyes and gray lizard-like wings. My jaw dropped open as I read about the ender dragon. I definitely wanted to see this boss in person.

"I want to tame one," I whispered.

"You don't tame the ender dragon, you defeat it!" Lonnie snapped the book shut under my nose. "And the only way we can do that is if we prepare our supplies, plan out our actions, and power through. Think you can manage that?"

"Prepare, plan, and power through," I repeated, waving my hands dismissively. I was distracted by a cow that had wandered onto the scene. I needed some leather. "Yeah, yeah, okay, I'll try."

. . .

I walked back to my home base. I needed time to regroup my thoughts. Villager Lonnie trailed behind me like a shadow, his expression like a mall mannequin's. Any signs of life I'd seen, or thought I saw, were clearly a trick of my mind. Another illusion, as it were. I decided to take a break and work on my shelter instead. Bare walls, dirt floor, and glassless windows were not exactly the homiest look. I added a bed and a pretty basic chest. It was just in time, too, because the light was beginning to dim, and I could use a second to think. I had an entire world at my disposal.

I had only gotten one of my torches lit when the sound of a zombie moaning rose up outside the house. Now, when you're playing the game on-screen, you've got to go out and look around to figure out exactly where this zombie is coming from, but in the VR world I knew exactly where it was. Just outside the window that faced south. One zombie I could ignore, but moments later there was the sound of another, and then another. They all seemed to have zeroed in on the house, and they seemed to be targeting me and not Lonnie. At this point he was standing stock-still in the middle of the room. He wasn't moving or speaking, just facing a wall. He must have taken off his goggles while still logged in. *A lot of help he is when I need him*, I thought sarcastically. And since I hadn't built more than the one room, and I hadn't gotten around to putting glass in the windows, I figured it was zombie-smashing time. I grabbed a sword and burst through the door, ready to go.

I didn't expect there to be so many of them.

Up close and personal, these VR zombies were more frightening than usual. I would have just ignored them normally. I tend to find zombie mobs more annoying than threatening. But I was suddenly excited for a challenge, and I had a hillside full of zombies just asking for a fight. I grinned as I started plowing through green guys with the sword like an Amazon warrior—in my head, I mean. I'm pretty sure I looked awful, and if anyone was looking at me play they might have died from laughter, but I was screaming and chopping, and generally having a great time until one of them hit me, and the energy bar at the top of my vision went down half a heart. I was mad, but I also laughed.

I lifted the sword again, determined to battle my way through. In all the screaming and chopping, I'd only managed to kill three of the mob that was coming my way, but it was three less I had to think about. I rushed forward into one near the front door, and green slime burst in pixilated arcs that fell on the ground and disappeared in seconds. I turned and targeted another that was coming up behind me. The same ooze spilled, so I turned to a third. But I was too slow. This one caught me by the arm, and I watched again as I lost health points.

The next time I tried to swing the sword, I could've sworn it felt heavier, and was hard to hold. That was an extra level of game detail I did not expect. But I did hold it up, and began swinging it as hard as I could, and then down the middle of the same zombie that had touched me moments before. It died, but I saw more and more of them coming up the hill. Maybe it was time to retreat.

I slipped past the splatter of my last zombie victim and moved into the trees on the hill, thinking it would make for good cover. No such luck. Because coming down toward me were a couple of skeletons. I dispatched the first one with a diagonal strike across the torso, but the other one managed to hit me with an arrow, knocking me back and ensuring that a second strike was impossible. This time I didn't need to see the bar to know I'd lost another heart. Maybe two. There was a total slowdown of my movements. It was like I was being rebooted on the slowest connection ever conceived. Basically, dial-up; but on, like, an old-timey rotary phone.

I was being taken down by one skeleton, and the rest of the zombie horde had figured out where I was, so I ran around the mob and somehow managed to make my way to the top of the hill. My energy level had a chance to revive somewhat, enough for me to sprint like a frightened kitten down into the next valley. I switched out my weapon for the pork I'd traded for earlier, and ate it to help my slowly depleting food bar.

I found myself panting, despite knowing that I hadn't actually run anywhere at all, that it was all just me moving through the animation of the game. Maybe it was the zombie horde, or the quick thinking, or the feeling of being attacked and having to defend myself, but I could feel the even pulse of my heartbeat in my ears out in the real world. It made a strange echoing sound here in the game.

More zombies and the skeletons were on the move, right in my direction. I didn't know what to do, and panicked when I realized Lonnie was still in the hut and I'd have to figure out how to get back to him, but then he showed up at my side. He must've logged back into the game!

I grabbed Lonnie by the arm and shouted, "Time to go!"

We ran until the terrain changed from lush green to an expanse of dull brown with a few patchy scrub plants. Desert. There was no cover here, and my energy was steadily going down since I had no food left, and I'd been under constant attack the last few minutes. The sky was starting to brighten, which was good news, but it wasn't happening very fast. Past another dune, I spotted what looked like a villager all in brown, dealing with its own throng of zombies. With my own problems at my back, I tried to go around, but they were moving too, and in moments we intercepted each other.

The what-I-thought-was-a-villager turned to me and yelled, "Stay and fight! I'll help you!"

Besides the muttering of the villagers and the zombie moans, I hadn't heard anyone speak in the game. I stopped.

"Don't just stand there, get your weapon out!" the player said again.

"Are you real?" I said, dumbly.

"We don't have time for this!"

The player came closer. This was when I realized they were wearing leather armor. They offered a trade—a wooden sword, for nothing in return. Best trade I'd ever been offered. I grabbed the sword, stood beside the other player, and started slashing as hard and as fast as I could. My leather-clad friend, though, was better, cutting through twice my number in the same amount of time. Between our work and the daylight dawning, we defeated our foes and found ourselves alone in the middle of a desert.

"I didn't know there was anyone else inside the game." The player put away the sword and said, "I'm Esme."

"Bianca," I said. "I thought I was alone in here too. But then I found Lonnie."

"Who?"

"My friend, Lonnie." I turned and gestured behind me. But to my shock, Lonnie was nowhere to be found. Sometime since we'd run into the desert, he had just disappeared.

"Oh, come on! How are you going to log out on me like that again, Lonnie!" I yelled into the air, like he could hear me from the game or something.

"Are you . . . okay?" Esme asked.

"No, I'm not!" I grunted, then calmed down a bit. "I mean yes, I'm fine. My friend was just here, though, I swear."

"There are a few of us around. He might show up again." She shrugged. "Everyone comes and goes as their treatment schedules allow. Gotta leave time for the doctors and the nursing staff to poke and prod you, right?"

"You're a patient in the hospital too?" I asked.

"Yeah, aren't you?"

"Yes, I was in a car accident." I paused, and then asked, "Have you seen a kid named Elon Lawrence? He would have come in the same time I did. About fifteen years old, dark skin, gray eyes?"

"I don't think so," Esme said. "How long ago?"

I realized I had been unconscious too many times to give an exact answer.

"I'm not sure, maybe a few days, maybe two weeks? We were both in the same accident." I quickly told Esme what had happened, how a car had come out of nowhere to hit us straight-on, how there was nothing we could have done about it.

"Ouch!" Esme said. "Did the driver run a red light?"

My stomach twisted and I felt a little sick. I didn't mention the part about the cell phone. I didn't want to think about how maybe it was us who ran that red light.

"Anyhow, just let me know if you see him," I said.

"Will do. One more thing, if you've only been here two weeks at most, how did you get the glasses so soon?" Esme asked. "They usually don't hand them out until you've been here at least a month."

"Some kid who came wandering into my room," I explained. "He brought me my own pair."

"It was probably A.J., right?"

"Yep. A.J."

She nodded. "He's our biggest recruiter. Always trying to get new people into the game so he can show off." She shrugged again. "He's a pretty sweet kid, though."

"So how many people play inside the game?" I asked.

"Right now? It's just the three of us," she said. "I think."

"You, me, and . . ."

"Anton."

"Who's that?"

"You'll meet him soon enough." She began to walk away toward the other end of the desert biome. I followed.

"So, what are you in for?" I asked.

"Chemo," Esme said, as if she were replying to my question with her favorite color. "We're hoping this round will be the one to kick the cancer out once and for all."

"Wow, I hope it works too," I mumbled. I felt like my words were totally lame and unhelpful. But I just didn't know what to say to someone with that kind of news.

"It's kind of my ultimate boss," Esme said, shrugging.

She frowned. For a moment, her stare drifted as if she was thinking about something else. Then she refocused on me. "How long have you been in the game?" She seemed concerned.

"Not long," I said. "It was night when A.J. came over to give me the goggles."

"Did you come out? Was it still night when you came out?"

"I haven't gone out yet," I said. "I'm sure someone will take the goggles off me eventually."

"So you haven't made an exit portal yet?"

"A.J. was serious about that exit portal method?" She just stared at me, so I continued. "I'll make it when I make it. I don't see the rush."

She stared me down and shook her head.

"This version of Minecraft is special," Esme said. "The goggles are reading our brain synapses. You know what that is, don't you? It's not just about clicking some keys on a keyboard."

"Yeah, I know what that is," I lied.

"So when beginners come in who don't know how to play the game, their thoughts can mess with the settings."

"I'm not a noob," I said sharply. "A.J. already told me stuff."

"Yeah, yeah, well clearly he didn't tell you everything. You're not much for thinking things through, are you? Word of advice, you're not ready. Log out, wait a few more weeks, and then the nice doctor will give you a pair of goggles and an instruction manual. Go back to your nice comfy hospital bed with the cartoon characters on the walls."

"My room doesn't look like that," I said. "My room's beige."

Esme paused for a moment. "How bad is it that they didn't even bother to put you in one of the rooms with the cartoon clowns?"

"Most of my body's in a cast. I got wrecked big-time," I replied. "That's why I'm here. In the real world, I can't move at all. And I can't figure out what happened to my best friend."

I felt an unexpected sob rising in my throat. I suddenly wanted to curl into a ball and cry about everything that had happened. I just didn't want to do it in front of a stranger in Minecraft. Luckily, it didn't seem like the avatars were that good at showing emotion. I quickly collected myself.

"So please, can you just show me around? I'm a fast learner, I promise."

Esme was silent, her avatar standing still as she thought about it.

"Okay, fine, follow me and do as I do. We're going to talk to Anton."

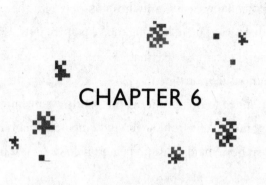

CHAPTER 6

I followed Esme through the desert biome, heading in what looked like no particular direction.

"Where are we going?" I asked.

"To Anton's lair," she said. "He and A.J. helped build a lot of the mods in this game. He can walk you through how to keep your brain from messing with the game."

"What do you mean, 'messing with the game'?" I asked.

Esme sighed, like she was talking to someone who was way dumber than she was.

"This version of Minecraft is manipulated with our brains . . ."

"Yeah, I got that part, loud and clear!" I snapped.

"It's also a shared realm, so all our minds are playing in the same playground."

"Okaaaay," I said, trying to follow. "So?"

"So?! Think of it this way: Say you walked into a sandbox and didn't know you had poop on your shoes. That just ruins the sandbox for everyone. Noobs who don't know what they're doing always have poop on their shoes. They didn't mean to bring it in. They just don't know to check their shoes."

"Well, that's why you're helping me," I pointed out. "I'll check my shoes."

She grunted. "For now."

She continued to stomp through the sandy terrain, and I actually felt hot, most likely from anger and embarrassment. I mean, it wasn't heat from the digital sun beaming down on our heads or anything.

"I should probably find something to eat," I said.

Without stopping, Esme opened her chest and traded me some pork for nothing. My health level went up. I said, "Thanks," but if she heard me, she didn't let on. We walked in silence for a while, so I tried to restart the conversation. "I could go for a real pork chop right now. How about you?"

"I don't eat much," she said. "In the real world, I mean. Nausea."

"From what?"

"Chemo makes me nauseated. Food, even the smell of food." She went a little out of her way to mine over a dune. I waited for her to continue, but she didn't, so I said, "I'm sorry."

"It's okay. You didn't know." She stepped aside so I could take some of the redstone she had uncovered for me.

"Thanks," I said.

"So, what about you?" she asked. "Give me all the gnarly details."

I tried to recall the long list of broken body parts Dr. Nay had recited when she was poking at my hologram.

"I've had a bunch of surgeries, and I'm probably going to be doing a bunch more," I said, trying to sound like it wasn't a big deal. Deep inside, my heart started pounding again. I hoped Esme couldn't hear it. I wondered if they would be able to let me stay in Minecraft while all that was going on.

"Wait until you meet Anton," Esme said, simply. "I bet he has you beat."

"Huh?"

"No matter how many surgeries you've had or will have, none of them have been as awful as Anton's brain surgeries," she said, like it was a point of pride. She then switched from her mining pickaxe to her sword.

"I should get better weapons," I said. "A.J. started me off with some pretty basic stuff."

"Yes, that would be good," she replied.

Over the next dune, there was a one-story house made of stone with glass and obsidian around the top, and a dense patchwork of cacti surrounding it except for a long path that led to the front door.

"Hold up," Esme said.

"Why?" I asked.

"Traps," Esme said. "Traps are Anton's thing." She moved forward, and I followed close behind. There were levers all along the sides of the path, and blocks of redstone, obsidian, lava, and TNT interspersed throughout. Exposed redstone wire joined them all together.

"It's pretty long and complicated," I said, actually impressed.

"If you don't know where to step," Esme said. She beckoned

me with her hand, and I followed close behind, mimicking her jumps from one block to another, even when it seemed like I was going to a block that would blow up in my face. She went from an obsidian block on the left, jumping over to the other side of the path onto a sandstone block that looked like it had a trigger attached, but it didn't go off. Next, she jumped onto a block of TNT, and turned back to say, "It's a dud." I nodded and followed. She moved off to the next block, more sandstone, jumped over some lava, and finally onto a short landing that led to the front door. I was relieved when I made it to the end of the treacherous path. Esme opened the door, and I jumped down, only not quite onto the landing that she'd just occupied.

There was an explosion. I turned back, and the entire gauntlet had been triggered in a cascade. Blocks exploded, lava erupted, and a series of sparks bloomed in front of my face.

"Get in!" Esme yelled. I stepped inside the house and she closed the door and backed away down a raised hallway as the lava burned at the front door, and seeped inside the room. I followed her up the steps to the hallway as the lava covered the entire floor.

"What the heck?" someone behind me said.

I turned around. A player in green came running from a back room toward us.

"What did you two do?" He ducked into a side room, and a moment later I could see him through the windows outside of the house. He went behind a cactus and fiddled with something, and the explosions stopped. He hesitated a moment, then went around looking at everything and shaking his head. By the time he had come back inside, the lava flow in the front room had receded to halfway across the floor.

"Who are you?" he asked, pointing at me.

"I'm Bianca," I said.

"Bianca," Esme repeated. "This is Anton."

"Well, Bianca, you just ruined days' worth of work," Anton said.

"Sorry. It was an accident."

"What did you bring her here for?" he asked Esme.

"It turns out—" she began.

"Jeez. Do you know how long it took me to do all of that? You can't just grab up random kids from the ward and bring them over. You should ask first," he snapped. "I'm not running a day care."

"I'm not a little kid," I said. But neither of them responded.

"First of all, I didn't grab her up to bring her here," Esme said flatly. "And second of all, she needs training."

"Yeah, no joke," Anton said, gesturing to the last of the lava and the ruined front door.

"A.J. dumped her in here before the doctors could talk about the program," Esme continued. "She knows zilch about keeping her mind focused and uncluttered by the real world. She could mess up the game at any moment, rewrite our mods, just like Andrea!"

"Who's Andrea?" I asked.

"Crap, you're totally right." Anton seemed to stare out at nothing, then mumbled, "Well, come along, let's get you into a safer space so we can walk you through the basics."

I didn't much appreciate his tone, but what were my choices? Esme and I followed Anton through a sliding glass back door, and there was an arch. Well, the remnants of one. It looked like this was where he kept his permanent exit portal.

"The heck?" Anton said. He walked around the broken arch. The pieces hung in the air as if there was something holding them together, but there really was nothing at all. I was a little happy to see that they hadn't been totally messing with me about needing a portal, but Anton looked pissed.

Anton moved from surveying his old portal to look at us, and stepped through the arch as if to make sure it really was ruined.

"This . . . is very bad." He turned to me. "Did you do this?"

"What? No," I said. "I just got here! I didn't do anything at all!"

"Remember what I said about poop in the sandbox," Esme said. "You may not know it, but your brain might have caused something in the game to mess up and break our portal."

I didn't know what to say. If I had messed something up, I didn't know what it was. I tried to remember everything that had happened, to see if I'd stared at some command thing for too long by accident.

"I'm not sure exactly what happened," I offered. "I had just gotten into the game, and I was exploring, then I met up with Lonnie, and then it was night and zombies showed up and—"

"Quiet," Anton snapped. "Let me think for moment."

We stood in silence, and after a while I asked, "So what's with all the traps? I mean, it's only a few kids in the game, right?"

Esme coughed, but it sounded suspiciously like a chuckle. "He has trust issues," she said.

"Inside a game?" I asked.

"No, outside of the game," she said. "His significant other is breaking up with him, and his parents are forcing him to play a sport he doesn't even like, which he's good at—"

"I *was* good at," Anton interrupted.

"Which he *is* good at," Esme continued.

"The point is, I rigged up my house because I knew I would have monsters mobbing it if I kept dwelling on the not-so-great real world stuff," he said. "You don't need to hear about that. Not now. There are other things we need to take care of."

"Like what other things?" I asked.

"Like warning anybody else who's come into the game since you got here," Anton said.

"We should find Lonnie," I said. "He's in the game somewhere, but his avatar is messed up. He looks like a weird villager and he can't talk. I last saw him in the forest biome."

"What does he look like, exactly?" Anton asked.

"He has a blue shirt with a white cross on the chest."

"I've never heard of a player porting into an NPC," Anton said. "And I've been here since the beginning."

"That doesn't mean it's not possible," I said. That player *had* to be Lonnie. Didn't Esme say that A.J. was a bit of a recruiter? "My friend was in the same accident that I was in. And he . . . yes, he was wearing a blue shirt then, too."

"With a cross?" Anton asked.

I wasn't sure. I blinked a couple of times trying to bring back the memory of what Lonnie had worn the night of the accident. I remembered the dark blue. And then there was his silver crucifix that he always wore. Was that the same as a white X?

"Yes," I said. "I'm sure."

Esme and Anton looked at each other.

"Maybe his goggles are broken," I continued, trying to think of ways Lonnie's avatar could be acting up.

Esme and Anton shared another glance. Then Anton shrugged.

"It's too early for theories," Esme said. "All we know is that you saw him recently and that he was acting weird. Things inside the game don't necessarily reflect things outside the game."

"You're right that we should look for him," Anton said. "I want to see him for myself."

"Good, then it's decided. Let's find Lonnie, fix his avatar, and then you can train us both in the ways of Minecraft mind control or whatever."

I turned to head out, but Anton blocked my path. "Listen," he said. "There's more you should know. There're uh . . . there're some other possibilities to consider."

"Like what?" I asked.

Esme moved forward. "Let's just find the guy first, okay? There's no need to scare her."

"Just tell me already," I said, exasperated.

"All right, all right. You should know about Andrea," Anton began. "This was when we didn't know what would happen when kids come into the game unprepared, and A.J. just lent her another pair of goggles like he always does. The few times she played the game she was fine, but then weird stuff started happening. Inventory would go missing for no reason, rare elements would fall from the sky."

"That last part was pretty cool, though," Esme interjected.

"What does that have to do with Lonnie?" I asked.

"Well, when we got out of the game, we found out that her dad got a new job and her family was moving. She was obviously upset about it, and her emotions started turning the game upside down. We tried to keep her mind off it as best we could, and it would get better sometimes. Not enough, though. So A.J. and I started talking about building mods to help prevent someone's issues from messing with the game. But then . . ."

"Then, she found out they were moving to a whole new country," Esme said dramatically, stealing Anton's thunder. "To Spain!"

"Oh." I immediately thought about how terrible it would be to know that I'd have to leave all of my friends behind and go to a new place where I didn't know anyone. How would I even make friends if I didn't know the language?

Esme nodded, seeing the conclusion forming in my brain.

"The next time she tried to play with us, our realm basically detonated. Biomes started moving around on us, noncombative mobs would start surging at us for no reason, and our home bases were totally wrecked."

"What happened to Andrea?" I asked, bracing for the worst.

"A.J. managed to calm her down while we fought off the mobs. We had to rebuild everything from scratch on a different server. She ended up moving, and she eventually made friends at her new school," Esme said. "She doesn't play in this realm anymore, but she still writes to us. She said—"

"Listen, the important part is," Anton interrupted, "that after that, we built mods so that any emotional messiness shows up as low-level things we can ignore or easily handle."

"We also make an effort to solve our problems in the real world," Esme said. "Before we come into the game."

"Lucky for you guys, I don't have problems in the real world, other than having to heal myself," I said. "Lonnie's fine too, it's just his avatar that's glitched."

Esme and Anton shared a look that I couldn't read.

"What I'm trying to say is that it might not be Lonnie . . ." Anton began.

"Of course it's him!" I yelled. "I saw him, he looked at me!"

I was tired of talking. Each second we wasted was another second my best friend was stuck in a villager body. I dodged Anton and ran off into the desert, in the direction of the forest biome where I had spawned.

"You have no idea what's happening," I called back. "You just want someone to blame. For all I know, you two are the ones messing with me!"

I was going to get to the bottom of things, starting with finding Lonnie again. It was always him and me against the world. I didn't need anybody else.

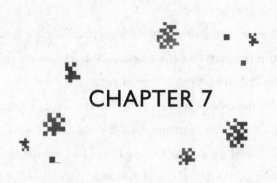

CHAPTER 7

Esme and Anton followed me out into the desert, and eventually I allowed them to catch up with me. They tried to talk to me, but I wasn't having it. The fact is, all I knew was that the villager *was* him, but there was no way to prove it until we made contact. I never responded to either of them, so eventually we moved along in relative silence, stopping occasionally to harvest whatever neutral mobs we came across. Night fell, and we encountered hardly any mobs in the desert.

"Listen," Esme began again.

"Nope," I said.

"I just want to prepare you," she tried.

"She doesn't want to hear it, Esme," Anton said. "Let her find out for herself."

"It'll be better if Bianca—"

"Esme," I interrupted. "Can we just get to the forest biome first, before we jump to conclusions?"

Esme slowed down, as if she was going to stop and let the two of us continue on our own.

"Whatever we do, we need to stick together," Anton said. "We can work through anything if we just work as a team."

Esme huffed and picked up speed again.

Behind some trees, I spotted a wolf. It snarled as I got closer, but it seemed a better companion at the moment than the two actual humans I'd found inside the game. I pulled out one of the bones from a skeleton mob we'd defeated, and offered it to the wolf. It walked away at first, bounding up a couple of levels on the hill, so I offered it a few more. It moved forward, eyeing me and the gift, and then it jumped closer, pounced on the bones, and they disappeared. I gave it one more. It made a low whining sound, and nuzzled close to my legs.

"I thought we were supposed to be looking for your friend, not taming pets," Anton said. He was right behind me.

"We are," I said. "But you said to prepare, right? We could use the backup."

I struck out again, with the wolf following behind. We moved rapidly down the hill until I came to the one-room house I'd built. Most of it was destroyed, as if someone had come through with TNT. Two walls were blown out, there was no door, and nothing inside. Even the floor had holes in it, dug down farther into the earth.

"It's basically a lean-to," Anton said, without an ounce of humor.

"I haven't been here that long," I said. "It was a basic shelter. I would've added to it eventually."

"I wasn't criticizing," Anton said.

"None of this is important now," Esme said. "Let's just find that villager."

I was about to turn around when I thought I noticed something moving in one of the holes in the floor. I went closer, and a cave spider skittered out. I tried to jump back and out of the way, but in my cramped home base there wasn't much room to move. I crashed into Esme and my sword came down on the spider's head. It looked toward me, as if it was seeing me for the first time.

"Watch it!" I yelled to Esme and Anton as I picked up my sword again and hacked at the charging spider. It broke into blue pieces and fell to the ground. I would have taken a breath, but no sooner had I dispatched that one than another, and another, came out. Esme rolled her eyes at me and said, "Really?" She and Anton flanked me and did more damage with their stone swords than I could do with my wooden one. But soon the broken house was spilling over with spiders, which proved too much even for all three of us and the wolf, who was getting in there attacking spiders as much as it could. We were pushed out of my shelter and backward toward the riverbank.

If there had been any time at all, I might have made a snarky remark to Anton about befriending the wolf, but I could barely catch my breath.

"What are you doing to the game?" Anton shouted at me, as one of the spiders attacked him.

"I didn't do anything," Esme and I said at the same time.

Anton laughed.

"Oh no, not you, Bianca. Spiders and witches are Esme's specialty," Anton said, as he skidded back. "It's pretty legendary when she gets jealous."

"Shut your face, Anton. I'm busy!" Esme said. She and I moved toward the river, cutting through the spiders as we went, but they were resilient, and required several hits to die.

"What? You blabbed all my secrets, so I'll tell some of yours," Anton said. He did a spin and swiped at another spider. It broke apart, but the river of spiders just kept pouring out of the house. Another enemy dropped in front of him. "Esme's unpleasant in real life as well, you know. She's pissed off most of the nursing staff, and her doctor, and hardly anyone ever comes to visit her. So when she says she's in here hiding from nausea, she's really in here hiding from loneliness."

Esme screamed and ran a spider through with her sword, and it felt like everyone, including the mobs, paused to watch her rage shatter the creature into a few bouncing blocks.

"Whoa," I said.

"I told you. Legendary." Anton turned back to the spider in front of him and resumed the battle. "They always show up when she's insecure."

"Whatever," Esme said. "I'm not the ticking time bomb here. She is."

The wolf, who I'd decided to call Howl, aided us in the fight. As another spider died, it dropped a couple of experience orbs, which Esme swiped quickly.

I tried to copy her moves and land a few hits on the mob in

front of me, but I wasn't as good. Esme dispatched it for me, so I ran over to help Anton finish off the last cave spider. That's when I noticed that he was down to half a heart.

"You got poisoned," I said.

"Didn't I say I'd get poisoned?" he said. He looked over at Esme. "Didn't I?"

"No, you didn't," Esme replied with an edge to her voice. She softened a moment later, though, and said, "Good thing we passed that mob of cows earlier. Here, take it." She gave him some milk from her inventory. It helped a little. His health bar, I mean. Not his attitude.

"The two of you are going to get us killed," he said. I frowned at his thoughtless reply, and he shrugged. "What? It's true!"

We were alone on the riverbank, holding our weapons, and looking around like another attack was going to happen any moment. Luckily the sun began to rise, and we lowered our weapons.

"So where do you think Lonnie is?" I asked. "Is there a place where most players spawn?"

They both looked at me, and then at each other, and nodded.

"Let's go back to where you first saw him," Anton suggested.

A rabbit hopped into view and Anton turned his sword on it.

"What are you doing?" I asked.

"I don't know if this thing is going to attack me next." He lowered and raised the sword as if he was getting ready.

He looked at the rabbit. The rabbit looked at him. And then it hopped away.

"Frightening," I said.

He growled at me, and then jerked his chin toward the village. "You saw your friend in there, right? Let's go."

"Before another bunny shows up," Esme said teasingly.

"Ha ha," Anton said drily. "Look, the game's gone weird."

Esme snickered, so I did too. In a moment, we were both openly laughing.

"Haven't you ever been spooked by something everyone else thinks is a nonissue?" Anton asked.

"No," Esme said.

"Pirates," I said.

"You know pirates don't exist anymore," Esme said.

"They definitely do," I said. "Everyone's been thrown off by Johnny Depp, but pirates exist and they're scary!"

"Maybe you're thinking of an amusement park ride," Esme said.

"No, they're still around," I said. "When my dad was a kid, he and his family were sailing their yacht between a couple of Caribbean islands where he grew up, and they were attacked." I felt a shiver run up my spine. "I only found out because I was playing pirate at the playground one day and his face went pale and he made me leave right away. I couldn't figure out why he was so upset. It was my mom who told me what had happened. His family was fine, but the pirates took everything they had on board. He was just a kid. It terrified him."

Anton looked like he was going to say something, but Esme interjected. "That's definitely scarier than bunnies!" She started laughing again.

"Fine. Laugh it up," Anton said. "But do you have any idea what other stuff is going to be messed up? Do you?"

I shook my head.

"How about you, Spidey?" he asked Esme.

She rolled her eyes, but didn't respond.

"Okay then, so let's just be prepared for whatever," he said. "I've read *Watership Down*. Those things cannot be trusted." He pointed at the bunny, hopping away in the distance.

"And by *Watership Down*, he means *Bunnicula*," Esme said.

I snorted.

The boat slid across the river. The scenery was seamless and beautiful, and I wished I could show it to my family. I wondered what they were doing at that moment, and as I stared at the water I remembered the feeling of my mother fiddling with my braids, and how nice it felt to get a big bear hug from my dad, and I even smiled a little bit thinking about how Carrie sometimes would crawl over to my bed to snuggle before the alarm went off at 6:30 a.m. on a school day. My heart lurched, and a deep chasm seemed to open up inside. I really missed them. And I missed Lonnie, too. If there was some way to get rid of all the painful feelings while keeping all the good ones, I'd do it in a nanosecond.

"What was that?" Anton asked.

"Nothing. I didn't say anything."

"You did," Esme said, turning on me. "Something about your feelings."

Maybe it was just the way avatars gave blank, unblinking

stares, but her face gave me a chill right then. She was scary. *What does she look like in real life*, I wondered. I guessed dark hair and eyes, since that's what she chose for her game skin, but sometimes people liked to switch things up.

"How long do you think we've been playing?" I asked, trying to change the subject away from my feelings.

Anton shrugged. "It's hard to tell how long you've been inside the game. Game time and real time don't often match up."

"Why?" Esme asked. "Are you worried?"

"No, I'm just wondering what my family is doing."

"They're probably still asleep," Esme said. "It's probably still night and A.J. is looking for another set of goggles so that he can play too."

"I hope he doesn't find one," I said. "I don't want to know what his problems are."

"Me neither," Esme and Anton said together.

"Jinx!" they both said.

Then, "Double jinx!"

And, "Jinxy jinx!"

Then they both bent over with laughter.

The boats jerked to a stop at the shore, and we all got out. Howl appeared by my side moments later, and I grinned at her before heading off to the village. Just like the last time, villagers gathered around to see what we were doing, and immediately began offering trades and making their usual muttering sound.

"Do you see your friend?" Esme asked.

"Not yet," I said. I moved past the villagers and into the town.

We walked past the shops and to the street of buildings filled with villagers going about their digital lives. Anton and Esme stopped to trade with the butcher, but I kept walking.

I spotted a villager in a blue shirt with its back to me, in the middle of a garden. I resisted the urge to shout for Esme and Anton. I wanted to talk to Lonnie alone.

"Hey," I said, keeping the tremble in my voice down.

The villager turned around. There was the white X.

"Lonnie?" I asked.

He didn't respond, only turned back in the direction he was facing before, and began to move off. I tried to stop him.

"Lonnie, come with me," I said. "I want you to meet some people."

He jerked to a halt, then walked back over to me. Esme and Anton looked like they were purposefully hanging back, as if they were a little afraid of what would happen next.

I turned to face them, Lonnie by my side.

"It's definitely him," I said. "It's Lonnie."

"Based on what? He looks—" Anton started to say.

"I just know," I said.

"How? He isn't talking," Esme said.

"His face. I know that face," I said.

The two of them looked at each other, but didn't say anything to me.

I knew it sounded crazy. He looked like an oddly dressed villager. But when he looked at me, I felt it. Just like the first time I saw him in the game.

"I've got to get him to come with us," I said. "His avatar must be glitching."

"But he's not playing," Esme said. "I don't think we can get him to come along."

"I'm not doing a single thing without him." I crossed my arms, or at least tried to with my avatar.

Lonnie turned and moved into a path between vegetable beds, away from me. He didn't respond to anything Esme and Anton said, but I wouldn't have either. They were talking about him as if he couldn't hear them. Maybe if I got them doing a mission together, Lonnie would wake up from whatever trance he was in.

"Bianca, I've been thinking," Anton said. "Maybe we should exit the game and meet in real life. You know, clear our heads for a while."

"But we just found Lonnie," I said. "Why don't we try to fix him?"

"Because I don't think we can," Anton said. "He's not participating. He's just—there!"

"Let's do a few missions together, you'll see," I suggested. "Lonnie's a genius at making up traps. You two will definitely get along."

"Bianca . . ." Anton's voice trailed off, like he didn't know what to say.

"Just one mission, to the Nether. Come on, it'll be fun," I said. "Either way, I'm not leaving until Lonnie and I get to the End."

Esme pulled Anton to the side. I could hear them whispering

urgently, but couldn't make out their words. After a moment they returned.

"It's fine," Esme said. "We can take him with us." She took a breath. "How much string did we manage to get from those spiders?" she asked Anton.

"A lot," he said.

"Then make some rope," she said. "Let's guide him with it."

"We can do that?" I asked.

"Yeah," Esme said. "A.J. put the mod in when I wanted to play as Wonder Woman, and he's never taken it out."

"That's awesome," I said with a grin.

"Could you get him?" Anton asked as Lonnie wandered off. I nodded and stuck near Lonnie, herding him so he wouldn't get too far as Anton crafted the rope.

"Do you think maybe Lonnie fell into a coma or something?" I asked. "Maybe in the middle of gameplay?"

Esme sighed. "It's possible, I suppose. Andrea's avatar also somehow stayed behind. We guessed it was because she didn't exit herself, so her skin got stuck inside the game, and it'd just wander around aimlessly."

"Weird. So is she still stuck in here?"

Esme shook her head. "No. After we rebooted the realm and came back, we couldn't find her again."

"Maybe Lonnie was put into this game so we could help him get conscious again." I knew I was grasping at theories, but it was all I had. "Maybe this is like group therapy!"

"Maybe, maybe, maybe," Anton said, mimicking me. "We

don't know what is really happening, which is why we should log off and get to the bottom of it in real life."

"You said yourself that no one is probably awake now; why don't we try something in-game first?"

Esme frowned and, after a moment of hesitation, asked, "You really think you need to play through to the End?"

I turned to look at Lonnie, and he turned to me as well. It was like he finally recognized me. I smiled at him and said to Esme, "Yeah, I really do."

Anton sighed dramatically and said, "Fine. You said we should go to the Nether? Well, let's go then." He put the rope around Lonnie to lead him, and pulled Lonnie out of the garden and back into the cobblestone street in front of the butcher's shop. "Back to the boat!"

Maybe it was the fact that we had what looked like a regular villager roped and were pulling him away, or maybe it was someone doubting the plan, but the rest of the village turned hostile the moment we got near the riverbank. They all turned on us, mercilessly raining down blows.

We ran for the boats, trying desperately to ward off the attacks, but we took several hits. Anton got the brunt of the blows because he was the one pulling Lonnie along.

We fell into our boats, crafting one quickly for Lonnie, and I pushed off hard, sending my craft spinning into the middle of the river. I felt triumphant, though, since there was no way the villagers could pursue us now. That was short-lived, as when I looked back, the villagers had gotten boats seemingly out of thin air and were following. I picked up the oars, righted the boat, and rowed hard for the other shore. Once there, we exited and looked up at the ruins of my house.

"We don't even have anywhere to hide," Anton said.

"There was a cave around the other side of that hill," I said, pointing. "I saw it when I was exploring the first time I spawned."

"Quick!" Esme said.

We ran around the base of the hill, but we hadn't gotten far into the cave before we heard zombies moaning. I started to dig through a different wall to circumvent the threat. As I went, I embedded torches in the walls. The other three, and Howl, followed.

"You know, they can follow the torches as well," Anton said.

"Yeah, but without them we'll never be able to find our way out," I said. "It might only be a game, but how would you like to spend some of your digital existence wandering around in a dark computer world?"

"He's afraid of the dark, so I'm guessing he wouldn't," Esme said with a snicker.

"I certainly am not," Anton huffed.

Esme didn't respond. She came to my right and started digging through as well. She hit a block, and it opened up to a tunnel.

"Nice work," I said.

Anton picked up one of the torches and followed Esme as she moved into the tunnel. Howl and I took up the rear. I could hear the sounds of the enemies we'd tried to escape, the groaning of zombies and the fizzing of creepers, getting closer each moment. Maybe the torches were not the best idea. But what else could I have done? We moved forward slowly, knowing that something else could pop into the tunnel at any moment. I stayed close to Lonnie as Anton pulled him with the lead.

I reached for Lonnie's hand, hoping I could feel it, when something struck me from behind. I turned and was face-to-face with a zombie. Ahead of me, Anton dropped the rope that he was using to lead Lonnie along, and pulled out his stone sword. We were surrounded in the narrow tunnel. He and Esme started slashing through the mob as I picked up the rope and dug through to another part of the cave. I luckily managed to pick up some iron ore as I tunneled and pulled Lonnie through with me. I was hoping Esme and Anton would follow behind, but they got cut off by two zombies that refused to die. Luckily, Howl was still at my heels.

"Go!" Esme called out. "We'll find you later!"

I kept digging through the ore, this time putting up fewer torches, so in places it dimmed to near black, and it was hard to tell which direction I was going in, or even if I was moving farther up or down into the hill. In moments, the darkness felt tight around me. There wasn't even the sound of Esme and Anton fighting to guide me in the right direction. I tried to keep digging straight ahead in the gloom, hoping that at some point I would exit into more light, but I was getting nowhere.

"Any idea which way is out?" I asked the wolf.

She stopped and licked herself.

"Time to use more of the torches again, I guess," I said to Lonnie. "I mean, we're far enough away. It's unlikely that they'd find us now, right?"

Lonnie gave no response.

I dug and put up torches and tried to find another tunnel, or some way out. I kept going, pulling Lonnie along with me, but everything ahead was darkness.

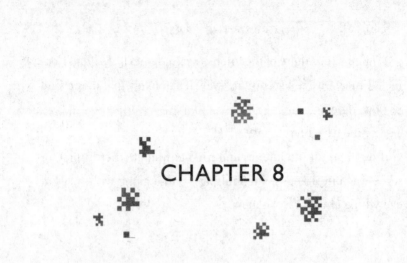

CHAPTER 8

I tunneled through until I came to a cross section cavernous enough that I could stick Lonnie in one corner and have a look around. The wolf followed close by. The cave didn't have an outlet, at least not one I could make out immediately. There was no way to know exactly what part of the hill I was trapped in. Any direction could mean trouble, but I figured up was my best bet because I'd hit light eventually.

"What do you say, Howl?" I asked the wolf. "Lonnie?" No response from either. "Well, here goes nothing," I said to both of them and neither at the same time. I started mining upward in a jagged pattern, making stone footholds as I went. The wolf bounded up with me, jumping from ledge to ledge. When I'd moved up far enough to lose the light from the torches below, I went back down and grabbed Lonnie, and dragged him up to a landing I'd created that was just big enough for the two of us. Howl watched from a spot a little higher up and on the opposite side of the hole I'd made. I dropped Lonnie's lead again and mined upward some more. There was light. I dug up faster and burst through to—not daylight—another cavern that was already outfitted with torches.

"Esme and Anton must have come through here," I said to Lonnie and the wolf. The torches were all on one side of the narrow path, which was a tactic I often used when I was digging through a cave, to remind myself which direction was in and which was out. Only, I wasn't sure which side they'd put the torches on to show "out."

"Well, the game makes everyone a righty, which means as they came through they'd put the torches on their right, right?"

Lonnie stared into the distance, and the wolf walked up ahead, and back again, tail wagging.

"Which means they would have gone in this direction," I said, pointing down the path.

The wolf followed my lead, and Lonnie came along mutely through the dark, winding trail.

I felt a chill, which I wasn't sure if it was just me feeling eerie about being inside the game, or me actually feeling a chill out in the real world where my body was. I blamed A.J., really. If that kid hadn't come into my room with his VR goggles, none of this would have happened, and I'd still be in the real world, in the hospital with my parents, and maybe someone would be ready to tell me what had happened to my friend. I took another look at Lonnie and tried to recognize something in his eyes, but they were the same dull, lifeless avatar eyes that everyone had.

"Are you there, Elon?" I asked. He always reacted when I called him that. He hated it so much. But it didn't work. To be honest, at this point, I'd take another attack to see if he'd help out. At least then I'd know he was thinking *something*.

There was an audible fizz as I moved around the next corner and came face-to-face with a creeper. The fizzing was getting louder, so I backed off with Lonnie in tow. The creeper exploded as I moved back the way I'd come, but behind me were two more.

The path curved ahead to the left, so I cut through the stone, hoping I'd catch the path at another point, and avoid the explosive creepers at our backs. I mined through, pulled Lonnie along with Howl crawling closely behind.

I moved faster, despite the fact that every now and then Lonnie would bump into solid rock.

"It's not real, so it doesn't count," I said, more to make myself feel better than anything else.

The path split into two up ahead, one leading up and the other leading to the right. But neither of them had torches. I had no way to tell which way Esme and Anton had taken.

"Heads or tails?" I asked Lonnie. It was our usual way of choosing stuff. The fizzing of another creeper got close. I chose to go up. It had worked before. There was a network of tunnels, and I kept choosing one and heading through any one that seemed creeper-free, but with Lonnie in tow I wasn't moving as quickly as I could have on my own, and pretty soon I was surrounded again. Howl snarled and snapped. I let go of Lonnie's lead and prepared to square off against the creepers pressing in. One on a far end popped and set off a chain reaction. As the one closest got ready to go off, I pulled Lonnie out of the way, but Howl jumped on the creeper, pushing it back and muting the blast. The mob was gone and Howl lay on her side on the cave floor.

"No!" I shouted, feeling the sting of tears in my eyes. The sight of her on the ground hit me harder than I would have imagined. She wasn't a real pet—none of this was real—but she'd sacrificed herself to save us. I shook my head and repeated, "None of this is real." Then I looked at Lonnie. Maybe some of it was . . . I hesitated a beat, but the moan of a distant zombie got me moving.

Illusion, illusion, illusion, I said to myself as we ran. *It's all an illusion.*

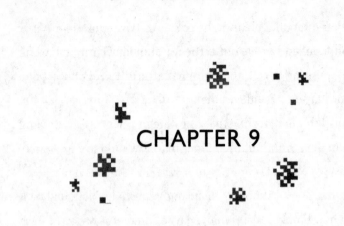

CHAPTER 9

I chanted to myself as I crawled up and away from the cavern. I pulled Lonnie slowly along. The light dimmed the farther away I got from the torches on lower levels, but I still moved upward, hoping with every strike that we would come to the surface. But cut after cut into the stone and dirt of the hill brought us no closer to escape.

"What now?" I asked Lonnie, expecting no response.

He obliged.

"Keep going? Wait for someone to rescue us?" I waited, thinking in the dim light. "There's no rescue, is there? We either get out of here on our own, or . . ." I paused to take a deep breath, then continued, "I'll get us out. I promise." I started moving again. "Prepare, plan, and power through, right?" I waited a moment to see if he would remember his motto, and then I started cutting up through the hill again. After what seemed like a few minutes, we burst through the surface and I pulled Lonnie out at the top of the hill. The light in the game was brightening. It was morning. While we had been underground, another day and night came and went.

This was a different hill entirely than the one near where I had spawned in the game. It was higher up, for one thing, and at the base of it was a large pool of water with green vegetation growing in patches all over it.

"It's a swamp," a voice to my left said.

I turned to see Anton putting his sword away. He had upgraded to iron. Esme came up next to him. She'd changed out her leather armor for iron, and she had new arrows.

"I know," I said. "I see you've had some time to make some improvements."

Esme initiated a trade and let me have an iron sword as well.

"Thanks," I said.

"Not that you were any help," Esme said.

"What?" I asked, taken aback.

"You abandoned us!" she said. "You left and you never even bothered to look back."

"You told me to go. You said you'd find me!"

"Forget it, Es," Anton said. Esme rolled her eyes and seemed anything but fine, though it was hard to tell with the avatar faces.

"Whatever," Esme said. "The fact is, we've been fighting while you've been hiding out inside the hill. We need to regroup."

"I haven't—" I began, but Esme had already moved away, and Anton followed her. They weren't listening. I followed grudgingly, tailing them at a distance until Anton turned around and gave me a look, then jerked his head forward like he wanted me to hurry up. I picked up speed, and a moment later Anton shouted with surprise. I looked up just in time to see a witch's potion sail past my face. It burst behind me, and I ran. Anton called to Esme. She skidded to a stop and pulled up a bow and arrows, which she launched down the hill at three witches, each coming at us fast. There was little vegetation on this side of the hill that I could use as cover, and Lonnie was slowing me down, but I kept tugging him forward, moving as fast as I could.

"Leave him!" Anton yelled.

A potion hit me and exploded. My movements instantly became slower. The health bar over my head dipped.

Anton ran toward me and whacked at the witch with his sword. I moved between Lonnie and the mob so that any attack would find me first. I tried to get hold of my own sword, but it was hard. It must have been a strong potion. Anton kept on hitting until the witch died. Then he picked up the fire-resistant potion and the gunpowder the mob dropped, and moved off to the next one.

Esme looked back at me, shook her head slightly as if I was some kind of disappointment, then turned back to her own witch fight. She had also changed to a sword, and had gotten in close. I watched helplessly as both Esme and Anton attacked the two remaining witches. I didn't see the fourth one spawn and head out of the swamp straight toward me.

Another potion erupted against my avatar's skin. I fell to the ground. Above me was Lonnie, vulnerable to attack without me shielding him, and my health bar was vibrating. I was down to a mere four hearts. My food bar wasn't much help. I had forgotten to eat anything since back before we'd taken Lonnie from the village, so there wasn't anything there to help me heal.

I pulled up the few supplies I had and ate a little. It did nothing to help my health bar. I was still low on food.

A moment later, Anton was over me, pulling me to my feet. He snatched the rope away from me and screamed "Move!" right in my face. Then he took off again, taking Lonnie with him. I followed as closely as I could, but I was slow and weak from the witches' potions. Another one hit me in the shoulder. My right arm went limp, as if it had been paralyzed. I couldn't pick up my sword if I tried. I did it with my left hand, but it was hard to wield, and clumsy. I heard a witch nearby, and turned as fast as I could, swinging the sword around with me. It caught the witch in the side.

"Esme, you need to get your emotions under control!" Anton yelled. "We can't just keep thwacking at mobs forever! We need to log off!"

"Not in mid-combat we can't," Esme called back.

"What happens if we die in-game?" I asked.

"When you hit zero life, you normally respawn. But if you've been playing for too long, instead of respawning, you get kicked out of the game and back to the menu until a doctor comes to check in on you and make sure you're okay," Anton said. "Considering you're not even supposed to be in here yet, they might just confiscate your goggles."

"I'm not going to get killed," I said in a low voice, then louder, "I'm not going to get killed!" as I swung the sword around a second time, catching the witch in the other side. It still wasn't dead. It aimed another potion at me. This time, I used all the energy I had left for one last mighty blow. That one did it.

The witch disappeared in a haze of fire and smoke, dropping goodies.

There was some redstone, lots of sticks, more spider eyes—we definitely did not need more of those—and string, but not one useful potion in the lot.

"How'd that work out for you?" Esme called back.

That girl was getting on my last nerve.

Another volley of potions came sailing over my head. They rained down a little too close to me, which told me that a) there were more witches, b) Esme must've still been angry at me, and c) I had a few more chances to stock up on supplies. Annoying as they were, finding a mob of witches was like going to the Mine-craft general store. I moved just a little bit faster this time, but both Anton and Esme were way ahead, cutting into witches with abandon. Then I had that same feeling again that someone was watching me. Anton had left Lonnie by himself. He was away from the witches and the fighting, but he was looking at me. And I could feel it.

I grabbed him and pulled him into a small cavern just at the base of the hill before the swamp started. Most of the witches were trying to attack Esme, which—I'm not proud of this—made me the tiniest bit happy. But with the two of them fighting, it was my chance to recoup some of the energy I'd lost in the fight. I pulled up my supplies and had something to eat. Mutton. As I watched my food and health bars go back up, I thought about whether I could just wish for things to show up in the game, like an unlimited supply of mutton.

Every game has cheat codes. And A.J. had said something about verbal commands, right? If I figured out the secret to this version of Minecraft, could I fix Lonnie just by wishing hard enough?

Out at the swamp, Esme and Anton were taking down witches and picking up supplies. I honestly wasn't sure if I could trust everything they said. Something told me they were holding back. Plus, if they were so great at keeping their issues in control or whatever, why were they still having to deal with Esme's mobs, and why'd they keep building Anton's booby-traps?

As soon as my health bar stopped vibrating, and my food points were up to nine, I left Lonnie in the cavern and stepped back out onto the bank of the swamp. I dove right into the middle of the fighting, picking up another health potion that a witch—one that Anton had killed—had just dropped.

"Sorry," I said. "I need that more than you do."

"Be my guest," Anton said, as he slashed through another witch.

The three of us mowed through the remaining witches quickly, but on this difficulty level, there were way more of them than even all of us at full strength could handle. I had the sinking feeling that we weren't going to make it. My throat started to close up just thinking about what that would mean. That everything would stop, fading out to black.

I shook my head. *There's no time to think like that,* I thought as I launched myself back into the battle. We were working so furiously, none of us had a chance to speak. This wasn't like regular gameplay, when you're on the outside and looking at a screen. Having witches press in on you from all sides triggers the same kind of sensations as when you're in a crowd and everyone's too close and all you can do is swallow your anxiety and try to find a way out. Only this crowd was trying to maim us, and it looked like they were going to succeed. I really wished we had some help.

Then there was snarling to my right, and one of the witches went down. More growling as I killed another witch and gathered the supplies. And then a bark as I pushed through to the last cluster of witches and saw Howl, who must've survived the attack.

"Hey girl!" I cried out. I couldn't believe that she'd made it, and that she'd managed to find her way back to me. I wanted to throw my arms around her, but a witch darting into my line of sight pulled my attention back to the battle.

Esme and Anton looked back. Howl took on the same witch I was attacking, and together we killed it. There were only two more, and Esme and Anton were taking care of those.

"I'd high-five you if you had hands, or we could even touch hands, but this'll have to do," I told Howl, giving her a bone. "How'd you make it out, girl?"

She licked herself.

"Well okay then."

Esme and Anton came back over, putting their swords away, and breathing heavily, as if it was real muscle work they were doing, and not just thinking about moving. But I got it. It was mostly the adrenaline that had us out of breath in here.

"You okay?" I asked tentatively.

"Yeah. Sorry about that, guys," Esme said sheepishly. "I thought I'd gotten over most of this stuff."

"Let's just get out of here," Anton said, "before they all respawn and we have to start over again."

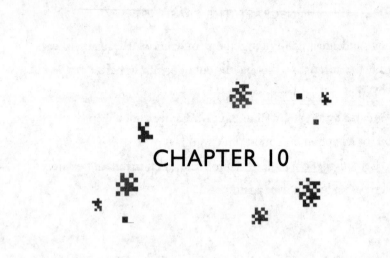

CHAPTER 10

Esme and Anton knew that they had to swing around to the right of the swamp to get back to the desert stronghold. I followed along with Lonnie on the rope, and Howl beside me. Esme kept looking back, and then getting close to Anton, clearly saying things. I tried not to let it bother me. But it did. I was tired of feeling like the outsider.

"Hey, Esme?" I called out.

"What?" she asked, already sounding annoyed.

"So, like, should we talk about your spiders or something?" I said in my most nonchalant voice. "Like, if you talked through your problems with us, we won't get mobbed as much?"

At this, I gestured to Lonnie and Anton.

"Oh, that's rich, coming from you," she scoffed.

"Es, be nice." Anton had paused as well, and looked back and forth from me to Esme. I had the feeling that if he could have gotten his avatar to smirk, he would have. "I agree with Bianca. Just air it out already. It's only going to get worse."

Esme made a stabbing motion at Anton. "I'd like to air out my fist in your face."

"For what it's worth, you're like a really great fighter," I said. "I don't think you have anything to be insecure about."

That stopped Esme in her tracks.

"Um, thanks?" she asked, suspiciously, as if she wasn't entirely sure I hadn't meant it as an insult.

After a long silence, Esme sighed.

"Fine. I was just living my life," she began. "Playing baseball, complaining about my siblings, and checking the bullies who messed with my squad. And then one day I started feeling sick, and I just wasn't getting better, and then there was a blur of doctors, and my parents' faces looked sadder and sadder. I would have to stay in the hospital for a day, or two days, or three. And then I would miss a whole week of school. Next thing I knew, I was practically living in a hospital, wishing my siblings were around to complain about or there was homework to distract me, or even a squad to stick up for."

She sighed.

"I mean, I knew the chemo was always going to make my hair fall out. I'm not a dummy, I've seen all the pictures," she began. "I just didn't think it'd happen so slowly. Like clumps at a time."

She paused as if she were struggling with her next words.

"It's worse this way, you know? I'd rather just wake up with a bald head and have it over with."

"Have you thought about getting a wig?" Anton suggested.

"Like an old lady?" Esme sounded unsure.

"It could be a cool color, like purple," I said. "Imagine rocking purple hair in the ward. It'd just be like a Minecraft skin but in real life."

"I guess I've never thought about it that way," Esme said. "That's kind of cool."

I nodded, glad to be of help for once instead of a drag on the team.

"Speaking of looking cool, I need new armor," Anton said. "Let's go."

He turned back to the path, and continued to his base. As soon as we got there, he started fiddling with the traps he had lining the path, and grunting again like he was in pain.

"You can make them again," Esme said soothingly. "You like that anyway."

We went into the house, and Esme got busy crafting arrows with all the sticks the witches had dropped. Esme and Anton were whispering to each other again.

"I really hate it when you two do that," I said. "It's irritating. If you're thinking something, why not share it with everyone who's here?"

"Meaning you," Anton said.

"And Lonnie," I said, as I deposited him into a corner of the room. Howl took up a position next to him.

"Right, Lonnie, who could turn on us at any second if it weren't for that rope," Anton said.

"Paranoid, much?"

"Paranoia is Anton's M.O.," Esme interjected. "Total paranoia." She jerked her chin toward the traps outside of the house. "Who else does stuff like that?"

"I don't know," I said. "Sometimes it's fun to set traps and demolish your friends' stuff."

Anton nodded enthusiastically.

Esme huffed. "No, that's not it. Some kid had checked him on the court and it made him a little paranoid."

Anton tilted his head. "First of all, no, I am not paranoid. Second of all, that was an illegal check and that kid should have gotten thrown out and the entire team disqualified for the whole season. They always play dirty. And third of all, that's why I don't trust anybody. Because nobody's worth trusting." He glared at Esme.

I whistled to cut the tension. "Sounds like somebody else needs to talk to the group."

"He never wants to talk about this stuff," Esme said. "That's why he built all those traps, to deal with the mobs he spawns."

"Can you not talk about me as if I'm not right here in front of both of your faces?" he shouted.

"Well, technically, neither of us are near each other," I said.

Anton aimed his avatar's face directly at me. If this was a different game and he had some kind of laser-beam eyes, I would be toast.

"We're together virtually," he said. "There isn't anything wrong with me outside other than I need to rest up."

Esme guffawed and Anton jerked away quickly. Clearly there was more to the story. I waited.

"He's not fine out in real life," Esme said. "He's hiding out in here, so of course he's thrilled to stay inside the game for as long as he can."

"Hiding from what?" I asked.

"His parents. He doesn't want to face them and tell them that he's not interested in basketball anymore."

"That's just an added bonus," he said. "I'm not hiding out."

"And!" Esme continued, her voice pitching lower as she gossiped with me: "He's also hiding from his girlfriend, who he's sure is going to break up with him the moment he's better."

"Really?" I asked, amused.

"Really," Esme said.

"Quit it, you two," Anton said.

"Look, we're all hiding out in one way or another," I said. "Basketball, nausea, broken bones, whatever it is. We might as well just play through it all in here. All four of us will play through to the End." I nodded firmly and moved next to Lonnie.

Esme turned slightly toward Anton, but seemed to catch herself before she looked him fully in the face. "I don't think there's anything we can do for him," Esme said. "He's been a lump in that corner since we got here."

"He's just going to slow us down," Anton said.

"It's better to leave him here. He'll be safe in the house, if that's what you're worried about," Esme said. "And there's a lot we have to do before we get to the End anyway. We can come back and get him."

"Listen, I owe Lonnie," I said. "He's always been there for me, even when we were little kids. I can't leave him behind now. That's not how we do."

Esme stepped forward. "Okay, I get it. But you have to be responsible for him the entire time. Okay?"

"Okay," I said, glad to finally have convinced them to let Lonnie tag along.

"All right, if we're going to play this thing, let's play."

"What's the plan?" Esme asked.

I thought back to what Lonnie had been designing all those days before the accident. He was trying to make it to the End in five steps. If we started building his traps, maybe Lonnie would recognize them.

"We know what we need to do," I said, trying to recall the designs. "We need to mine the supplies to make a run through the Nether, and then we need to make an end portal, go through, and kill the ender dragon. That's it."

"Okay, easier said than done," Esme said. "We are low on supplies, we're going to be dragging around a player who will need our protection, and who will be slowing us down at every moment."

"The first part of the plan is we're not splitting up," Anton said. "I think we also need to get supplies for a group exit portal in everyone's inventory."

"We probably have enough blocks to make a basic portal, right?" Esme said.

"Right, but we should have extra materials on hand. We'll also need diamonds to make weapons and armor," Anton said. "But as long as we've been playing, I haven't found many diamonds."

"There are diamonds back at the hill," I said. "We should start there. We'll also need a diamond pickaxe for the Nether run."

"Right, the Nether run," Anton repeated, as if he still wasn't convinced of my idea.

"Wait, wait, wait," Esme said. "Before we go, let's make all the weapons we can."

"And get our health and food points back up to full," Anton added.

"Right, smart ideas," I said.

Esme smiled. "I know you're not much for planning, but see? It's not so bad."

Ugh. She was so irritating.

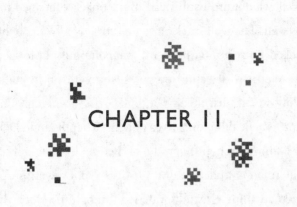

CHAPTER 11

The light in the game had gone dim by the time we left Anton's to go hunt for diamonds. Once again, Howl stayed at my heels as I pulled Lonnie along, and Anton and Esme took the lead. Our goals were clear: collect materials for two portals, one for the Nether and another for the exit out of the game. I knew which one I wanted to complete first.

As we crossed into the desert biome, a line of endermen appeared on the dunes, ominously dotting the horizon ahead of us. Endermen are usually neutral mobs. They only attack when you stare at them. But this group seemed to be gunning for us, arms outstretched in attack mode.

"You know what they say about best-laid plans," Esme said, sighing. She unsheathed her sword and got in a defense position.

"We need endermen pearls, anyway," I said, following suit. "Might as well start now."

I pushed Lonnie behind the three of us as the mob started

coming slowly toward us. Instead of waiting, we stepped toward them as well. The wolf stuck close to Lonnie, following behind.

I picked up speed, gripped my weapon, and ran to face the closest enderman. It came straight at me with no hesitation. I swung my sword, just missing it, and giving it enough time to reach me. My health points took a big hit when it landed a blow. So big, I almost thought I could feel the life draining out of me. The enderman pounded me with its fists. I put my arms up, unable to do anything else, and watched through my blocky hands as my health points dipped lower and lower. I tried to get away, but I couldn't escape. Howl ran over to help and took a hit from the enderman. She fell over, just like she had inside the caves. I worried that this was it for my wolf pal, but she thankfully stood back up after a few moments.

I heard a victorious whoop and watched as Esme finished off one of the endermen. Anton had also beaten his opponent, and I felt momentary shame that I couldn't take mine on alone. Anton ran over to help me, and delivered a couple of blows, distracting the enderman long enough that I could pull out a shield. No sooner did I have it up than the enderman turned back to me and started hitting again. This time I used the shield to cover myself, and swiped at it whenever I saw an opening. But it just kept on coming, relentless, and fear started to trickle into my veins. Anton attacked again from one side, delivering an impressive hit while Esme pulled out her bow and got it from the other. Finally, the last enderman dissolved to nothing.

Howl and I stared at each other from opposite sides of the dissipated enderman.

"I've never seen endermen behave like that," Anton said. "Bianca . . ."

"I've never seen anything like any of this," I said, cutting him off. "Attack bunny, remember?"

"Right. Attack bunny," Anton said.

"We've got work to do. Come on," I said, walking away before he could push the subject. We continued toward the hill, but when we got to the top it was clear the landscape had reset. The hole I had made was gone, and I couldn't figure out exactly where it was I'd come out. We also didn't want to get too close to the swamp full of witches, no matter how many supplies we could get from them. We moved a little bit away from each other, mining separately to widen the search area. I dug down until I came to a giant spider that scrambled out of the hole I'd just made. I screamed for help. Both Howl and Esme came to my aid. Esme jumped on top of the spider and aimed an arrow at its head, as I whacked it with a sword. The wolf attacked one of the spider's legs. The spider fell back into the hole and we tumbled after it. A few more hits later, the spider died under Esme's feet as she landed in front of me and Howl. We were inside the hill, in a tunnel, and we were surrounded again.

At least this time, it was a smaller mob than we'd met so far.

Anton jumped in to join us, bringing Lonnie with him. He pulled a couple of the spiders away as Esme and I faced the brunt of the attack, but in moments the spiders were gone, and we'd collected webs. I was going to leave the spider eyes behind, but Esme took them up.

"I'm collecting them," Esme said in response to my quizzical look. "Spiders show up when I get upset, so I'm keeping these to remind myself not to let everything get me down."

"You know," I began. "You've been through a lot. It's okay to be upset about that."

"Yeah, it is okay to be upset," Anton added. He cocked his head at me. "Bianca, maybe with the endermen . . ."

"I'm not spawning the endermen," I said sharply, although I felt some doubt starting to creep in. "We . . . we need to get going." I walked away, picking at the blocks of the floor, feeling Esme's and Anton's silence pressing in on me. After a moment, they caught up.

We continued to dig until we hit the mother lode. Diamonds. Each of us mined and gathered.

I was loading up my inventory when I thought I heard the faint sound of barking from a cave up ahead. "What's that?"

"More wolves?" Esme asked. She looked at my companion. "Seems like a weird place for them."

"Girl?" I said to the wolf. "Are those your friends?"

Howl whined.

"Does that mean yes?" Esme asked. "Are they wolves, or"— Esme and I looked at each other, excitement on our faces as we shouted—"wolf pups!"

I ran ahead, putting up torches as I moved in the direction of the wolf pups. The tunnel widened and we turned into a larger cavern with black and red walls and a litter of three wolf pups bounding around one another in the middle of it.

"Smart dogs!" Anton said. "They found us some obsidian!"

"This should be enough to make the exit portal," said Esme.

"Or the nether portal," I reminded everyone.

The pups moved to Howl, jumping and yelping.

Anton and Esme set to work mining as I bribed the pups with a few bones.

One of the pups snarled at Lonnie. "Good pooch," I said soothingly. "Nice doggie." Lonnie turned to me, and for a moment my heart stopped. I wondered if Lonnie would respond. But after a few seconds he hadn't moved, or made a sound, or even acknowledged that I was there.

"Let's go," I said to everyone.

Anton stopped mining and held out his fist, which I guessed was supposed to be a thumbs-up. I showed him mine, too. "We can go topside and build our exit—"

"Not so fast," Esme said. She swung a torch around the cave, and we all looked up. Above us were endermen lining the walls of the cave.

"Again?" Anton said. "Don't look at them. Maybe they'll leave us alone this time!"

I regretted not having crafted myself a bow and arrows, instead relying on the old faithfuls of axe and sword, because it meant I'd have to let them get close enough to hit—which meant they could hit me, too. I pulled out an iron sword and waited, hoping Anton was right, and ignoring the thought that maybe I *had* created the mobs. After a few seconds, though, I couldn't resist and peeked up at the endermen, accidentally making eye contact.

They rained down on us like black hail. Anton growled and charged at one toward the back of the cave, while Esme fired arrow after arrow into the crowd of them. I hacked my way through at one side, away from Esme's arrows and Anton's flailing. The endermen were huge, their presence as suffocating as the darkness in the cave had felt. It was almost as if any one of them could blanket my entire body and absorb me into them at a moment's notice. Then I took a hit. I instinctively moved back and away, but stumbled into another enderman behind me. I got hit again, so hard, my avatar spun around and I felt dizzy and nauseated. My health points were low. The bar was vibrating over my head once again. I wanted to shout to Esme and Anton for help, but they were in no position to do so. Another blow. I turned to face the enderman, slicing through its body with my sword, and then pivoted immediately to strike the one at my back. I screamed as I slashed. Howl and the pups helped with the attack, and then both the endermen were gone. I picked up the experience points and turned to attack another, taking hit after hit until it, too, dissipated, and I collected the ender pearl it left behind.

Straight ahead of me, Anton ran through one more of the endermen while Esme had moved to hand-to-hand combat with the final two. Anton spotted me across the cave and came running over.

"This isn't supposed to happen." He looked wildly around the cave. "We didn't even really look at them. Why did they attack?"

I looked away.

Esme stood over the last enderman, watching it disappear. She collected another ender pearl, then came to where Anton and I were standing. "That was unlucky," she said, glancing at me.

"We got some good stuff from the fight, though," I said, pulling up my inventory and taking stock of what I had.

My pulse picked up speed as I realized that we would finally have enough ender pearls for the eye of ender, one of the key items that would show us where the End was. Now we just needed to collect blaze sticks from the Nether to activate it.

I quickly constructed my diamond pickaxe and swung it around for good measure.

"Next stop, Nether!" I said, feeling triumphant.

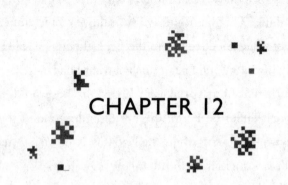

CHAPTER 12

"Where are you going?" Esme asked.

"The village," I said. "We need more supplies, and they have supplies. Seems like a good place to stock up for our trip to the Nether."

"You mean you're going to raid villagers?" Esme said. Then she tilted her head. "I approve."

"The two of you would make great mercenaries," Anton said. "You seem well suited to that kind of work."

Esme and I laughed as we set off around the hill. Lonnie stumbled after us, and the wolves bounded around us. Across the river, the village still looked about the same as the last time we'd seen it. Esme crafted boats for us and we took off across the water. I smiled at a wolf pup who was looking at me, then turned to Lonnie.

"Remember that time we crawled under the fence and into your neighbor's yard to pick their strawberries?" I asked.

Esme and Anton both looked back to see if Lonnie would respond.

"Remember how we made it all the way to their strawberry patch, but instead of picking them and running like you told me to, I started eating them on the spot, and then their tiny dog came out of the back door and chased us all around the yard? Remember that?"

Lonnie turned away from me and looked out over the water, his boat drifting a few feet away from mine.

"It's good to know that following directions has always been a problem for you," Esme said as she paddled.

"It wasn't a solid plan," I said.

"It sounds like you *ignored* the plan," Esme said. "And how did that work out for you two?"

"When we ran, we dropped a bunch of the strawberries, and the rest of them squished against our shirts as we crawled back under the fence."

Esme went, "Huh."

Anton chuckled. "Worst. Recon. Ever."

"We were eight and ten," I said. "It's not like we were an elite team or anything."

Anton laughed again. "No. Hardly."

Esme pulled up to the shore near the village, and all of us clambered out. This time, there were no villagers to greet us.

"Weird," Anton said.

"All the buildings seem to be fine," Esme said.

"Let's just go in and look around," I said.

We went up the small embankment and found the garden to the south side of the village.

"Leave your friend here," Anton said. He pointed to a fence we could tie him to. Then he looked more closely at my face, and added, "I mean while we check things out. Not permanently." He rolled his eyes.

"He's not a pet," I said. "We can't tie him to a post and go off on our own."

"You don't think he looks like a pet with you leading him around?" Esme asked. "This will make things go faster. We won't leave him behind or anything. Really."

I grudgingly tied Lonnie to an end post, and the pups happily kept him company while Howl came along with me, Esme, and Anton. Esme spotted the butcher inside the shop and went in to start making trades, but the villager didn't have anything that would help us. We tried the blacksmith, but there was nothing to trade there either.

"What is going on with this crazy game?" Anton said.

"These are all new glitches," Esme said, turning to me. "Bianca, you need to start talking."

"Listen, I don't have anything to confess," I said. "I'm just here to help Lonnie fix his avatar."

"What about you in the real world?" Esme said. "I know you don't want to go back to your hospital bed where you've been mashed to a pulp and your best friend is probably . . ." At this she paused, and Anton herded her down a path that was a little bit away from me. The two of them put their heads together like they were talking. I was totally uninterested in what they were saying. I was sick of being blamed. I had no more control over the game than they did.

A few moments later, Anton and Esme came back.

"Listen, I'm sorry that we're on your case all the time about this," Anton said. "But we've been doing this awhile now, and this is the best way we know to work through our problems—by sharing."

"Then what about yours?" I asked. "Why do you have to build traps all around your house like that?"

"Me?" Anton asked, surprised by my question. "Ha, where to even begin? Okay, if I tell you why I build the traps, will you promise to exit the game with us when we ask you to?"

"Depends on how bad your problems are, I guess," I bluffed. I had no plans to leave the game without having fixed Lonnie first.

Anton kicked around some dirt blocks.

"Before all the brain injury stuff, I was on track for a basketball scholarship," he said. "It was a huge deal for my parents. They're so proud, you know? They want me to set an example for my brother and sister. And basketball was my ticket to college. But now, I don't know anymore. It's all up in the air. I've missed too many practices and too much school. And . . ." He paused for a long while. "There's also the fact that while I'm good at basketball, I don't really love playing. There was a part of me that was glad when I took the hit and woke up in the hospital." He looked away from me and Esme before finishing. "So skeletons like to attack my house a lot when I start worrying about what I'll do when I have to go back to school. But I've learned to anticipate and manage it with all the traps.

"They're easier to deal with than Esme's mobs, at least," Anton finished. "They're only interested in tearing my house apart."

"What are their names?" I asked. "Your siblings, I mean."

"Oscar and Tara," he said.

"Older or younger?" I asked.

"Both younger. I'm supposed to be taking care of them." Anton paused. "That hasn't been true in a while."

"My little sister is Carrie," I said. "Carolyn. I miss her, too." I felt a wave of sadness rising through me. Carrie was no gamer. But she actively tried to get into every game Lonnie and I played, just so I'd pay attention to her. I always shooed her away, but now I wished I hadn't done that. I took a breath, surprised at the sting behind my eyes. I was glad avatars didn't cry. When Lonnie and I were done taking down the ender dragon, I promised myself, I'd exit the game and tell Carrie I was sorry for being mean and ignoring her. "What do they do when you're in here? And by 'here' I mean the hospital, not this game."

"They do their regular stuff, tae kwon do, ballet," Anton said. "My parents don't want them to think I'm the focus of all their attention or anything, so they try to keep them doing all the stuff they were already doing before I got sick."

"How long has it been?" I asked.

"About a year," Anton said. "It's a long time to have my life on pause." He took a deep breath before continuing. "Now what do you say, Bianca? How about we meet in real life? Esme and I can come to your room."

I turned to look at Esme, and noticed an exit portal behind her. While Anton was telling his story, Esme had created one that all of us could travel through. It was a carbon copy of the one that was broken at Anton's place. The sight of it made my stomach knot with worry.

"We need to go now, Bianca," Esme said, gently, as if she were trying to calm down a rabid animal. "It's probably almost morning. I have a chemo treatment first thing. You should come with us."

I knew I should. It was the logical thing to do. But out there—in the real world—there were real-world things to deal with. Questions I'd have to answer. But in here, no one was asking anything. No one but Lonnie knew, and he wasn't talking.

"I don't want to leave without fixing Lonnie first," I said. "I'm going to make my way to the Nether."

"What for?" Esme asked. "What's the point?"

"We had a plan," I said. "Get everything we need to get to the End and take on the ender dragon to fix Lonnie." My voice cracked a little, but I forged ahead. "We're supposed to go on a run to the Nether now, that's the next step. You said we'd stick together." I looked at Anton, and then Esme. "We made a plan, and I'm going to follow it."

"By yourself?" she asked. "That's total insanity."

"Come on, Bianca, we'll come back later and play it through with you." Anton was edging closer to me. I noticed that Esme had a rope in her hands now, the same kind that we'd used to tie up Lonnie. If they thought they could drag me through the portal, they had another think coming.

I backed away from them slowly. Before I could turn to run, Esme had lassoed me, pinning my arms.

"No! I'm not leaving! You can't make me!" I screamed. I thought about the TNT I had in my inventory, and how I needed a distraction. It suddenly appeared and detonated instantly in front of us. We were blown back in different directions. My health bar took a major hit. The rope disintegrated from around my avatar, as Anton and Esme were thrown back into the exit portal. They disappeared behind the diamond blocks. Just when I thought my troubles were over, the portal began to shake and turn completely black. It wasn't inky like an obsidian block, but like someone had pressed delete on all the color in the world. To my horror, the darkness began to surge toward me, swallowing up the wolves in a yawning chasm. Pixels were falling away and disappearing into the black. The game was closing.

I knew there was nothing I could do if the game shut down, but I admit, I panicked and reacted with the first thing I could think of. "Lonnie!" I called. "We have to get out of here."

Lonnie turned to look at me.

"Lonnie!" I screamed. "Run!" I waved my hands and pointed toward the boat.

He took a slow, uncertain step in that direction.

"Right. Run!" I shouted.

Then I noticed everything around me was turning dull. In some places the pixels all but went out, leaving behind tiny square holes with nothing behind them. The entire village, the few villagers, the wolves, all of them started losing their color, pixel by pixel. The edges around the game had blackened to char and were beginning to fall away like perfectly square panes of glass. The entire world faded from view. I felt alone in a vast space of nothing. It felt like a void—no color, no sound, no feeling. It was like a blank test space that no one had coded yet. I couldn't even see myself. I wasn't sure if I was really there—wherever *there* was—or not. I tried to speak, but nothing came out. I didn't even know what I would have said. My mind felt dull, too, like even it had been wiped out.

A moment later a blinding light appeared. I squeezed my eyes shut, then tried to open them again slowly. The light was still too bright, but it was reminiscent of the goggles' lobby menu. I didn't want to leave the game! Just as I was about to say something, I was plunged back into the void.

After several minutes everything started to come back into view. The world around me populated slowly: a few blades of grass, the brown of the shore of the river, a few cubes of blue popped up and were joined by others in varying shades. A moment later the ground appeared, and my feet with it. I was standing on a patch of green next to a few squares of brown. The fence slowly solidified next to me, and then my hand, and the rope I was holding. I didn't even know when I had managed to grab it. The end of the rope hung in midair a moment, and then Lonnie slowly appeared.

The garden came back. I wasn't sure if anything had changed there, so I turned to the village. The butcher's shop appeared, and the butcher. I looked across to the stone road where Esme, Anton, and I had stood moments before, but they didn't reappear.

I waited, hoping with every moment that my friends would show up and everything would be fine. If I had fingers I would have crossed them. Instead I held Lonnie's rope, and looked around feverishly as the village repopulated. But even after everything had reappeared—the river ahead of me, and the hills beyond—Esme, Anton, and the wolves I had tamed never came back.

I pulled Lonnie back to the boats, which had miraculously respawned in the same place, and took him across the river. Night was coming and we needed to go somewhere safe. We got out of the boats and started to wander upstream, around the other side of the hill. On the way, I gathered supplies from a couple of chickens and a passing cow. It was enough to manage our hunger levels for a while, but I knew I'd need to get more. A couple of zombies dotted the hillside, and I sidestepped them rather than fight. They seemed content to lumber on without much fuss, and I let them. We trudged through flowers and dirt and made it to a stone ledge on a hill. I cut a little farther into the ledge and put up a shelter on the overhang. The stone of the hill was to our backs, and the front of the house faced the river. To get to us, mobs would have to climb up the face of the hill, and I'd hear them coming with enough time to mount a defense if I needed to.

There were enough supplies to make a single room with a bed. I'd break it down in the morning for wood, and craft a bow and arrows. Without Esme and Anton, I would have to get through the game alone.

I left the bed to Lonnie and looked out the window at the village lit up downstream. I hoped Esme and Anton weren't too mad at me. But there was a part of me—and it was a bigger part than I'd ever admit to anyone—that was glad they weren't around to nag me about opening up with my feelings.

I pulled up the inventory. There was enough material to make an exit. I could do it, I could exit the game, too, and see how they were doing. But then what about Lonnie? What about the plan he had so meticulously laid out, the plan that I was trying now to follow?

"Prepare, plan, power through," I said aloud. I decided that I would see this through to the End. I racked my brain to remember what the next steps in Lonnie's plan were. There was a fortress I needed to find in the Nether, one made out of nether bricks. Once I got there, I had to kill blazes and collect their sticks. I felt like I was forgetting something key. Didn't Lonnie say there was a trick to this?

"Lonnie, can you remember how you wanted to take down the blazes?"

Lonnie lay flat on the bed, eyes staring up at the ceiling. I'd come to expect no response by now. But there was something about Lonnie's pose that made my stomach knot. I didn't want to linger on it too much.

I walked outside the hut, opened my inventory, and placed all the obsidian blocks in the shape I needed—a window four blocks wide and five blocks high. Stepping back, I used my flint and steel. The pane of the window glowed purple.

The nether portal stood before me, beckoning me to walk through.

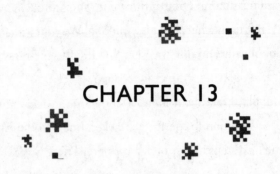

CHAPTER 13

I stepped toward the portal when a little memory niggled in the back of my mind—the image of Lonnie shaking his head at me, smiling.

I looked back in the direction of where Lonnie was. Was he reaching out to me somehow?

"Lonnie?" I asked no one in particular.

"When we get to the Nether, it's going to be fire-and-brimstone levels of epic," Lonnie's voice floated into my head. "We're going to need this."

The memory sucked me in like a vortex. The sensation of falling in midair overcame me for a second. Before I could even open my mouth to scream, I was back in my own body from weeks ago. I was looking down at my computer screen at a digital snowball.

I tried to jump up, but nothing happened. I was stuck in a movie version of my life, watching everything happen in playback mode. Lonnie's face appeared in another window on the screen, his bright red headphones pinning down his short afro. He needed a haircut. He almost never let it get that long. We were video chatting that day because Lonnie was sick with the flu. Sickness never stopped us from playing Minecraft, though.

"A snowball?" I heard myself ask.

"Yeah, they are going to deal the most damage to the blazes," Lonnie said. "Get it? Ice cools off the flames."

"And let me guess, we're going to need to build another crazy contraption to make snowballs."

"Bingo!" A *ping* went off in my email inbox. I opened the latest message from Lonnie. It was a guide to creating snow golems, which basically looked like blocky snowmen with pumpkin heads. These were the mobs that could produce snowballs for us.

The instructions read: *"In order to create snow golems, make snow blocks by stacking the snowballs into groups of four, and putting a pumpkin on top."* Seemed simple enough. There were also rules about where we could build snow golems and where we could keep them. We would also have to stack the snowballs into snow blocks so that we could transport more arsenal into the Nether.

"Ugh, Lonnie, this looks complicated," I said.

"No pain, no gain," he responded. "Here, I'll start off making the golems for us to show you. Can you just build us a shelter so that if it rains, they don't all melt?"

"Hey, I have a better idea. Why don't we go to the football game on Friday night?" I asked. "It's the big homecoming one, isn't it? And our schools are playing against each other! We're officially rivals! You can introduce me to all your high school buddies and—"

"Bianca, are you even listening to me?"

The world went dark after that question. I stood motionless, my heart thumping with regret. That was the last conversation we would have before the ride to the homecoming game. I would forget about building what Lonnie asked. Those snow golems were probably all puddles now. I had let my best friend down. I didn't want to be there. I didn't want to be in the real world.

"I want to be back in the game!" I shouted. I squeezed my eyes shut. It was like a black hole had opened in my mind and I was struggling to stop myself from getting sucked in. I didn't want to see what was on the other side of it. I didn't want to know what would happen if I let it take ahold of me. I thought I might shatter into a thousand pieces. "Take me back!"

I opened my eyes and I was back by the nether portal I had built. It was daylight and I let out a big sigh of relief. Lonnie was standing beside me now, looking at me intently.

"Thank you for the reminder," I whispered to him. "And . . . and I'm sorry for not listening before."

I needed snowballs. I climbed up to the top of the hill and, surveying the realm around me, spotted a cold taiga biome at the limit of my vision. There would be plenty of snow for snowballs there.

I gestured to Lonnie. "Follow me."

As we trekked across the landscape, I began to feel a lot better.

For the briefest of moments, this was just a game. It was a regular day, and we were the kids we used to be when we played in our own homes. I had made the right decision not to leave the game. I was better off sticking with Lonnie, just like he had always stuck by me. I owed him that much. It was always him and me against the world. There was no reason to change that just because I met two other people one time in a game. Esme and Anton were not even that nice to me anyway, always whispering out of earshot when they thought I couldn't hear, and blaming me for the endermen attacks.

I did not know how long we would have to travel. But I knew we had to cross the desert biome again in order to reach the colder one. Every once in a while I would reorient myself to make sure we were headed in the right direction. I saw that we were about to pass Anton's house again. Only this time some big commotion was happening in that direction. As we got closer, I scouted ahead.

"Check it," I said to Lonnie, pointing to the top of a sand dune. "Slime mob."

As we moved closer, a couple of skeletons showed up. The combination of their clacking and the hopping and squelching from the slime made a terrible chorus. Anton hadn't had time to reset all of his traps, so there was nothing stopping them from overwhelming the house, destroying what he had probably spent days to build.

I instantly felt guilty. It was my fault that his traps were all deactivated. The least I could do was vanquish these mobs for him.

Taking out my sword, I charged in, giving my best warrior yell.

I bashed through the little slimes that were at my feet while keeping the skeletons away from Lonnie. A huge slime hopped toward me, one of the big size-4 ones. I kept slashing though, cutting it down by half and half again, and then collecting slime balls. But more huge ones popped up, surrounding me.

I tried to move more quickly through the slime mobs and the horde of skeletons that kept popping up from the sand, but nothing was reducing the number of attackers. One of them got Lonnie and he fell down the side of the dune. None of the other mobs seemed to notice him there, so I left him where he was and continued fighting. A slime got me from the left, and I watched my health points go down as I staggered back, away from the fighting. But there was a zombie behind me, which punched me and drained more of my health points. I slashed it a few times until it died. It left behind an iron shovel that I wished I could use to bash the skeletons' heads in, but I put it away for later. I turned back to the slime mob, which seemed to have gotten smaller.

The last couple of attacks had moved me down the dune a bit closer to Lonnie, so I fought to get back on top and move the fighting away from him. Even I knew that having the high ground would give me the advantage. For that, I'd need to fight through this seemingly never-ending horde. As Anton had said before, these mobs were legendary.

I pulled up my supplies and took out sand, flint, and gunpowder. I ran off, around the side of one of the really big slime cubes. Just as it turned toward me, I threw the TNT I'd made on the ground between us. The blast made a crater going straight down.

The slime moved toward me and fell into the hole. A couple of smaller ones followed.

The skeletons were a little harder to corral but a couple of them fell in too. As they dropped, I delivered fatal blows with my bow and arrows. Then I gathered slime balls, bones, and a potato as they went down.

"We can't leave you alone for one moment, can we?" said a familiar voice behind me. I twisted around and was surprised to see Anton and Esme standing there, armored up like they were about to make a run to the End.

"What are you guys doing here?" I asked. "I thought I had . . ."

"Blown us out of the game with TNT?" Esme chimed in. "Yeah, you definitely did that. Locked us both out of the game."

"Luckily, the doctor on duty this morning let us back in," Anton said.

"Did he say anything about Lonnie?" My heart beat wildly.

"Bianca," Esme said slowly.

The pounding in my chest was unbearable. I could feel each thud of my pulse like a drumbeat, and it only hit harder when Esme said my name like that. "It's okay," I interrupted. "If the doctor didn't know anything, I mean. Every doctor doesn't know every patient, right? And besides, we should be focusing on the plan here. Next steps and all that."

Esme stared at me for a long second before saying, "Yeah, next steps. We think we need to visit A.J.'s place. He's created most of the complex mods in here."

"Why his house?" I asked. "A.J.'s just a kid."

"Just, nothing. A.J. has all the cheat codes, and knows way more about this game than we do," Anton said.

"So, where is he now?"

"He keeps rebuilding," Esme said. "Always someplace new. He likes to blow up the stuff he's made and start over again when the world resets, and he spawns in a new location."

"Which means he's hard to find," Anton said.

"Which way, then?" I asked.

"Last I checked, he started a big fortress in the taiga biome. That's probably our best bet."

"Great, I'm headed there anyway," I said, glad that this new side quest Esme and Anton were forcing on me would take me where I already wanted to be.

We moved north, following the river until it turned. We skirted the swamp and, before it got dark, worked together to put up a house on the side of a hill, overlooking a valley. The going was slow. I did most of the work, still feeling pretty bad for when I kicked them out of the game. But when it came to the traps, Anton wanted to put them together himself. It was going to take a while, so I decided to use the time to scrounge up some more supplies.

I moved to the next hill and started mining down. There was a seam of coal inside that I followed, putting up torches as I went. I found and kept some sand, too. I mined all the way through the hill and came out the other side to a plain that was flooded on one end with a lake, on which a little island of what looked like weeping willows stood. I suddenly wished for real water, a real island to lie on in the sun. I longed for soft lines, my mother's face looking into my own, my father's hand rubbing my back in that way that always made me feel better, the tangle of Carrie's limbs when she climbed into my bed. My entire family was out in the real world. But I couldn't log out. I didn't want to, not until I finished what Lonnie and I had started.

It was starting to get dark. Time to get back.

I hurried back over this new landscape to the three-floor house we'd made in record time. "That'll teach them I'm no noob," I said aloud as I got close to the house, and Anton stepped out, waving me over to the side. I was going to ignore him when I remembered that he was big on traps. I followed his directions and found a small door cut into the hill itself. It led to a tunnel that opened into the house.

"Look at this," Anton announced. "We found redstone in the hill." He slumped against a wall. Lonnie stared out of one of the windows. The darkness had settled in, and I waited for the mobs to start attacking. I handed Esme a diamond sword we made from the haul on the hill, and took up a position near the front door while she replenished her food points.

"What if we don't find A.J.?" she said. "He might not even be in the game today. The doctors have been in his room a lot lately."

"He came into my room rocking his 'gamer for life' pajamas and Minecraft slippers," I said. "I have a feeling that kid is always in the game."

There were the sounds of zombies and slimes nearby, but none of them ever made it all the way to the house we'd built. It felt nice, to actually be able to pass the night in relative safety for once. As light came up again, I breathed a sigh of relief.

When all of the mobs disappeared, Esme said we should get some food. A mooshroom had appeared on some grassy terrain in the valley below, and she went after it. I stayed near the house, and chased around a couple of chickens and a rabbit for meat and eggs.

"Want to help?" I asked when I noticed Lonnie had followed me. I held my hand out to him, and he came along.

"I'd feel better if you put the rope back on him," Anton said.

"No," I said. "You guys were right before. If I want to get my friend back, I have to start treating him like my friend, not a pet."

I looked at Lonnie, and he turned back to me in a way that made me wonder how much of him was in there, and how much he might have been holding back. Anton cleared his throat, ending the moment, and said, "We should probably get going."

We found another forest biome and built the next shelter there, inside a thick copse of trees. This time we went wide instead of high. The two rooms on either end were set to explode, depending on where you stepped, thanks to some clever wiring by Anton. The inner rooms were where we would stay. In the event of an attack, we'd have plenty of time to escape via a tunnel Esme and I dug that led to another thicket of trees. Between the wired-to-explode house hidden in the trees, the tunnel, and the next set of trees as cover for an escape, we should have been fine.

Should have been.

After the tunnel was built, Esme and I made our way back

through it to the house, hopping over one carefully hidden pressure plate that was our last-ditch effort if we were overwhelmed and still needed to run. I looked back at our handiwork when we got to the house again. Not going to lie, I was really impressed with what we had done.

"Pretty cool, right?" Anton commented.

"Yes, Anton, your traps are the best around," Esme admitted.

He grinned. "Anything that comes even remotely near is going to get blown sky-high."

Night came quickly, and we hunkered down in beds to make it pass more quickly. But as soon as we lay down, there were explosions from the front and sides of the house. I ran to the nearest window and watched as a mob of zombies got blasted to smithereens. I was just about to celebrate when another wave surged forward. More explosives went off. I held my hand up and Anton slapped me high-five. But there was a third wave, which included a creeper, and the mob had gotten dangerously close to the house.

"Time to fall back?" I suggested.

"Nope," Anton said with confidence. "Wait for it."

Two of the zombies went for the door while a third went around to the side of the house. I worried about the door, but I knew the traps would keep anything back.

As the first of the two zombies got near the door, there was the click of a trigger, and then the sound of a low whistle that got louder and louder, and then *bam!* Both of them got smashed by an anvil. Anton laughed. The third zombie off to the side kept moving until it hit a pressure plate and was immediately blown up.

Anton turned to us, clearly pleased with himself.

But the creeper had hesitated near the zombies at the door, and with both of them gone, and the two traps set off, it entered. It didn't know it was a booby-trapped room. It took a couple of steps forward, somehow missing the triggers, and I held my breath.

"No way will it miss them all," Anton said.

"I think it's time to fall back like Bianca said," Esme suggested. She started putting away supplies, and led Lonnie toward the escape hatch.

The creeper was still coming. It still hadn't tripped any of the traps.

"How is that possible?" Anton asked. "I was sure that I'd—"

"Doesn't matter now," Esme said. "Let's go!"

All four of us made our way down the escape hatch. I stayed behind a beat to close it tightly as Esme went on ahead, lighting up torches so we could see our way through, and so we wouldn't accidentally trip our own trigger. I saw when she helped Lonnie jump over it, and Anton followed. But I felt a cold wind at my neck, and looked back in time to spot the creeper coming toward me. I wished I still had Howl. She was a real scrapper and had come in handy in every close fight I'd had so far. Instead I turned and ran, hopping over the pressure plate and running to catch up with Esme, Anton, and Lonnie. Before we made it to the exit, the trigger went off and the blast from the explosion knocked us to the ground.

We made it out to the trees. I was grateful to see the flat, squared-off clouds in the night sky.

"Do you see this?" Esme said. "There's a path here."

There was a thin trail that wound through the trees, but it barely qualified as a path. "I'm not so sure," I said.

"The world doesn't generate this way," she said. "I've been playing in here long enough to know what's a path and what isn't."

I looked at Anton for confirmation, but he only shrugged. Lonnie trudged behind Esme and I took up the rear again, trying to make note of exactly which way we were headed in case we needed to double back.

We walked until daylight again, moving pretty consistently upward. There were more rabbits up this way, which we saved for meat. Through a little tangle of bushes, I spotted another gray wolf, and moved in closer. "Hey," I said. It looked at me briefly before running away.

"What?" Esme asked.

"Did you see that wolf?" I asked.

"No," Esme and Anton said together.

"It's just, I was thinking about Howl, and then all of a sudden, here was this wolf, and—"

"And there are plenty of wolves in the game. It's not a coincidence or anything," Esme said sarcastically.

I scoffed and walked ahead. We moved on to a high, rocky cliff that overlooked a frozen biome. Down below was a large building near a lake of solid ice. I got excited just looking at it.

"That's it," I said.

"How are you so sure?" Anton asked.

"It's weird and complicated," I said. "Exactly the kind of space a kid would build. It reminds me of A.J. Besides, what else do we have to do? It's not going to kill us to look."

"Famous last words," Anton added.

"It's pretty far down, though," I said, looking over the side of the cliff.

Anton pushed me aside. "It's Minecraft," he said. "You can literally cut away steps on your way down."

"Right," I said.

"Well?" he asked. "Those stairs aren't going to make themselves. And you're the one who wants to check out the house." He gestured over the cliff.

"Oh come on, Anton," Esme said, exasperated. "We're all in this together."

He groaned but walked over, pulling out his pickaxe to help me create a staircase in the side of the cliff. Esme also pitched in, and I smiled, grateful for their help. I could almost feel the relief rising through me that I wasn't alone, that they were actually going to help me follow through with the plan.

I glanced over at A.J.'s fortress. A.J. was the one who got me into the game to begin with; surely he had the cheat codes to fix my friend.

"Not much longer now, Lonnie," I said, as I cut another step down through the frozen rock.

CHAPTER 14

"Oh come on, A.J.! What is this nonsense?!" Anton threw his arms in the air.

There was a wide river of lava separating us from what looked like a much more ambitious gauntlet of protections than Anton had on the desert house.

"What? Because he put protections around his home base?" I asked. "You did the same thing."

He walked a little way to the left. "Look at that, it's redstone wiring."

"Exposed?" Esme asked.

Anton moved a little farther along, ignoring Esme's question. "Those are pressure plates. I'm sure of it." He lay down on the ground and crawled forward, looking toward the side of the house. "Yep. Definitely pressure plates, and they go around this way . . ." He trailed off and set to running. We followed him to the side of the house where it became clear that what we were looking at was a complicated array of levers, trapdoors, and pressure plates attached to who knows what, arranged in an elaborate labyrinth that surrounded the house entirely.

"How old is this kid again?"

"Eleven," Esme said.

"He's a genius," Anton said, and he was actually serious and sounded like he was in awe.

"A.J. has way more time on his hands," Esme said.

"More time than we, who are stuck in hospital beds, do?" I asked.

"Even though he's younger than us, A.J.'s been at the hospital way longer than any of us," she said.

"Whoa, that's harsh." I couldn't imagine what it might be like to spend most of your life sick. Dr. Nay had told my parents that I was looking at three months in the hospital and then half a year in rehab. In my mind, I was preparing myself to spend Christmas looking at a beige ceiling. I'd miss the rest of my freshman semester.

I shook my head and surveyed the field of traps we'd have to navigate. "I don't think even you could make this, Lonnie," I whispered.

Lonnie shuffled along the back end of the house, staying near us, but then he turned and moved away. I ran to catch up with him and corralled him back to where the rest of us stood.

Esme looked on silently as I managed to get him back and wedge him between the two of us so there was nowhere to go.

"What if Lonnie's like that forever?" she asked. "What then?"

"He won't be," I said with more conviction than I actually felt. And then I added, "I'll make sure of it."

"How?" she asked.

"I'm his oldest friend," I said. "If anybody can bring him back, it's me."

"The question is, what are you bringing him back from?"

"He's my best friend," I said. "I'll bring him back from anything."

She nodded, looking hesitant, and walked away after Anton. He was whistling and muttering under his breath, pointing to parts of A.J.'s defense system as if Esme and I were still paying any attention to him at all. During a longer than normal pause in his running commentary of how awesome all of A.J.'s traps were, Esme offered a noncommittal "Uh-huh," and Anton started up all over again.

I remembered getting a shovel from one of the mob drops, so I used it to dig up snowballs as we circled back to the front of the house. I would need these for my attack on the nether fortress.

"So," I said. "How do we get inside?"

"I'm sure I can figure it out," Anton said. "It's just going to take some time."

"We know where not to step," I said. "Anywhere there's redstone wiring is going to be a problem."

Anton chuckled and shook his head. "You really are a noob! Do you think a kid who could make this wouldn't know to camouflage every trap?"

"Except he didn't," I said.

"Except he wants you to think he didn't," Anton said.

Esme grunted. "You mean there are decoys."

"Exactly," said Anton.

Suddenly she seemed almost as enthralled with A.J.'s traps as Anton was.

"Listen, none of that helps us to get inside," I said.

"Just wait," Anton said, exasperated. "I can figure it out. Even with the decoys. Clever little kid."

I took a turn around the house again. I was sure Anton would eventually figure out how to get into the house, but, in the meantime, it had been daylight for a while and I expected night to rise on the digital tundra soon. I didn't want to be exposed when the mobs came out. We needed to avoid that at all costs. I didn't think Lonnie would survive another attack with no way to defend himself. I needed to find a place to stash him, so I decided to do my own recon.

The house rose several floors. About five floors up, there was a glass enclosure that looked like there was plenty of foliage on the inside. A greenhouse, maybe. The bottom floors were mostly windowless—more defenses, I guessed—so the greenhouse might have been the best natural source of light in the house. And based on the way Anton kept going around and around muttering to himself, lying flat on the ground, squatting, and looking at the labyrinth of traps at every angle, it was the only way to get inside.

"Stay here," I said to Lonnie. I had an idea, but it would require me to go it alone. Lonnie looked at me, and when I moved away, he didn't follow. I smiled at him, then turned back to the greenhouse.

Although it took me a minute to puzzle out, I was pretty certain I could make out a clear path up to the greenhouse. If I could follow it precisely and not touch any other part of the ground, then I could get right up to the side of the structure and knock out one of the cubes on the first floor and get inside. I took a deep breath, then jumped to a raised, snow-covered block.

Nothing happened, so I jumped to the next area, and again, no traps went off. I laughed and looked back at Lonnie, who was still standing where I'd left him, watching me successfully navigate A.J.'s booby-traps.

"Stop!" Anton yelled as I jumped to the next block. He and Esme started running toward me, and it felt like time slowed down as I landed. I felt rather than heard the click of a hidden pressure plate, and then time sped up.

There wasn't much time to react.

Esme grabbed Anton, and tugged him away.

I turned and sprinted back the way I came, not bothering to watch where I was stepping anymore, and tackled Lonnie. We fell to the ground and skidded away, but it wasn't far enough.

A.J.'s traps triggered with spectacular force. A series of flaming arrows flew toward us. Most stuck in the ground, burning in place, but a few of them hit us. The sharp stab of the arrow piercing me was bad enough, but the fire . . . I started to crawl away, but Lonnie sat where he was, pinned by three arrows that hit his legs and arm. I tried to pull him away, but another volley of arrows rained down. I put my arms over my head and hoped for the best. Then there were a series of explosions, so loud that they left my ears ringing. All four of us crawled away from the blasts just as the ground behind us fell open like a trapdoor and disappeared into a lake of lava.

It was the first time I was really feeling anything inside the game. And it wasn't good. I realized this could be an effect of being inside for too long. My mind was creating sensations that weren't really there, but it wasn't time to leave yet. I couldn't. Not now.

I continued crawling back into a snowbank that thankfully put out all the fire from the arrows. Esme and Anton were still approaching when a third volley came at us. This looked like flaming balls that fell like black hail, hard and fast. They sank into the ground, sizzling as they melted into the snow, then exploded pixels of dirt. I pulled Lonnie up onto the snowbank with me, and tried to yell at Esme and Anton to get out of the way. My throat felt strained, as if I were screaming at the top of my lungs. Still, neither of them moved. Maybe they couldn't. I didn't know. It suddenly occurred to me that their hearing might have been affected by the first set of blasts as well.

I pulled Lonnie to the other side of the small rise, then ducked for cover. A blocky hand grabbed hold of the top of our paltry snow shelter, and I grabbed it and pulled. Esme tumbled over, and then Anton. She was saying something to me, but I couldn't hear. She looked like she was shouting. Anton's face was twisted with pain. Only Lonnie appeared relatively calm, despite the bright red wounds that bloomed on his body.

Esme pulled herself to standing a few moments later and looked over the rocks. She turned back to Anton and told him something else. He nodded, and shifted his body to the right, leaning out so he could see the house. He nodded again, and she pulled him to his feet.

I pushed my way up and looked at A.J.'s house. The triggers had all stopped firing, but there was an enormous gray crater where I had been jumping earlier. I pulled Lonnie gently along to survey the damage. The house, amazingly, was totally unharmed even though the crater was huge. The kid was impressive, I had to admit. He probably had a future in demolition.

All four of us stood over the crater, looking dazed, not moving, until Esme walked up behind me and shoved me into the hole. I fell against a rock. A shard hit my shoulder and sent me spinning down another level, rolling to a stop just before another drop that led to the lava lake. I got to my knees and looked up. Esme screamed at me, but I couldn't make out anything she was saying, even though—good news—my hearing was already coming back. It was incredible how quickly people healed inside the game. If only it were that way on the outside.

I waited until Esme walked away from the hole to climb out. I wasn't an idiot.

When I got out, Lonnie was the only one waiting for me at the edge of the crater. Esme and Anton sat against the same snowbank we'd used for cover, talking between themselves. Lonnie's hand reached over and brushed against my own. I looked into his eyes, searching for signs of the friend I had out in the real world. He tilted his head, the way the real Lonnie sometimes did when he was waiting for me to figure something out. I knew what that thing was. I would have to confront Esme and Anton at some point.

It was better to get it over with.

I moved closer to them, taking Lonnie with me as backup. "I didn't know that was going to happen," I said.

Esme looked up, narrowing her eyes. "Why?" she asked.

I had no idea what she meant, so I waited.

She stood up. "Why didn't you know that was going to happen?" she asked. She stepped closer as she talked so she was right in my face by the end of the question.

I took a big step back. "How could I know?"

She laughed. Anton frowned, and Lonnie looked at me in that same head-tilted way.

"I was figuring it out," Anton said. "You could have waited."

There were a lot of good responses to that. I could have said, *I know, I'm sorry*, or even *You're right*, or maybe *I'm a giant idiot and I wouldn't be offended if you abandoned me here*. But instead, "You were taking forever" is what came out. "I needed to find a place for Lonnie to be safe."

Anton got to his feet with a little difficulty and glared at me. Esme stood next to him, as though she was there to support him in case he wanted to lay into me too. She eyed me angrily, but then turned off toward the house.

"What's the point?" she asked. "It's not even worth it." She let Anton lean against her shoulder as they went.

Lonnie looked at me once, then began to follow them as they skirted the edge of the crater. I let out a huff of frustration before I followed them.

Anton carefully examined the wooden door and frame as if he thought it might be explosive too. This time, I waited. I had learned my lesson. Then Lonnie pushed Anton aside, opened the door, and stepped into the house.

I cringed.

Nothing happened.

When I opened my eyes again, Lonnie was standing inside a large room looking back at the rest of us as if we were stupid to think that a kid who'd spent that much time on defenses outside the house would think he *still* needed another trap at the door.

Anton looked annoyed. But he stepped inside. I followed exactly in Esme's tracks, not wanting to cause any more trouble than I already had. But as we followed Anton moving carefully around the ground floor rooms, we all relaxed more and more. A.J.'s house was something of a funhouse with a few practical items thrown in.

Exactly like something out of an eleven-year-old's imagination.

The first room had a large fireplace crackling in one corner and a waterfall streaming in the other. Against one wall was a bookshelf, and a table with a lamp. I picked up one book that said RULES on the spine. Inside it said:

1. Don't play with the chickens.
2. Don't touch the levers.
3. Don't go to the fourth level.
4. Don't use the ladder.

I read them out for everyone to hear. Lonnie went up a couple of steps into the next room but Anton stopped him before he got too far inside, saying, "Hold up," and pushing past him. This next room was smaller than the first and packed with crates lining the floor against one wall. Anton went through each one. They were filled with A.J.'s supplies. There was a bed in the opposite corner and a ladder near the foot of the bed leading to the next level.

"Don't use the ladder," I repeated.

Esme put her hand on it anyway, as if she was testing it out. "It seems fine."

"There must be another way up," I said. I moved around the room looking for another passageway, but there was only a door at the back to the next room, which had stone floors and a series of levers against two of the walls. Anton studied them carefully.

Esme put a foot on the bottom rung of the ladder, and tested her weight on it. "Still seems fine."

"Don't," Anton whispered fiercely. His eyes cut to both of us. "Neither of you move a muscle."

"Nor a pixel," I said, attempting a laugh, but another sharp glare from both Anton and Esme sent me looking around the room as if it was the most fascinating assemblage of digital landscape I'd ever encountered. I turned to Lonnie and asked, "Do you want to sit?"

"You remember sitting, don't you?" Esme said, mocking.

"Shhh!" Anton sniped. "I'm trying to figure this out."

"Yes, sitting is very distracting," I said.

"Getting blown up in this game definitely *is* distracting," he said. And when he noticed me rolling my eyes at him, he muttered.

"Do you honestly think he'd set traps inside his own home base when the outside is so well guarded?" I asked.

"Doesn't matter," Esme said. "You need to work faster, or I'm going up the ladder."

"No, you're not," I said.

"You will want to get on this ladder too," she said as she pointed out the window.

Outside, it was getting dark, which wasn't the worst thing. No, the worst thing was that a horde of zombies had appeared and circled the building and the blast hole, and they all seemed to be looking in at us, getting closer every moment. The noise from when I triggered A.J.'s traps must have alerted them to our location. And there were a lot of them. Dozens. Nope. Hundreds. Line after line of digital mayhem approached.

I looked at Anton and said, "Hurry up!"

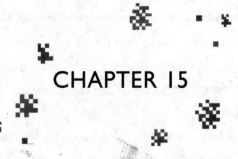

CHAPTER 15

"Do something!" I said again. I pushed Lonnie down into the chair and looked from Esme—who still had one foot on the lowest rung of the ladder and two hands firmly on the sides—to Anton, who was now lying on his stomach looking at what appeared to be a small crevice between the floor and the wall.

"It's a false wall," he said.

"And?" I asked.

Esme still hadn't changed position, but she had out her bow and an arrow aimed at the door and the growing darkness outside.

"Well?" I asked again.

"Hold on," Anton said impatiently.

Esme stepped away from the ladder and positioned herself next to the bookshelf with the arrow still pointed at the door.

"Maybe we should use the ladder," I suggested. "It's the only way out of this room."

"And I'm telling you it isn't," Anton said again. "But if you say one more word, I'm not going to tell you what that way out is, and you can deal with all of *them* alone."

The horde was pressing in, moaning. A few of the zombies managed to navigate around the craters, but most of them were falling into the holes I'd made at the side and front of the house. But so many more kept coming and falling in that soon the holes would be filled; I imagined the rest of the zombies crossing to the door by crawling over the backs and heads of their fellow ghouls.

"Have you ever seen anything like this?" Esme asked. "Ever?"

"No," I said. "What do we do?"

"Hold on," Anton said.

"They're nearly here," I said.

"Just a minute," Anton said in a higher, squeakier voice.

"We're toast," I said.

Out of the corner of my vision, I saw Esme back up a little and get to one knee. Her bow and arrow were still pointed outside of the room, but whatever she was aiming at seemed to be a whole lot taller now . . . or higher. *Aren't zombies supposed to be small?* I wondered. *And what is that whistling sound?*

"Anton?" I asked.

"What?" he snapped.

An explosion rocked the outside of the house and blew the front door in. It skidded against the floor toward us and stopped mere inches from Lonnie's feet, separating him from me.

Zombies poured into the room. I leaped over the door and grabbed Lonnie. But instead of following me blindly as he'd done before, he pulled his hand away and darted toward the door opening that was nearly clogged with green creatures.

They overwhelmed him quickly and surrounded me, too. I took a few swings at them with a diamond sword, but there were way too many.

"Got it!" Anton said. I saw him look up and around, and the smile on his face slid to fear and then frustration. "I was nearly there," he said sadly.

"Where?" I asked. "Maybe it's still good," I said.

Esme fired arrows into the crowd. The zombies required multiple hits to go down, and more and more were coming. I continued slashing with my sword while pushing Lonnie backward, away from danger. I turned to see where Anton and Esme were, but a zombie hit me, sending me sprawling. My body felt leaden as I hit the floor, and I didn't know if I had the energy to escape the approaching zombie, but then someone dragged me away. With a surprising amount of speed, I was pulled back toward the wall where Anton had been working, and then somehow through the wall to the other side. I could still hear the zombies moaning and moving through the space, but for some reason they didn't follow. I looked up to thank either Esme or Anton for saving me, since—let's face it—they owed me no favors, and found myself looking at Lonnie. It could've been a trick of the light, but it almost looked like he smiled at me, as if he recognized me. Warmth flooded my chest.

"Lonnie?" I said.

He shuffled back into the darkness of whatever room we were

in, taking his maybe-smile with him, his face hidden in the shadows.

"You saved me," I said. He looked at me briefly, then turned away.

Esme and Anton were also off to the side, looking on silently.

"You saw it, didn't you?" I asked, excitement sending my voice to a higher octave. "He's getting better."

Esme sighed heavily, clearly not convinced. Anton completely ignored me. He lit a torch and surveyed the small narrow space.

"He saved me," I told them.

Again, neither of them bit.

"He did," I whispered.

Then Esme said, "Sometimes the brain can play tricks on the eye."

Esme's comment and cold stare seeded dread in my stomach.

"I found the way up," Anton said, interrupting the fear moving through my veins.

Outside, there was the sound of scraping and then another series of small explosions.

"Since when do zombies know how to use explosives?" I asked.

"I think that was the ladder," Esme said. "Sounds like it came from the same part of the room."

"Good thing we didn't use it, then," Anton said. "And that we waited for me to figure things out."

Anton had found what was little more than a crack in the wooden wall panel. He fit himself into it, and was immediately sucked up, like in one of those pneumatic tubes at the bank.

Esme pushed Lonnie in next, and then she followed. I entered last, and was whisked up through what felt like an elevator shaft without a floor or walls. When it stopped, I stepped forward into a lighted room—the greenhouse I'd been trying to break into when I set off all the traps. Esme spotted me staring out at the destruction I'd created.

"It would've been cool if you'd actually made it, I guess," she said.

I didn't know what to say. *Thanks* seemed like too much, and *yeah* seemed like too little. "I'm sorry I didn't" is what I finally said.

She nodded slightly at me, then turned away to explore the room.

If I hadn't thought that A.J. was impressive before, with the multilayered traps and bombs he'd created to keep everyone out of the house, I was definitely impressed now. We were standing inside an extended greenhouse that was meticulously planned out. Fruit trees surrounded the floor on three sides, and at the center were rows of edible plants in boxed gardens with clear paths between them. The kid could have survived in here for weeks without ever having to leave. Between this and the traps outside, he could hold out like it was the end of the world. Some parts of the greenhouse had glass flooring that looked down on other parts of the house.

"Glass floor, Lonnie! See?" I said, excited.

"It's like a fort. Some kind of hideout," Esme said.

"Looks like he was prepping hard-core for some big mission," Anton said.

"The End, perhaps," I suggested. I looked around, hoping this place would have everything we would need.

Anton's eyes flicked in my direction. He wandered over to a perfectly square strawberry patch and gathered some to eat. "It's amazing in here. How did he even make these in-game?"

Lonnie moved up to a tree and picked an apple. I chuckled. Only in a digital world could any and every fruit grow at the same time. I started stocking my inventory. I would need food once I got to the Nether.

"I don't know how he did it," I said.

"Very careful planning," Esme said. "Over a long period of time."

I whistled. My life was on pause at age fourteen thanks to the accident, and would be for a few months. But what if your entire life had been set on pause? Minecraft was probably A.J.'s only way to escape.

"What else is there?" I wondered.

Anton touched a place between two of the trees against the long wall, and a door opened. "Let's see."

"Come on, Lonnie," I said, fully anticipating I'd have to go over there and grab him and make him follow, but he looked up, and came right over, as if he understood. I froze, not wanting to do anything that might throw him off, but what I really wanted to do was cry or laugh or scream or shout to Esme and Anton that I'd been right all along. Instead, I stood still and waited for Lonnie to walk up beside me. I smiled just a little, and walked ahead through the door that Anton had found, with my best friend following.

He was coming back. I was sure of it.

"He's not," Esme said drily.

"What?" I asked. "I didn't say anything."

"I know what you're thinking," she continued. "You called him and he came, right?" She paused, perhaps waiting for me to respond with a nod or an actual yes, and when I didn't do either, she went on. "You think he's himself again. He isn't." She moved off into the new room without further explanation.

It was another food room, only this one was filled with chicken coops, and sheep and pigpens. There were plants in this room as well, though many fewer than in the other one.

"Don't play with the chickens," I reminded them.

"What do you think will happen if we do?" Anton asked.

"I don't want to find out," Esme said. She stepped toward a sheep pen, picked up one of the sheep, and began to shear it.

"You're going to have to do more than that to convince me that what I said was happening really isn't," I said. "Why else would he come when I call him?"

"It's A.J.'s coding," she said simply. She finished shearing the sheep and put away the wool, and placed the sheep back in the pen, where it baaed along with all the rest. "He's just responding to your voice commands. You think this is Lonnie, and that he's reacting to you, but he's not acting on his own."

"He is acting on his own," I insisted. "I've seen it, he's been communicating with me through my memories."

Esme put up her hands as if I had just proven her point. "Hey, I'm just trying to warn you, the game doesn't work that way."

"The game *I'm* playing does," I said. "Why won't you believe me? Why aren't you helping?"

Esme looked at me, dead serious. Her voice, however, was gentle as she said, "That's exactly what we're trying to do." She took a deep breath. "Your friend Lonnie is gone, he was never checked into the trauma ward or the children's ward. I don't know what else to tell you, but he's not here with you right now."

I looked at Lonnie, hoping he'd do something to prove her wrong. But he was simply standing there. Then I looked over to Anton, but he was far away from us on the other side of the long room, gathering supplies and muttering. I could only make out "great," and "genius," and "get out of here." There was no help to be had from him.

"You're wrong," I whispered, moving away from her and taking Lonnie with me.

We moved up one level to what looked like a sleeping floor with carved wood walls, a couple of beds, and two tables. Then there was another room with a library, complete with a trampoline in the middle, maybe for reaching the highest shelves, and finally a random room of what looked like the frameworks for portals.

"Nope, he's a kid all right. I mean, a genius kid, but definitely a kid." Anton reached into one of the portal frameworks and his hand disappeared.

"Don't do that!" Esme shouted.

"I can feel something," he said. He pulled his hand back and in it was an orange, which he immediately ate, and laughed. "This is amazing! Seriously, what mods are these?"

Looking at the portal, I had a sudden thought. "Do that again," I said. "But on my count." I went back to the greenhouse and shouted, "Now!" I looked at the orchard to see if Anton's hand showed up there. Sure enough, I found it near a high branch of one of the orange trees. I climbed up and slapped him high-five.

"Was that you?" he called.

"Yep!" I said.

"That's so cool!" he called back.

I returned to the portal room, where Esme and Anton were trying out some of the other arches.

"How did he do it?" Esme asked.

"The kid can do anything, I guess," I said. I was feeling more and more hopeful, especially given the portals didn't seem to have any exits where they led. Only entrances. It was a clever way to get around, for sure. Only A.J. would know how to use them.

"Well, great as this is, he's obviously not here," Esme said pointedly. "There are no cheat codes to get. So now what?"

"We should wait for A.J. to get back," Anton said.

"That's a waste of time," I said. The longer we waited, the more Esme was going to try to convince me to abandon my quest. "I have all the materials for a nether portal, why should I wait around?"

"We're supposed to stick together, remember? That was the promise we made to each other," Anton said. "Or do you break those as often as you do plans?"

"Listen, you don't know me or Lonnie," I said, feeling an angry heat rise in my chest. "I don't have to keep promises to you!"

"What about you?" Esme looked at Lonnie. "What do you think about Bianca's inability to face the truth?"

"Don't do that," I said.

"What?" Esme asked, putting her hands on her hips and staring me down.

"Don't talk to Lonnie like that."

"Like what? I was only asking him a question. Engaging him in conversation. The same as you've been doing since we dragged him along. Isn't that what we're supposed to do? Try to get him to respond?"

"That's not what you were doing," I said. "You were being mean. Don't do that to my friend."

"I'm trying to be your friend, Bianca! I'm trying to show you the truth! He wouldn't know if I was being mean to him or not, because he's not even there!"

I don't know when I got over to Esme and pushed her to the ground and started to hit her with my fists, but she was back up on her feet a moment later, punching back. And she didn't feel like a twelve-year-old. I put my hands up to shield my face, hoping the blows would end soon, and a moment later she stopped. I looked up, expecting to see Anton pulling her off me, but it was Lonnie. He had picked her up and moved between the two of us. She backed off.

A moment before, I was nearly convinced that she was right, and that my friend was gone. But now, I didn't know what was going on.

"You two need to stop," Anton said sharply, but he looked directly at Esme. "This isn't how we work through stuff, and it's not going to help anything. And anyway, we should get moving. We've been in here two days already."

"Two?" I said.

He nodded. "You guys haven't been paying attention to the light, but I have." He pointed outside, where the light was just beginning to brighten.

"It's only been one night," I said. "I'm sure of it."

He shook his head. "Two. When we got to the house it was just before nightfall. Then we had the zombie attack and we found the way up here. And while we've been exploring, an entire day and night went again." No one moved for a few beats, and I was scared they were going to suggest we leave the game again.

"Are you two coming with me to the Nether or not?" I didn't like how my voice wavered when I asked the question, but I had to know.

"We're coming," Anton said, eyeing Esme carefully. "Let's just gather some more supplies."

"How much of it can we take?" I asked, considering a raid on the kid's stores. It seemed kind of rude. "Can we just take his stuff? Won't A.J. mind?"

"That's the game," Esme said. "Either you're playing it, or you're not."

"Fine," I said. "I'm giving you one more day to gather what you need before Lonnie and I head into the Nether, with or without you." I stormed off to the greenhouse where I moved through the apple trees, gathering up all the ones that had dropped.

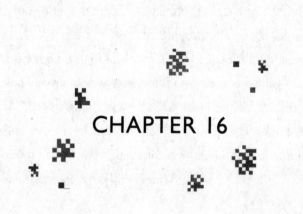

CHAPTER 16

I double-checked all my supplies to make sure we had what we needed for the Nether. I had plenty of snowballs collected. I repaired my diamond pickaxe, and grabbed a bow and arrows from A.J.'s arsenal. I loaded up on torches and buckets. I'd even enchanted my armor to add Fire Protection. My inventory was close to full by the time I finished.

Anton, Esme, and Lonnie sat waiting for me outside the orchard in the small panic room filled with chests. They were also armed to the teeth. Anton and Esme had even figured out a way to attach more arsenal to Lonnie, who now had his own armor. As I walked in, I caught the tail end of a conversation between Esme and Anton.

"What happens when you cross over to teenagerhood?" Esme asked Anton as they started enchanting their armor. "Why does everyone your age get all weird and angsty?"

"High school is like being in *Jumanji*," Anton said. "You get tossed into the jungle and you have to figure it out on your own, and if you don't, you'll get trampled."

"Lonnie didn't seem to think much of high school either," I said. "He said there were just different types of mobs and bosses."

"He sounds like he knew what he was talking about," Anton said, his tone softened with something that resembled sadness. For a moment, I wondered what it would be like if all four of us were just regular kids playing Minecraft. Perhaps we would all be friends.

"We need to keep playing our way out," I said, getting back to the task at hand.

"Great," Esme said. "Too bad A.J. never showed up. He would have been a good player to have on our side."

"We'll be fine just the four of us. We've been fighting off mobs like crazy ever since we got in here, we're good. The Nether has nothing we haven't seen already in the Overworld," I said. I gestured at the stack of chests. "Now let's open those babies up and see what's inside."

Anton shook his head. "No can do."

"Why not?" I asked.

"These are empty, and that one is an ender chest."

How didn't I see that before? The chest was black with purple particles hovering all around it.

"I think we've done all we can here," Esme said. "It's time to go."

She started for the hole in the floor to get out.

"Don't forget, the only way for us to survive this is for us to stick together," Anton said. "If I make a portal for us to leave, we *all* have to go through it this time."

"Fine," I agreed. Lonnie had made so many improvements since the last time Anton tried to get me to leave that I had to believe he would be fixed by then.

As Lonnie descended, he looked at me and then down into the hole like he was asking if I was going to follow. "I'm coming," I said. He seemed satisfied enough to climb down.

We regrouped in the greenhouse. Esme located a couple of regular chests and raided the few supplies inside. A.J. was clever enough to have stored all the good stuff in the ender chest, it seemed.

"Last call to check your supplies," I said. "Once I build the portal, I'm going through whether you're ready or not."

"Wow, you got bossy," Anton commented.

"I prefer to think of it as leadership qualities, thank you very much," I corrected.

I chuckled, and Lonnie turned to me with a smile. It was exactly the kind of thing we would have found funny, you know, out in real non-Minecraft life. I was reminded that Lonnie had also mentioned we would need a fishing rod in order to pull the blazes into melee range. I shook my head in amazement; Lonnie was somehow communicating with me through telepathy. I was sure of it. How else had he been able to plant all these memories to help guide me in our quest? Then I caught a scowling look from Esme, and I stopped.

Anton clapped his hands together and rubbed them like he

was an old-school cartoon villain without the thin twirly mustache. "All right, let's do this! Once we finish this trip to the Nether, it's off to the End, and then we're outta here!"

I was going to explain why we should maybe wait to leave and instead find a fishing rod, then stopped. There was a chill inside the room. I looked around, searching for the source of it. Outside the window, in the places not messed up by the blasts I had caused, the icy tundra stared back. Nothing appeared different, but it almost felt like someone had come into the house and left a door open. The chill came over me again.

Anton had already exited down the suction lift. Esme had moved on to another room, looking for more stuff to raid.

I walked carefully around the greenhouse, searching. A little way down the path was something shadowy standing between two apple trees. It turned.

An enderman.

With a white scar slashed across its face.

I heard my own breath sucking in, and then the sound of my own scream. I pushed Lonnie out of the way, knocking him into the carrot garden. A chicken flapped across my vision, blinding me for a couple of seconds. When it was gone again, the enderman was closer. I pulled up my inventory and took out the diamond sword.

"This isn't going to work," I called at the enderman. "You don't scare me."

But something about the enderman's scar chilled me to the bone.

It came, as fast as ever, straight toward me as I thrust upward with the sword. I caught the enderman's arm. It staggered back a step, but then reached around with its other arm to strike me. I ducked. My health points were still low. I had to be careful. The enderman took a side step and came at me again. I moved as it moved, and slashed with the sword again. This time I struck its torso. The enderman's arm flashed out, lightning quick, thwacking my face. The blow burned like fire. I pulled back, then ran in, with the blade of the sword held parallel to the floor. Another stab. Another swipe from the enderman. Another smack that made my arm feel like it was aflame.

I crashed to the ground, and felt the hard floor against my knee. The enderman raised its arms again and I caught sight of the white scar. That was when I realized that I had seen the scar before. In the accident. The person in the other car, he'd had a slash across his face the same way this enderman did. Only it wasn't white. It was red. I shook my head to get the image of the gash on the other driver's face out of my mind, but I couldn't.

I was out of energy. The room felt like it was spinning around me. Then I realized I was being turned and dragged away. It was Lonnie, pulling me away from the enderman. But who was going to stop the enderman from attacking him? I lifted my head just enough to see Esme aiming with her bow and arrow. By the time Lonnie had gotten me to the lift, Esme had delivered a final shot and the enderman broke apart.

Lonnie and I stepped into the lift. It whisked us down to the first floor. Anton was there, and he looked horrified.

"What's going on?" we both asked each other. We both answered at the same time too, which meant neither of us heard what the other one had said.

Anton held his hands up. "It's night again," he said. "So you know what that means."

I looked behind him, at the rows of endermen outside the house.

"There was one inside," I said.

Esme burst through the false wall in front of the lift and looked at the three of us. "Why are you standing here?" she asked. "We have to run."

"There's nowhere to run," Anton said.

I pushed Lonnie in his direction. "We'll buy you enough time to craft the nether portal. Go!"

Anton hesitated, but grabbed Lonnie after a moment, and went back into the lift. I moved with Esme toward the front door. The line of endermen faced us. Two, no three, rows deep. It was going to be a massacre, and we knew it.

"What now?" Esme asked.

"Keep firing and hope for morning," I said as I loaded my first arrow.

"What about that guy back there?" she asked.

"I'm going to pretend you didn't remind me about him," I said.

We both aimed at the crowd and began to fire.

The arrows weren't helpful. There were too many of them coming. What we needed was—

"Look what I found!" Anton was behind us again. He and Lonnie had TNT. He lobbed the bombs over our heads as we kept firing. Most of the endermen were starting to slow down. But some kept coming through the remnants of the blasts, and as the smoke cleared they were still advancing.

We had used up all of our arrows. Esme started to break apart anything made out of wood, to craft sticks. Anton caught on and got as many feathers out of our supplies as he could, then went back upstairs to raid the chickens.

"There isn't enough flint," Esme announced.

In the middle of the line of endermen, still heading toward us, was one with a white diagonal scar on his face.

"No," I said.

Esme looked up. "No way."

We pulled back. Esme fired arrows behind us as we moved as far back into the room as possible. We had one last TNT bomb.

"Take cover," I said.

We moved behind the broken bookcase and I tossed the bomb at the wall. The blast threw us back a little farther, and buried us under rubble, but we were mostly unharmed. There was some kind of cave behind the wall we had blasted open. As we scrambled for it, Esme accidentally dropped a small object. It went skidding on the ground away from us and came to a stop just at the lip of one of the blast holes. A shulker box. Esme groaned when she realized what she'd done, then moved carefully toward it as it teetered on the edge of the hole, grabbing it as soon as she was close enough. I breathed a sigh of relief and said, "Good save!" She smiled and we kept moving.

Inside the cave, we followed a narrow path at Esme's feet that led deeper down into the earth. At one point the path narrowed to a thin strip, and to our left were the gaping holes in the ground that I'd created with my blasts. I was still trying to puzzle out what had happened with the scarred enderman. How had it reappeared? And why did it have that scar? Esme stopped suddenly and I bumped into her. There was a lake of lava beneath us, and I could feel the heat of it searing my skin.

"What if we get stuck?" she asked.

"An entire mob of endermen are behind us," I said. "Do you really want to go back that way?"

"Good point," she said.

We stepped forward and were rocked by a blast that came from somewhere over our heads. "What was that?" Esme asked.

I suddenly remembered A.J.'s warning about the chickens and Anton going to get feathers. "Chicken bombs?" I suggested.

"We better keep moving," Esme said.

We went deeper, and with each step, I dug down, ruining the path.

"You know they can teleport, right?" she asked.

Yeah, but I'll take every precaution I can.

We stepped around a corner, and entered a glittering cavern.

"Diamonds," Esme said.

Without a word, we both jumped off the path and began mining. There were more than we could carry in the shulker box, so we maxed out what we could, and continued on. In another cavern, a mob of zombies moved toward us. I had an idea, and hacked away at the low ceiling. My intuition paid off, and a load of gravel came tumbling down, between us and them. No fighting necessary.

"Nice! How did you know that would work?" Esme asked.

"I just . . . had the idea. I thought I'd try this and see if it would work, and it did. Anyway, I'm tired of hand-to-hand combat, aren't you?" I asked.

She shrugged.

After a few more steps, she said, "We need to get out of here."

"How?" I asked.

She pointed up toward the top of the cavern. I nodded. We slowly started picking our way up the dark rocks, planting torches as we went to light the way that we hoped was out. It grew cold again, and we hacked up and out of the last bits of rock, to blinding white on the other side. We'd reached the surface of the tundra. I looked back toward A.J.'s house and found it far in the distance, gray and beige against the white snow. The cliff and forest were behind us. Somewhere between the house and the forest were Lonnie and Anton.

Esme and I started for the forest. Neither of us wanted to go back to the house, though we never said that. We just started hiking away from it. Esme pointed to a narrow ridge, like an undulating shelf above our heads, and we climbed up to it. It made for a good vantage point. A.J.'s house was to the right of us, and straight ahead was the spot from where we'd seen the house in the first place. It was like going backward. I was annoyed that we had been separated. We'd had a good thing going in A.J.'s base with all the food and supplies.

We got to the place where I had started cutting down into the rock to make a path for us to the house. But the boys weren't there. We went back up into the trees and climbed them to be able to look around, but there was nothing. Finally, I put my hands to my mouth and called out, "Lonnie!" but Esme shot me a hot look that got me to stop before I even got to the "*ee*" at the end of his name. She jumped down from her tree and moved away from me, clearly annoyed. I jumped down after her and followed.

"Just when I think you're finally getting better at thinking things through first . . ."

"We couldn't find them. What was I supposed to do?" I asked.

"Not draw the mobs' attention to us! Could you do that?"

I didn't say anything. I was tired. And irritated. Plus, maybe she was right.

There was movement ahead, and I pointed, nearly saying something, but remembering not to at the last moment. Esme held her hand out as if she wanted me to stop moving, so I did, and she went on ahead. Then there was a garbled shout, and she came back running my way. Behind her was the scarred enderman, and behind it, Anton and Lonnie.

Esme took out a sword and got ready to face off. She walked around it, and it turned, following her, putting its back to me. I understood what Esme was doing. I took out my own sword and approached the enderman from behind. Now at the enderman's left side, Anton pulled out his own diamond sword and got ready. The enderman swiveled to look at each of us, and then it chose the most vulnerable to attack—the person I was most hoping it would ignore—Lonnie.

We broke formation, piling on the enderman, striking it with as many blows as we could manage before it turned back on us, and now that we were closer, it got several good punches in. I felt weak. From the sluggish movements of Anton and Esme, I knew they felt the same. Lonnie was lying on his side, not moving. I started slashing again, screaming at the top of my lungs. The three of us got into a bit of a rhythm, each of us swinging in succession until the enderman had enough of us, and the purple particles around it started to go inside. It was going to teleport, but I wasn't going to let it get away so easily.

I got in close, preparing to chop the fleeing mob with all of my might. I was so angry that it had somehow reappeared, that its scar reminded me of the accident, that it had chosen to attack my best friend. Before my sword could land, it disappeared in a swirl of purple pixels, and I screamed in fury.

Teleport, my frenzied mind shouted. Suddenly, trees disappeared, pixel by pixel. Ground cover. Dirt. Rocks.

Everything.

CHAPTER 17

When the game world rendered again, Lonnie reappeared next to me, holding my hand. In his other, he had a shulker box. Then Esme and Anton reappeared, looking none the worse for wear.

"That was insane!" Anton whooped. "I've never teleported *with* an enderman before!"

"I don't think that's what happened," I said cautiously, remembering the thought—the command—I had before we'd disappeared.

"Ugh, I feel dizzy," Esme complained. She plopped down on her back to stare at the sky. "Give me two seconds."

I looked around for a moment, terrified. But luckily, the enderman didn't reappear with us. Whatever mod or cheat A.J. had put in this game must've required my command to be more specific, and I was calm enough now to be thankful for that. We were near a river. It was like no part of the world I'd encountered so far, with a lush forest of tropical trees and flowering plants in reds and oranges. It curved around on both sides, making me think it was some kind of island, rather than one huge landmass. There was a boat in the river, and off in the distance was another shore, which I guessed was the mainland.

"I don't recognize this place at all," Anton said. "Where are we now?"

"It's definitely a jungle biome, wherever it is," Esme added.

"Great, I love getting lost in the jungle!" I sighed, took a breath, and tried to rein in my frustration. "You okay, Lonnie?"

Lonnie nodded and surveyed the landscape around us. Then he moved forward and started cutting down trees, making a shelter. I didn't want to jinx it by saying something, so I just helped. He was always better at making things than I was anyway. It was better to follow.

"Good idea, we should put up a base as soon as possible," Anton said, acknowledging Lonnie's actions for once. "When we go over into the Nether, we need to protect the portal on both sides from mobs."

"Good going, Lonnie," I said loudly, emphasizing his participation to both Anton and Esme. Esme rolled her eyes as Lonnie got to work on crafting a table, and a bed, which would be handy if we wanted nights to go faster. So far, we hadn't used that tactic enough.

"We should check our inventory. Did we lose anything?" I asked. I was worried that maybe we had suddenly reset the game without meaning to. I calmed down once I saw that all my food remained intact. I moved my extra flint and steel to the front of my supplies. We would need it to reactivate the portal from the other side to get back to the Overworld.

Then I went to count up my obsidian. I should've had a huge amount from what we'd collected up to this point. I should have had enough for three portals, really. So my stomach twisted in a sudden panic as I saw that all those inventory slots were now empty.

"Oh no," I said. "No, no, no!"

"What is it?" Esme asked.

"My obsidian! It's completely gone!" I racked my brain for how it could have happened. My thoughts immediately went to the scarred enderman that had attacked us. Could he have done it? Could endermen steal now?

Anton opened the shulker box to inspect the goods. A.J. had stockpiled it with a lot that was useful. Food, flint, redstone, a couple of pieces of obsidian—though not enough for a nether portal—some triggers, wool, and paper.

"Well, there're some blocks here."

I wanted to burst into tears. I had worked so hard for that obsidian and now we had to start all over.

"It's okay," Esme said, seeing my face. "Obsidian's not so rare. I'm sure we'll find some more in this biome. And once we do, we'll make the portal and get what we need from the Nether, no big deal."

She was right. I nodded and tried to calm myself down.

"Okay, so we need blaze rods to eventually make eyes of ender, nether wart for potions . . ." Anton's voice trailed off as he and

Esme wandered away, lost in their planning. I let them go, taking the moment alone to focus on my own next steps. I needed to find obsidian.

As soon as Lonnie was finished with the inside of the base and I was sure he'd be safe there alone, I moved to another part of the island to hunt for obsidian. Anton and Esme had disappeared, probably still talking through every detail of the Nether run. I explored and mined, finding coal easily enough, and dug through a tunnel that seemed to lead under the water. Eventually I chose to stop rather than risk hitting a rock that would flood the entire thing with me in it.

I got back to the house, telling Lonnie about my finds: more coal, some flint, and redstone. He nodded and made some grunting noises. I was excited. He was improving. Even Esme and Anton were noticing it. A sudden wave of exhaustion swept over me, and I staggered to the side of the room and leaned against a wall. We'd been going nonstop, and I needed a rest.

Lonnie came over, looking worried. It was the first time I recognized real emotion in his face.

"Hey friend," I said. "I'm fine. Don't worry about me."

Lonnie made a sound, like he understood, or was trying to communicate something.

"I just needed a minute," I said. "I know we have to get moving." I took a breath. "Where do you think the obsidian is on the island, Lonnie?"

Lonnie made a sound again, which of course didn't help at all, but I was grateful that he was there, at least. And I was glad that the others hadn't managed to convince me that this wasn't him. He was coming around. This was working. Now all I needed to do was get us out.

"I'm going back out there," I said. "I won't be long."

But the island was larger than I'd thought. As I moved along the terrain, mining as I went, I thought it might not be an island at all. It might be a long peninsula. I moved methodically side to side, but as far forward as I went, there was no other shore. I moved into a thick growth of bushes and trees, and began to dig down. The island seemed to have nothing but coal, and a few cuts of diamond. I had enough to craft a diamond pickaxe, but there was no obsidian to use my diamond pickaxe on.

I didn't realize how long I had been out of the house. Darkness descended quickly and I was forced to make my way back. I was exhausted, and wished for real, actual sleep. The kind where I could close my eyes and see nothing at all. My brain felt like it was alight with fire. I thought that was my imagination until I saw a burst of flame ahead of me. I was under attack.

I turned toward three witches that laughed at me from a tree above my head, raining down potions in vials of purple and orange. They burst ahead of me. I ducked under another tree and ran, trying to draw them out. The first one took the bait. It dropped to the ground and began to chase me.

Since I'd scoured the landscape earlier, I knew exactly where to go. I ducked behind a short, squat tree as the witch ran past me, then I got behind the witch and started hacking. I almost laughed out loud when I saw what she'd dropped: a fire-retardant potion, and glowstone dust.

I doubled back and started to look for the second one, but I had gotten turned around while going after the first witch. As I stepped through the trees and grass, I came upon a tall, sharp hill. There was no way to climb up without digging out steps; then I saw that the other two witches were on either side of me. I was cornered. The first witch had probably been a decoy. And I had fallen for their trap, thinking that they had fallen for mine.

"Smart," I said out loud. But that didn't stop them from coming.

They pelted potions, and I warded them off with my sword as best I could. Then I charged the closest witch—the one on my right—slashing until it died, dropping sticks and glass bottles. I turned to the last witch. It seemed to be smiling. It came at me with such force that I got knocked over onto my back. The witch kept coming, hitting me with everything it had, until I couldn't move at all. I wished I hadn't gone out by myself, and as the witch prepared to strike me again, I flinched. But the witch never attacked.

I could hear a scuffle nearby, and when I got up, I saw Lonnie delivering a hard right hook to the witch before she dissolved. He grabbed my hand, and we ran the rest of the way to the house.

As soon as we got inside, we piled into the beds, and in seconds it was daylight again. Lonnie had saved me. For a third time.

He got up first and came over to where I lay. He held out his hand and pulled me up. I felt the warmth of it against my own palm.

"Thank you," I said.

He squeezed my hand and nodded.

CHAPTER 18

"Mommy!" I was six years old again, at the playground. I stood on the edge of a wooden platform, waiting to launch myself onto the monkey bars. I had a new trick that I wanted to try. I was waiting for my mom to turn around so I could show her my big girl moves.

"Mommy, Mommy look at me!" I shouted again. But my mom was too drawn into a conversation with our neighbor Doreen, the one with the flamingos in her yard. They were looking at something on her phone. I shrugged and leaped onto the first bar. I dangled from the tips of my fingers, feeling the weight of my body pull me down.

A boy eight years old watched me as I swung back and forth, trying to build up momentum.

"What do you think you're doing?" he asked, his gray eyes looking warily at my efforts to kick my legs and pick up speed.

"I'm going to flip and land on my feet," I grunted. "Just like they do in gym-matchsticks."

"You mean gymnastics," the boy corrected me.

My fingers started to go numb. I loosened my grip and dropped down to the ground in a squat. All my plastic barrettes clattered near my ears, and I brushed my braids out of my eyes.

"Stop distracting me!" I said. I rubbed my palms together and climbed back up to the platform to try again. "Stranger!" I narrowed my eyes at him.

"My name is Lonnie, and I can already tell you're going to fall big-time."

"Shut up, meany-pants," I responded with my hands on my hips. "You don't know anything!"

"If you want to do a flip, that's not how you do it."

"How then?"

"First you should dangle upside down with your knees hooked onto the bars," he said. "And then you swing forward and grab the bars and let your feet loose."

"That doesn't sound as exciting as my way," I said, scrunching up my nose. "Why should I believe you?"

"Because I know about physics," Lonnie said matter-of-factly. "I learned about it in school."

I narrowed my eyes at him. "You're not old enough for that class."

He hesitated, then said, "Whatever." He turned away, pulling a tablet from his back pocket and turning on the screen.

"What're you playing?"

He glanced over his shoulder at me, still a little stung that I called his bluff. "Minecraft. Do you know what that is?"

"Yes," I said, sticking out my bottom lip, as if that somehow made the lie more believable.

He spun back toward me. The bright green pixels and gray lettering of Minecraft booted up on the tablet. "You sure?" he asked. He let me have a look at the screen.

"Maybe I know a different one," I said softly.

Lonnie smiled. "It's like a building game, but you can also do lots of cool things like fight monsters and set traps." Lonnie pulled up his house and showed me around what he'd already built in his realm. I was easily impressed at that age, since what Lonnie had built was nothing more than a one-room shack with some redstone-powered carts that could take him from one end of the house to another.

"Let me see that," I said, reaching for the tablet. "You should build some decorations for your house, it looks really ugly."

I tapped around the world, surprised at how easily I could manipulate the ground with a shovel. I started digging straight down.

"Not bad, newbie," Lonnie said.

"What's that?" I asked.

"Somebody new to the game."

I nodded. "You won't be able to call me that tomorrow," I said. "I won't be new then."

"You're right," Lonnie said. "So what should I call you tomorrow?"

"Bianca," I said. "That's my name."

"Well, Bianca, maybe we can play together sometime."

"I'll have to ask my mom first, but I guess that's okay," I responded. "Does that make us friends now?"

Lonnie shrugged. "Yeah, I guess so."

I beamed brightly at him, displaying all three gaps in my teeth. "Then you should watch me do my epic flip!"

"Wait, Bianca!" Lonnie began, but I was no longer listening. This time, I took a running leap off the platform. I extended my arms to catch the first bar, but my hands missed the moment to grasp. Suddenly I was hurtling through the air with no way to catch myself.

I opened my mouth to scream, and closed my eyes, which was a very dumb thing to do. The next thing I knew, my body collided with something soft and warm and I heard someone yelp in pain.

Even when he didn't know me, Lonnie was there to catch my falls.

"Can you talk now?" I asked, looking at Lonnie's avatar, and thinking we were a long way from that playground.

Lonnie shook his head.

"But it's you," I said.

He came over and rubbed me on the head like he did when he was in a good mood.

"What happened to you?" I asked.

Lonnie arched one eyebrow up and looked at me.

"Right, I guess it doesn't matter," I said. "What matters now is that you're finally getting better."

He gave one definitive nod, then picked up the shulker box and started for the door.

"We still need to find obsidian," I said.

Lonnie pointed out the door to a boat that hovered just off-shore.

"Right," I said. "We could use that to get back to the mainland."

Lonnie's head tilted as he looked at me.

I looked out the window, wondering where Anton and Esme had gotten to. "Well, I could make a quick mission. It would save a lot of time," I said. "And since you're better, there's no reason to leave you here."

There was a part of me that felt good about leaving Anton and Esme behind. I was tired of them doubting every move I made, and yelling at me every time I messed up. I thought it would be good to be on our own again, Lonnie and Bianca alone, where I could mess up and at least the person reading me the riot act would be someone I knew, someone I could trust.

We climbed aboard the boat. He looked knowingly back at me, looking more Lonnie-like, and giving me the same steady stare that he did out in the real world when he disapproved of something I was doing.

He knew. He knew exactly why I didn't want to leave. He had probably known all along.

"Once we get to the End, I'll log off," I said. I didn't know if I'd be ready to face the real world by then, but his unblinking gaze got me thinking that I'd at least have to try.

I started to navigate us to the next strip of land, and tried to convince myself that I meant what I'd said, but deep down I knew I would do everything I could to hold off going back to the real world. But there was time, wasn't there? How much time, I didn't know.

I shook that thought off and concentrated on steering. Once we were on the other side, I took out the diamond axe and started bashing through things, hoping to hit obsidian or even lava that I could divert water to. Lonnie tagged along but didn't help with any of the mining. I talked to him the entire time, but my one-sided conversation quickly went from enthusiastic and encouraging to doom and despair the longer we went without finding what we needed.

Lonnie pointed to a crusty-looking gray stone hill ahead, and I headed there, hoping I'd find lava beneath it. Lonnie stood aside as I dug down and hit lava with just a few short strokes.

"Jackpot!" I declared. I poured water over the lava. It sizzled and turned immediately into obsidian, which I dug into with the pickaxe with the enthusiasm of an enderman with a grudge. I kept going until I'd made fifteen obsidian blocks, which were ready to be assembled into a portal right at the side of the rocky hill.

"This is it, Lonnie," I said.

But Lonnie wasn't standing near me anymore. I ran back down to the water, near where the boat was, then back to the first set of rocky hills we had come to, and climbed to the top to look out over the landscape. Nothing. Lonnie had been there, and then he was gone. In an instant. Like he'd been snuffed out of existence.

I turned again and followed the river farther down than where we'd come in, with panic rising in my chest. I found him past a curve in the path, and ran to catch up.

"What are you doing?" I asked. "I got all the obsidian we need. It's time to go."

But Lonnie didn't budge. He stood looking out over the water, peacefully, then turned to me and seemed surprised to see me there, and then was confused about why I was out of breath.

"I got it all ready," I told him as I held my hand out. "We have to go. Are you ready?"

Lonnie looked back over the water as if he wasn't ready to move just yet, so I went next to him and looked out too. I listened for the sound of the waves. It was there, but so was the tinkly Minecraft music that I'd tuned out since I'd landed inside the game.

He squeezed my hand and looked past me, toward where Anton and Esme were still waiting in our old base. I sighed and said, "You're right. We won't leave without them. I wanted some time with just us, but we'll go back for them before we leave for the Nether. They're our friends, and we don't leave our friends behind."

Lonnie smiled before moving over the sand on the shore of the river and then up onto the grassy plain toward the hills. Watching him walking, for a moment it seemed like the vibrant blue of his shirt flickered, and momentarily he was a shadow of himself. There, but not there. More like the memory of a person than the real thing. Like a ghost.

I shook my head. It was just a trick of the light. I went back to the plain, and while I put the portal together, Lonnie stayed close, but his attention was elsewhere. He looked all around, but never in my direction, not even when I talked to him directly about getting out and eating ice cream at that place we liked on West Elm Road. I even tried teasing him about starting to borrow his car once I was old enough to drive and getting control of the satellite radio station. For a moment it was almost like he'd been at the beginning of the game, when I wasn't really sure if he was there or not. My frustration bubbled up; it was like every time we took a step closer to the End, he took two steps back.

Is what Esme said before true? Is Lonnie really—

I shivered and shut that thought down. Besides, there was another possibility . . . I could be creating all the diversions myself. I'd been tracking how things seemed to happen in reaction to me, and what Esme and Anton had said about the mods they created to protect the game from noobs. The game could be reacting to what I feared. Either way, there was nothing I could do but play through. Shaking my head, I focused on building the nether portal instead. I only needed some flint to light it. I opened up my inventory to check, but there was no flint inside it.

"You're kidding," I said. I checked and rechecked the contents of the box. Still no flint. Esme and Anton must have taken it, or it got left behind at A.J.'s house, although I could've sworn it was in the box before. I took a deep breath and considered my options.

"What would you do?" I asked Lonnie. "Should we go back to get Anton and Esme now, or find some flint ourselves?"

He glanced at the ground, just as I'd hoped.

"Mining it is," I said.

I left the obsidian portal frame where it was as the two of us went a little farther inland. I dug everywhere I could, looking for some gravel, and turning up nothing. Most everything here was sand and dirt. We kept moving farther in until the water disappeared behind us.

"I'm sorry," I said out loud, though really I was just saying it to myself, as in *I'm a sorry excuse for a human being,* or maybe *I'm sorry for being a complete idiot that day in the car and getting us all hurt.* But it could have been both. Actually, it was both. Definitely.

I smashed everything I saw with the diamond pickaxe, leaving literally no stone unturned as I ran through the digital countryside in search of some gravel.

Lonnie tugged me in another direction when we hit a patch of trees.

"Do you want to go this way?" I asked. "Your guess is as good as mine."

He led me down a couple of levels of dirt and rock and into a shallow plain, at the base of which was gravel.

"Genius. You are a genius, and you have always been a genius," I said.

I mined as fast and as furiously as I could. I dug so far down, the valley was no longer shallow. Lonnie stuck close to me as I worked, and it was only when I got about half of the way through that I realized he had been steering me in a methodical path all along. We had mined in one square grid, then moved to another, and then another.

"I see what you did there," I said.

Lonnie didn't respond, he just gently moved me to the next section. I kept going.

The thing about mining gravel for flint, of course, is that you're not very likely to find flint. And it seemed even more unlikely now. Nothing we really needed was going to come easy. I could either deal with it, or get mad and walk away.

Lonnie paused and looked right at me, as if he wanted to say something, or he was trying to bore a thought straight into my brain. I stepped back, out of his line of sight, and his gaze didn't move. He was looking at a rock behind me. I moved to it and mined down, almost expecting there to be flint. There wasn't. Once again, I was reading something into Lonnie that wasn't there. I turned and threw the axe, hitting another bit of gravel. When I went to pull it out, there was something behind it. Black. For a second I got super excited, thinking I'd accidentally hit some flint. But it was coal.

"I give up," I called up to Lonnie. "There's nothing here. We're going to have to look someplace else."

Lonnie stamped the ground where he was standing.

"No," I said. "There's nothing here. We really have to go."

Lonnie looked back over the plain. I still had a long way to go to go through all of it with Lonnie's method. But all I wanted to do was hack it up to bits, hoping that by sheer force of luck, I'd hit what we needed.

He stamped again.

"Okay, okay," I said. "No problem." I started to dig in the spot where he had been standing. I went down two levels, and there it was, black flint.

I couldn't help but grin and hold up my hand for a high five, which Lonnie happily slapped.

We rushed back to the spot where I'd made the frame, and I ignited the portal immediately. It glowed purple with swirling patterns splashing out of the border and all around us. It looked so much deeper in person than it did in the game, like we would be diving into an ocean, and we would need to hold our breath to be able to get through.

Lonnie put his hand up, trying to touch one of the purple swirls that came out at us.

"Lonnie, not yet! We have to go back for Es—" I called out. I tried to catch his hand, but lost my balance, and pushed him closer to the portal, which was the exact opposite of what I'd intended to do. He turned and grabbed me, maybe to help me, or to help himself, but before I knew it we had both fallen through the portal, disappearing in a moment.

The shulker box with a good chunk of our supplies was left behind in the Overworld, along with our friends.

CHAPTER 19

I wasn't expecting the heat to feel like a blast to my face. I raised my arm to shield myself, and hit Lonnie in the process, pushing him forward down a slope of deep brown soil and toward a lake of bubbling lava. I reached out and grabbed him back as I calculated the risk of leaving him there for the length of time it would take me to return to the Overworld, grab the shulker box, and get back to the Nether. Anything could happen in a few seconds. But without the flint, there was no way to relight the portal if it went out. I'd have to risk it.

I let go of Lonnie and turned back to the portal. Above us, a ghast came screaming down, tentacles waving, cutting off my path. I pulled out my bow and took a few shots, missing terribly, but at least the ghast flew away for the moment. But a stray shot from the mob blew out the portal fire in the process.

It took me a couple of seconds of staring at the empty portal for the following to sink in: we were stuck in the Nether.

The ghast came around again, flying upward in an arc and then diving down toward us. I could see it huffing, getting ready to blow. I knocked down Lonnie and held him there as the ghast sent a fireball straight at us. I wondered if this could ignite the portal, but realized it could also fry us in the process. I pressed us both flat against the ground. It whizzed over our bodies, and I felt the singe of it whisk past my skin. I got up, pulled Lonnie along with me, and ran down the slope toward the lava.

"Where's that potion of Fire Protection when you need it?" I asked aloud. "Oh right, it's back in the shulker box that I didn't bring with us."

The ghast dipped and turned and came around again, faster this time, its gray face like the cold, hard mask of death.

"When I tell you to jump, you're going to have to jump, Lonnie." My heart beat hard in my chest and my legs trembled as I pulled out my sword. "Ready?" I asked as the ghast bore down on us. I waited until it was within striking distance, then shouted, "Now!" I jumped backward over the rivulet of lava while wildly swinging my sword, landing a few good blows while pulling Lonnie backward with me, hoping I wasn't dragging him, because if he didn't jump on his own I would be pulling him to his death by liquid fire. But he landed just a microsecond after me on the other side, as the ghast died, plowing face first into the lava and becoming nothing more than motes of smoke. I yanked Lonnie out of the way as its crash landing sent some lava our way, but not quite fast enough to save myself. My leg burned as if someone had slashed it with hot iron. There was no time to worry about it. It would heal. Everything in the game healed eventually. And we had to move on.

Why exactly didn't I use the potion on myself *before* I lit the portal to the Nether? My armor had fire resistance, sure, but it wasn't enough. For that matter, why didn't I wait to get Anton and Esme before I lit it up? I braced myself for the fact that they would nail me on that later. There was no excuse.

"Hindsight, right?" I said to Lonnie.

He looked confused, of course. He didn't know what was in my head. I kept moving.

We were on a slope now, with heat on all sides and the ghostly puffs of ghasts on the periphery of my vision.

"We're going to have to move faster, Lonnie," I said, but Lonnie was already picking up the pace.

A mob of ghasts swirled high above, pale against the orange-black sky. They looked like they were conferring, planning their next move against us. Up ahead was a rock formation that looked like a portal—curved up and over in an arch—which might provide cover. I steered Lonnie in that direction, keeping him at my side except for in those narrow passageways through the rock, or over thin paths with lava on either side that forced me to go ahead of him.

We made it to a long, knife-thin ledge. Just before us was the rock formation and a slight refuge.

The ghasts turned as one, and barreled toward us.

We ran. It looked like a straight stretch to the arch, so I went full-out with Lonnie following close. But what looked like a direct path, wasn't. I saw the edge of the cliff nearly too late, and we skidded to a stop. Well, I skidded to a stop. Lonnie lurched over. Somehow I managed to get my arm out, grabbing his hand as I dropped to the ground. He dangled over some burning rocks as the ghasts did a flyby with a couple of fireballs strafing us for good measure. Luckily, none of them hit us. I pulled Lonnie back to safe-ish ground and we got to our feet. We immediately got to work building a bridge that we could use to cross the chasm.

We moved as I lay the stones across, going as fast as we could with the ghasts coming around for another pass. We weren't going to make it. Instead of continuing with the bridge, I stopped and moved behind Lonnie, facing the oncoming ghasts, and put up a quick wall between us and them. Then I pulled Lonnie against the wall and waited. I heard the explosion of fireballs against my back. But they didn't break our shelter. We were okay for the moment. I continued with the bridge and got us both across to the ready-made refuge of the arch. I quickly built some walls around us for more cover. This time when the ghasts came around again, there was no target to hit.

I waited awhile until I was sure they had moved off, and then I broke down the walls and looked out.

"Welcome to the Nether," I said.

I checked my inventory for what supplies I did manage to bring in with me. I had my armor, which would be some protection. I put it on Lonnie. If I got hurt, I wasn't sure that Esme or Anton could do anything to help us out. *All of this should have been thought out before you even got here*, I scolded myself.

We needed a base. I moved us into a nest of rocky protrusions, and past lava pouring down the side of a cliff like the most unpleasant waterfall you could imagine. I started to dig into the rocks, looking for a way to carve out a home base that would withstand anything the Nether had to offer.

I discovered a small cave of intertwined passageways, and went with Lonnie inside. We had to duck to move through, and I had enough torches to keep the path lit ahead of us, but it wasn't ideal. I mined upward, and the space opened up, exposing us to the same three ghasts that had come for us minutes before. I pushed Lonnie down a different path as the ghasts came lower. One of their tentacles waved inside the hole, but it was too small for them to get any closer.

"We need a plan," I whispered.

"Bianca making a plan. That will be a first," someone said from the darkness.

I spun around and set a torch near where I'd heard the voice. It was Anton.

"How did we guess that you would try to sneak off and come into the Nether on your own," he said. He was wearing glowing blue armor that shone purplish or greenish depending on which way he turned.

"I was going to come back for you two after I'd made the portal, but we fell through and then the portal went out. It was all an accident, I swear! I wasn't going to leave you two behind."

Anton paused, considering me for a moment, before he nodded. "It's okay, I believe you."

"Thanks." I smiled at him, and then asked, "Where did you get that wicked-looking armor?"

"You mean this enchanted diamond armor with Fire Protection?" he said smugly. "I'm a master enchanter."

"What?" I asked. "When did you even have time to get supplies, let alone do some serious enchanting?"

"I'm pretty awesome when people just give me a little time to work my magic," he said smugly. Then he paused and frowned at me. "Did you seriously come in here with nothing?"

"I told you I didn't plan it this way," I said.

"No, you never do," Anton said.

I felt heat rising in my chest that was some combination of embarrassment and disappointment in my inability to think things through. "I'm sure I can craft some iron armor," I said.

"And put some enchantments on it," he added.

"Well, no," I said. "Those got left behind too."

"How?" he asked.

"In the shulker box."

Anton shook his head.

"And I only have enough supplies for one suit of armor," I added.

Anton laughed in disbelief. "Okay, well," he said, taking a deep breath. "Maybe today is your lucky day."

He had an inventory of enough supplies that both Lonnie and I could get enchantments and protections placed on our armor. Anton even dropped a projectile enchantment that I could use on mine.

"Thanks for helping me," I said, feeling like a first-class idiot.

"What about him?" Anton asked.

"He's responding to me more now," I said. "It's definitely him. And he's nothing like your friend Andrea."

"Except he doesn't talk," Anton said.

"Well, yeah, right," I said. "But he communicates."

"By grunting?"

"There are a lot of nonverbal ways of communicating," I said. Anton frowned.

"You understand everything that's going on, don't you?" I asked Lonnie. But he was staring off ahead into a section of cave wall, and didn't respond.

"Yeah, I see what you mean," Anton said, slapping Lonnie on the shoulder. "Nonverbal."

I didn't have time to argue, and I wasn't sure why Lonnie had suddenly gone comatose again. What mattered was getting the supplies we needed to get to the End.

"Look, I know Esme and I have been giving you a hard time about everything, but trust me, you really deserve it sometimes," he said as I finished up with the armor.

"I know," I mumbled. "Why'd you come find us here? You can exit anytime you want."

Anton shrugged. "We said we'd stick together, remember?" he said. "We're back to the original plan: get through this part of the game and get the stuff we need to get to the End."

"I'm hoping you managed to make more than this armor?"

Anton smiled. He put his hands on his waist in what can only be called a Wonder Woman pose.

"So what you're saying is, you have a ton more stuff," I said.

He raised his eyebrows twice. "Yep. And it's all in a shulker box that Esme brought with her."

"Where is she now?"

"Fighting. Like usual," he said.

"And you're . . ." I prodded.

"I was providing a distraction. This is not me hiding or anything. I am executing a well-timed plan that she—" Anton dove past me and ran, shouting, "Argh! I forgot!"

Lonnie and I followed closely in Anton's steps as he moved through the maze with a speed that told me he'd probably created it himself. We barely managed to keep up.

"Fun, right?" I said to Lonnie.

He looked at me, and then ahead at Anton again, keeping up better than I was. How could Anton not see that he was different now, better?

Anton made a sharp right that nearly doubled back in the other direction, but as soon as Lonnie and I made it around the bend, he screamed and turned back. Anton practically trampled us trying to get past. Behind him was a mob of zombie pigmen. They weren't quick, but they were close.

"This way!" Anton shouted. He made another zigzag turn into an even lower passageway. We were pretty much crawling at this point. But this time none of us lit any torches, so we were feeling our way through in the dark. I listened for the gentle scraping of Anton's body against the sides of the rock, and for Lonnie following behind me.

Rock scratched against my body and snagged my skin as we

continued to move through. I resisted the urge to cry out. My leg was still in pain from the lava burn, and I still hadn't recovered all my energy from the witch attacks on the island. Moving was uncomfortable to say the least, and extremely painful to say the most. Craning my neck back to make sure that Lonnie was following along wasn't exactly helpful either.

At some point Anton stopped, and I bumped into his armor, which also hurt.

"Shhh!" he hissed.

"What?" I asked.

"Hear that?" he said.

I caught a glint of light from his armor, and saw that he was pointing up. I looked where he was gesturing even though there was nothing to look at, just rock above us. Then I heard what he was talking about. There were feet moving on the rocks over our heads. And they were moving hard and fast enough to send out little puffs of smoky dirt whenever they stomped the ground.

"Zombie pigmen?" I whispered.

Anton nodded.

The footsteps halted, and sounded like they were milling around, probably looking to find us.

"Are they always that organized?" I whispered.

"They are now," Anton said. After a few moments, he whispered, "They're moving off."

"Shuffling, more like."

"Whatever. Let's go. Esme is going to be pissed."

"When is she not pissed?" I asked.

"Correction," he said. "Esme is going to be more pissed than usual, which means we're in a lot of trouble."

"Not me," I said. "I just got here."

"Bianca, when are you not in trouble with Esme?" Anton asked.

I didn't have a response to that, and Anton wasn't waiting for one. He led us out where I was happy to not be breaking my back, neck, and legs from constant crouching, and down to a narrow bridge. On the other side of it, Esme was battling huge magma cubes. Several of them were springing up around her, hopping and attacking, with a horde of zombie pigmen around them. Esme was surrounded. But she was well-equipped, wearing diamond armor like Anton's and attacking them with a diamond sword.

She chopped one magma cube in two, then turned the other way and pierced straight through a zombie pigman all in one stroke.

"The passageways come up on the other side of where she's standing," Anton explained. "If it had worked, we would have been able to take them from both sides."

Instead, Esme looked like she was struggling. She grimaced with every swing of her sword. I ran ahead across the bridge, leaving Lonnie with Anton, and slid into the fray, positioning myself on the other side of Esme so we could take on the magma cubes from two sides. She hacked at a large one and it broke into two smaller pieces that moved off in opposite directions. Esme left me to the smaller ones while she took on another large magma cube.

With my enemies dispatched, I collected the magma cream, and turned toward a zombie pigman.

Esme moved toward me and spun around so we were back-to-back. By then, Anton had come up to supply reinforcements.

"What happened?" Esme shouted at him.

"Best-laid plans," he said with a shrug. That seemed to be enough for Esme, who ran at a magma cube and jumped over it, slashing at the same time. It split into four smaller pieces instantly as she landed on the other side of it, breathing heavily, with her diamond armor glinting.

Anton came up after her, cutting each of the four cubes down and taking the cream into his inventory.

They were a well-oiled machine.

In moments, all the zombie pigmen had shuffled off, and the magma cubes had bounded away. Maybe they decided they needed less dangerous prey. Esme and Anton high-fived and laughed. For a moment, I forgot why we were there. I was just thrilled to have gotten past this hurdle. But then I spotted Lonnie stuck between some blocks that Anton had probably used to trap him so he couldn't get away, and I went to free him.

"He's not like he was," I said. "It's really him. He's in there. He can help us."

"He's slowing us down," Esme said. "You should have left him in the Overworld."

"That wasn't an option," I said. "He fell through."

"There is always an option," said Esme. She shook her head. "You just won't listen. You're too stubborn."

"And who exactly do you listen to?" I asked.

Esme walked away in a huff, and the rest of us fell in line behind her.

"Where are we going?" I asked.

"We made a base. It's not far from here," Anton said in a low voice.

I shuffled behind, sticking close to Lonnie and putting a little distance between us and the others.

"Look who's excited to share our supplies again," Esme said snarkily over her shoulder.

"Don't mind Esme," Anton said. "When you took off the last time, she actually was worried about you. Thought the scarred enderman might have gotten you."

"She saw the scar too?" I asked. Until now, I thought maybe I had imagined it. The image of the jagged line across the enderman's face resurfaced like a terrible nightmare.

"Yeah, we all did," Anton said. "Why, do you know something about it?"

"No, nothing, I thought it was just weird-looking too, that's all," I deflected. I wasn't ready to talk about the resemblance to the guy in the other car. It would bring up questions, ones I wasn't ready to answer. I put up all the mental barriers that I could around those memories.

Lonnie and I moved faster toward Esme, leaving Anton to catch up behind us.

CHAPTER 20

Despite our iron armor and my Projectile Protection, Lonnie and I were still vulnerable in the Nether. I moved us in between Esme and Anton, with Esme in the lead and Anton bringing up the rear.

Ahead of us, Esme lit netherrack, lighting our way through the darkness, and moved slowly enough to detect incoming enemies, which she conveniently dispatched with her arrows. Just in case they decided to attack.

"Scars are a weird thing to see on the mobs," Anton said, trying to bring up the subject again. "Even mine don't—"

"I don't want to talk about this," I said, getting annoyed. "I can't explain it and neither can you."

"I don't believe you." Anton pushed further. "I saw your face when I mentioned the scar. You recognized it."

"So what if I did?" I said.

"Bianca, remember what I told you about the witches and how Esme manifests them with her anxiety?"

"Yep, and you've got literal skeletons after you."

"Right. So, yours are endermen. There's something you need to deal with that's creating endermen, and this one in particular. The only way to get rid of it is to talk through what happened." He put a hand out to try to stop me, but I turned my body to slip past and kept on walking. "This place doesn't hide us from the real world. Not really. Everything we're dealing with out there, we bring in here."

I picked up the pace and moved farther away from him. "I don't know what you're talking about. I don't have anything to process." I felt a throb of pain in my head, and ignored it. "And it doesn't matter. What matters is trying to get to the end of the game."

"You two!" Esme called from up ahead. She jerked her head toward a mob of zombie pigmen. "Think you can handle that by yourselves?" She was looking at me, but I guessed that she meant me and Anton together. My eyes flicked to Lonnie. "I can babysit for you," Esme added.

For some reason, this babysitting comment put me over the edge. All the abuse she'd piled on me since the beginning of the game hadn't done it, but that—an insult designed to hit both me and my best friend in one blow—fueled some combination of rage and pride that made the following possible: I pulled out a diamond sword and axe and strode off in long steps down the path, gathering speed into a run, then jumped as I reached the mob. I brought the axe and sword down in simultaneous swipes, catching two of the creatures in the process. I landed on the other side and wound up behind them. So I turned and struck them again from the back, bringing both the weapons together in a clash of metal and sparks. Then I finished the two zombie pigmen off with a third blow. I picked up the rotten flesh and moved on to the next two, slashing, cutting, and stabbing my way through. By the time Anton caught up, I'd put away the flesh of four of them and was working on a fifth, leaving only one for him to take out with an arrow that he shot from a short distance away. My anger now vented, I put away both the weapons, and grabbed Lonnie from Esme in the space of two long strides.

"Yes. I think I can handle it."

Esme raised her eyebrows and gave Anton a look. "Well, look who's finally decided to play the game."

It was the final straw.

I let go of Lonnie's arm, and turned to face her. "I've been playing," I said, seething again. "Same. As. You." I took another step forward. "This isn't just a game for me, either. I'm playing through. Maybe not the way you want me to, and that's fine. Lonnie and I can make it on our own."

With that, I tugged Lonnie out of the relative protection of the two people in the whole place who had any gear with enchantments that we could use to stay alive, and I marched off into the darkness, not even bothering to light my way.

"Come back!" Anton called. "She doesn't mean it!"

I heard Esme snort with disdain.

"She does," I said.

"She's a jerk sometimes," Anton said, jogging to catch up with me.

"That's the first accurate thing I've heard you say," I said.

"Hey. I'm trying to help." Anton sounded genuinely hurt. And when I didn't stop walking, he added another "Hey!"

"What?" I whipped back, swinging Lonnie around with me, and then had to immediately help him up off the black, gravelly ground.

I faced both Esme and Anton, silhouetted against the black and orange background of the Nether. I suddenly felt exhausted and frustrated and angry all at once. I would have cried if I could. And that somehow also made me ticked off. I dropped my eyes to the ground, wrestling with the warring emotions of how much I was experiencing was the game, and how much was me creating things in the game. I knew that my friends were trying to get me to open up about my feelings, to talk about what happened that night of the accident. I knew it would probably help clear things up. But I also knew I wasn't ready to talk yet, and I was tired of fighting with Esme and Anton. A distant part of me finally realized I couldn't put off this conversation forever, and if what I'd brought from the real world into the game was making things so much more difficult, did I really have a choice? It was time to grow up and deal. So I took a deep breath and prepared to speak.

I lifted my eyes again to find Esme shooting a flaming arrow in my direction, and Anton running toward me hard, with a sword held up over his head in both hands and a grimace on his face.

Before my shocked brain could force me to respond, or move, he was directly in front of me, and brought the sword down just to my right as I felt a sharp pain. Something sharp stung me from behind. I fell forward into Anton's chest. He kept moving, and I slipped off him, and rolled onto my back. Then I saw what had prompted Esme's attack and made Anton come running: right in front of me was a group of mean-looking wither skeletons with their swords held high.

And I had been hit.

Lonnie was still standing, and he turned to one of the wither skeletons with nothing but his hands, and started to whale on it. The skeleton seemed startled, getting smacked from behind, but Lonnie kept up a relentless pace of punching, so it had no opportunity to retaliate.

Meanwhile, Anton killed one at close range by slicing its torso, and one of Esme's arrows found its target, destroying the third one. Then both she and Anton turned back to the first, which was struggling to stand up because of Lonnie's beating. Anton took it out with one sword blow. He looked at Lonnie, as if he was seeing him differently. But since Lonnie didn't respond, and didn't reciprocate, Anton held his hand out to me and picked me up off the ground.

"Did you see that?" I asked.

"Yeah, I did," Anton said.

I looked at Esme to see if she'd noticed. She was staring at Lonnie, frowning, then she shrugged. "I still don't know," she said.

"I do," I said.

We regrouped near Esme. I stared at Lonnie, the speech I was going to deliver before the attack turning to ash in my mouth. I didn't know what to say, and luckily Esme had already moved on to something else.

"If there are wither skeletons around, there must be a fortress," she said to Anton and me. "It was actually helpful, drawing them out like that."

"You mean just now when I was bait?" I asked.

"Yeah, exactly," Esme said. One side of her mouth cocked up into a crooked smile.

"I'm glad I could be useful."

She laughed and simply moved on to the next phase of the plan she was laying out.

We needed to build a bridge to get over a thin rivulet of lava. It might have been possible for the rest of us to jump over, but even I wasn't sure Lonnie would be able to execute that wide a jump. Esme decided we should stay close to where we had drawn out the wither skeletons, so making a bridge and staying close to our current location was our best option.

A few steps ahead, the dark reddish brown and black dirt of the landscape turned a different shade of brown. It was a grayer color and had no tints of red or orange in it. As we got closer, I could make out faces in the pixilated shades that looked like they were in agony, mouths fixed into screams.

"Soul sand," I said.

Esme stopped short and turned to see it.

There was the equivalent of a large lake of soul sand a few steps away. Anton moved into it first, and immediately slowed to a crawl. He mined it as he went. I followed, gathering as much as he did. Esme stood with her bow resting against her shoulder, ready for anything that might pop out and kill us.

Lonnie stepped forward, as if he was coming to help, but Esme pulled him back to her and held on to him until we had finished mining. I was grateful that she didn't do so with a snide comment this time.

We finished mining and returned, pulling ourselves slowly out of the muck. Anton was the first to make it to regular Nether ground, and he held his hand out to me to pull me the rest of the way. I took it, already feeling the effects of both the weight of the sand and the hit from the wither skeleton. I winced as he got me out.

"You're hurt pretty bad, but we don't have any potions to help you," Anton said.

"How long do you think I have?" I whispered.

"In this game?" He looked at me as if he could evaluate my strength with a look, then he shrugged. "We're going to have to adjust the plan. Soon you won't be strong enough to help us get all the materials we need for the End."

"I'm fine. It's not so bad," I said. "I'm going to power through to the End."

"So, you're not going to say anything to her?" He glanced at Esme. "She should know you're hurt."

"What's the point?" I asked. "I'd only get more sarcasm."

I walked up to where Esme and Lonnie were waiting. When Esme took off in silence, I followed without even a glance back to Anton. Moments later, a black hill came into view. It rose up as we moved forward, looking like it was cut to resemble a face with a gaping mouth. Both Anton and Esme trudged toward it. And then I realized that it was their home base. I stopped, but no one else did, and Anton bumped into me. I picked up my pace, trying to pretend where we were headed didn't scare the pants off me, when Anton said, "It's pretty intimidating. I know." I nodded, and moved along.

The mini fortress Esme and Anton had built was cozy for two, but a bit of a logistical nightmare for four. We broke down a few of the walls, and expanded using cobblestone and nether brick. A couple of curious ghasts flew by, as if trying to decide whether to attack us now or later, but the brick would assure our safety—so long as we stayed inside the fortress, at least.

One of the ghasts came down low, its dangling tentacles nearly within reach. I scrolled through my weapons to choose a bow and arrows, when Esme pulled me inside, with Anton following.

"I could get it," I protested.

"That's not the point," she said. "You're not thinking. Again."

I frowned, trying to understand what she meant.

Anton jumped in. "We're going to need all our supplies to get to the End," he said. "We need to hold on to as many as we can now."

"So why not just tell me that's what we're doing," I asked. "Would it have been that hard to say, 'Hey, we need to conserve the supplies'?" I walked away, shaking my head.

"It shouldn't have been that hard to figure out," Esme said. "It's pretty obvious that we need to conserve as much as we can. There are four of us and we're sharing the few supplies we've got."

"And all I'm saying is that a little heads-up would have been helpful. If there are new rules that you're making up, Your Highness, maybe you could clue in us commoners."

Esme stomped toward me and peered real close into my eyes. I count it as a mighty show of bravery that I didn't even flinch. This, of course, seemed to make her even more angry, and she stormed off to a back room.

Anton looked like he was going to say something, but I waved him off and turned back to finishing up the expansion of the mini fortress.

"Do you want to help?" I asked when I noticed Lonnie tagging along. I gave him one of my pickaxes and turned him in the direction of a wall we needed to smash.

"Nothing could possibly go wrong," Anton said, as he layered a part of the ceiling with nether brick, observing us from the side.

I rolled my eyes at him and turned back to Lonnie. "Go ahead," I said. "Try."

Lonnie looked at me and then at the wall, and moved forward, bumping into it.

"How about like this?" I said, and I demonstrated by breaking part of the wall.

Lonnie mimicked me, and I heaped him with praise.

Anton came around to where we were working. "It's like he's a puppy that's finally pooped outside," he said. "I'm sure that makes him feel awesome. I'm kind of glad he doesn't understand much. I mean, we can't have his self-esteem go through the roof and turn him into a diva."

"This is hard enough," I snapped. "It's just, sometimes it seems like he's there, but sometimes . . ."

"Most times," Anton corrected.

"*Sometimes*," I said again, "it seems like he's checked out, and

I'm worried that if I don't do everything I can to fix him, Lonnie will hate me forever."

Anton put his hand on my shoulder. I felt the pressure of his squeeze and the warmth of his hand. "The truth is, it's nice that you're doing everything you can do as his friend," he said. "It's kind of great. I wish I had a friend who'd stick with me like that." He turned to walk away, then paused and added, "Sorry if I've been a jerk. Sometimes I can't turn my sarcasm off." He turned back and looked at me for a couple of seconds before he continued. "The first time I played the game, I stayed in here too long, and when I got out, my legs were stiff from not moving, so the nurses hid the goggles for a while. They said they'd been calling me, and they were sure I was ignoring them. But I wasn't. I just was so into the game that I'd tuned them out."

"I know how that is," I said. "I don't even need the goggles to tune people out when I'm playing, usually."

Anton chuckled. "Well, yeah. What I'm saying is, it's really easy to lose yourself in the game."

I suddenly felt warmth running through my body, as if someone on the outside had pressed in close to me, or had pulled a blanket up to my chin. "Yeah," I said. "I'm sure you're right."

"It's easy to forget that this version of Minecraft is so immersive," Anton said, as he threw his arm out and looked around. "But you can't stay here forever."

"What if I want to stay," I said more than asked. "What if I just don't want to deal with whatever is waiting for me on the other side?"

"We will still be there on the other side," Anton said. "You're not alone in here or outside."

"Lonnie always stuck by me, even when I was little," I said. "And we promised we'd always be there for one another." I took a deep breath.

Esme came back, looking hesitant. "I'm sorry to interrupt," she said, and I was surprised that she did sound genuinely sorry. "But we've got to go to the nether fortress and gather all the supplies we need so that we can get out of here and back to the Overworld. We have to go now, and we have to be fast. You're fading," she said to me.

"What? I, no—"

"We don't have any milk to cure the wither effect," she said grimly. "Did you think I wouldn't notice? And I can't see your health bar anymore. It's bad. I hate to say it, but the time to talk is later. We have to get you out of here."

Anton raised an eyebrow at me, waiting for my response.

"Well?" she asked. "What are you waiting for? Get your stuff and let's go. It's time to raid that fort."

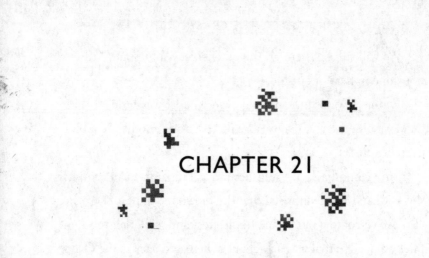

CHAPTER 21

It's a good thing that whatever was connecting our brains to the game had not incorporated tastebuds, because I imagine that rotting zombie pigman flesh is not a culinary delight anyone would go out of their way for. But I munched on it anyway, taking the chance of getting food poisoning since it was the only sustenance we had left, as we moved toward the fortress. Luckily I didn't get sick, and of course, thinking about actual culinary delights immediately gave me the idea of making a restaurant in Minecraft that specialized in Minecrafty dishes that I could construct once we got out of here.

"Hold up," Esme said, forcing my scattered thoughts to focus back on the mission. She put her hand out military-style, as if we were soldiers in formation behind our commanding officer. She drew her sword and each of us followed suit, holding them up and reflecting the orange light of the Nether.

A group of wither skeletons came up on our right. I immediately flinched, not prepared to take another hit, armor or no.

"Just don't move," Esme said. "Maybe they'll go right past us."

"That hasn't worked before," Anton pointed out.

"Shhh!" Esme hissed.

Anton zipped up, and I nodded once to acknowledge Esme's instruction, then held my breath, worried that even that slight movement might set them off.

The wither skeletons moved toward us, marching in a jagged formation but all moving at the same pace, with the same dead look in their faces as they came closer.

I breathed. I had to. But nothing happened. Their movements were unchanged.

Even when they looked in our direction, it was hard to tell whether they saw us or not. And it looked like they were going to pass us just to the back of our line. The first wither skeleton shuffled past on the black dirt, and then a second got up close to Anton without turning to look in his direction.

I relaxed. This was actually going to work.

One of them got close to me. So close that I shifted just out of the way to avoid brushing against it. *This is almost too easy*, I thought.

Lonnie chose that moment to turn and scream, sprinting toward the skeleton. His fists were up, and I tried to get between him and the skeleton, but he was flailing and punching, getting me, the wither skeleton, and even Anton when he tried to intervene.

Every single wither skeleton turned in unison. It was as though they were seeing us for the first time. So much for too easy.

I slammed into the closest wither skeleton, sending it careering onto its back. Then I grabbed hold of Lonnie's hand and ran.

By then, Lonnie had somehow gotten tangled up in another wither skeleton's ribs, so it got dragged along. Lonnie kept trying to punch his way out and I tried jabbing it with the tip of my sword, but between the running and Lonnie's flailing, I wound up hitting him a couple of times. Not my best move, I'll admit.

The wither skeleton brought its sword down and I shielded Lonnie from the hit, absorbing the stinging pain in his stead, but I could feel my energy sap. I wasn't sure how much longer I could keep this up.

The skeleton pulled up again, readying for another blow. I lashed out desperately, catching this one in the side of its chest. It tumbled away as Lonnie and I fell backward. I tried to get to my feet, but I was moving incredibly slowly. I thought at first that the blow from the first wither skeleton attack was finally catching up with me, or that I'd gotten another hit in this attack, but hadn't noticed. I called to Lonnie for help, but he was also moving very slowly. I looked down. We were standing in soul sand. And we were right near the edge of it, close enough for another wither skeleton to reach out and attack us if it wanted to, without getting into the soul sand itself.

"Anton!"

"I'm busy, Bianca!" he called back.

"Anton!" I screamed again.

This time he looked back, narrowly missing being cleaved in two by the wither skeleton he was battling. Near him, Esme smashed a skeleton to pieces with her bare hands, then knelt and switched weapons to her favorite: the bow. She stayed in place, aimed, and sent three successive arrows toward Lonnie and me.

Each of them lodged in the wither skeleton's back, and it flopped forward into the soul sand, just missing us, before disappearing in a swirl of pixilated dust.

I worked my way out of the soul sand trap, then yanked Lonnie out as well. Anton grunted as he killed off the last wither skeleton and struggled out of the soul sand, holding its head like Yorick from *Hamlet*.

"Alas, poor Wither," he said with a grin.

I laughed. It reminded me of the year before when my sister's drama club did *Hamlet*, and in the middle of the *where be your gibes now* speech, there was the very audible clatter of the skull's plastic jaw falling on the stage floor. Suddenly, Carrie's scene was the comedy hit of the night, but she had been furious that everything hadn't gone perfectly.

Nothing ever goes perfectly, Carrie, I had told her.

That was too true.

"Hold on to that a minute," Anton said, handing me the wither skeleton's skull. Then he turned to Lonnie, helped him pull up his limited supplies, took off his helmet, and put the wither skull on Lonnie's head.

I shuddered. It was like looking at the Grim Reaper. There was even something about the mouth that made me feel it was opening and closing, like it was casting a silent spell. I wished I could take it off, but I knew its use. With the skull on, Lonnie might be ignored by the mobs in the game. Or at least maybe long enough that they wouldn't immediately attack him, or us. As horrifying as it looked, it was a good strategy.

"Ready?" Esme asked.

"I've got him," Anton said, so I followed Esme in the direction that the wither skeletons had come.

The fortress appeared on the horizon, a looming castle complete with towers and turrets and surrounded by lava that poured out of holes in its walls in gloppy gushes, filling pools in a cavernous lake that was so far below I wasn't sure anyone could reach it. Torches lit up the walls in ruler-straight lines, showing the path into the fortress, and the vast outline of the building. As we got closer, details on the fortress came into view. There were archways with elaborate patterns, buttresses coming out of the walls like steadying hands with fingers grabbing hold of the earth. Steps were carefully cut into patterns of rising and falling levels—which would make a straight charge from the outside impossible—that was almost like artwork. Although the castle was tall, it was also spread out and looked like a hulking monster, crouching, waiting to explode out. And when we got close enough and looked down into the depths where the lava pooled, it seemed like it might really have been a colossal creature that could attack and crush us into ash beneath its fiery feet. Everything about the fortress— the high, spiked towers like spiny ridges along its back, the gaping opening at the front that looked ready to snap shut and consume anyone who got close enough—seemed designed to dissuade anyone from entering. As we moved toward it, Esme hesitated at the bridge that would take us to the large mouth of a front door.

"It doesn't look so bad from far off," I said.

Esme nodded in agreement, then strode off bravely across the rock bridge, straight toward the entrance.

"This is exactly what it wants," I whispered to myself. "An easy meal." But I followed her anyway, though admittedly a good few steps behind.

When we got to the huge open door, I looked back, and Anton and Lonnie were coming as well, but had only reached the start of the bridge. Anton waved me on, and I thought, *Sure. I would wave you on too if I could hang back a bit.*

We entered a large room with tapestries hanging on immense walls that looked like they went three levels up. The room was lit with candles inset into the stone and a huge candelabra ablaze with what might have been a hundred more candles. The higher levels had archways cut into the walls, like inset balconies, while the floor we were on had a few doors surrounding it. Esme walked across the empty room over a few crisscrossing layers of carpet, and went to the nearest door on her left. She opened it, and there was a long hallway leading away from the room, but no other openings from the hallway that we could make out from where we were. She went to each successive door, and found nearly the same setup. Leading away from the room, every path was a long, dark hallway that led who knew where.

"We could split up," I suggested.

Esme shook her head. "Better to stay together. If we get separated and we need help, it's going to be bad."

"Okay, so which door?" I asked.

She shrugged. "Pick one?"

"Me?"

"You," she said. "If it's a bad one, I will blame you for picking it, and if it's a good one, I'll take all the credit for leading us there."

"A win-win," I said.

She smiled. "Exactly."

"Look, Esme," I said, seizing the moment alone with her. "I'm not trying to make things difficult. Really."

"I know you're not," she said. "I know I can be—"

"Harsh? Abrasive? Inflexible?" I suggested.

She chuckled. "Yeah, those. Having something to do that makes logical sense is exactly what I come here for. I know if I follow a plan, things are going to work. But outside . . . everything the doctors and my parents try is unpredictable." She stepped into the hallway and grabbed one of the torches to take with us. "Can you imagine what that's like?"

"Imagine knowing that you caused all the pain that the people closest to you are in. That it's all your fault. My parents, my sister, Lonnie. Even the other driver. None of them would be hurting if it wasn't for what I did in one moment of being a total idiot."

Esme blinked at me twice, before continuing on. Just when I thought she was going to let this line of conversation go, she added, "I'm not really mad at you, Bianca. I'm mad that this is the only place where I can feel like I'm in control of myself again. And sometimes, I guess I try to be too controlling of others in the game."

"Once we log off, I can get someone to roll me over to your room," I said. "I'll find some way to bring the sword on the outside, and I'll tell the doctors that the next time they don't do right by you, they'll have me to answer to."

She smiled weakly.

"Too bad real life can't be more like a game." She waved her hand dismissively and added, "Whatever. Not important."

"It's important. All of this is important. Just because it's a game doesn't mean it's not significant," I said. "I'm sure about that."

She briefly laid a hand on my shoulder and nodded before moving ahead. The hallway opened up onto a wide landing with two paths leading in different directions where the floor dropped away, so they were like bridges leading to other parts of the castle. Esme went on one of them, and I went on the other.

"Bianca, look down," she said.

Beneath us was a crisscrossed network of pathways and stairs leading down to the belly of the castle.

"How are we going to find the blaze spawner?" I asked. "It could be anywhere." I rolled my eyes and happened to see that the crisscrossing paths were above us, too. "Look, Esme!"

"Ugh."

"Now what?" I asked. "Maybe we *should* split up."

"Definitely not now. It will be too easy to get lost. At least if we have each other, one person can remember the way we came so we can get out again, while the other person focuses on finding the blaze spawner, and keeping any of the mobs away."

"I suppose I'm the one who's going to be figuring out where we are and how to get back?" I asked.

"That's right, Dora. You're the map." She moved off along her own path, and I had to run back around to catch up.

"How do you even know this is the right way to go?" I asked. "You're just guessing."

Esme stopped short, and I bumped into her. She pointed up at one of the walls on the other side, near the ceiling of the fortress. "See that?" she asked.

"What?"

"Look. That glowy yellow thing coming out of that wall?"

"Oh."

"Oh," she said, as she ran off again.

"We can't know that it's the blaze spawner," I said.

"We'll find out when we get there, won't we?" she said. "And it's as good a place as any to start." She picked up her pace, making me have to run full-out to catch up.

On the other side of the bridge, the door opened into a room that was nearly as stark as the first one we'd entered. Esme found a far door that led to a stairway, and she took them two at a time. I was moving a little too slowly to do that. I knew it was probably because of the blow from the wither skeleton, but I did my best to keep up.

The floor above was elaborately decorated with paintings on every wall; actual windows, even though they only looked out on other parts of the castle and highlighted the dark rat-maze we were in; and detailed furniture that reminded me of the Gothic artwork on all of the archways. There were no other exit doors, though.

Esme walked back out of the room, looked up at the next level, and then reentered the room.

"Maybe there's another way," I said.

She shook her head. "No, it has to be here. None of the other bridges lead close enough to the room with the blaze spawner."

We went back to looking through the windows at the rat-maze, and then feeling up the walls inside of the room.

"Maybe it's designed to be misleading," I said. "This room is the closest, but there's no way to get to the blaze spawner from here. We have to go back and try one of the other paths."

She narrowed her eyes at me for a moment, then nodded agreement. I led us back out to the bridge, and across it, down the next hallway, until we came to what looked like an identical room.

"Did you bring us the same way?" Esme shouted, sounding frustrated.

"I didn't. You saw that I didn't!"

"So, all of the rooms are the same, then," she said, deflating, sounding tired and defeated.

"These two are," I said. "We can't know about the rest of them. There are lots of variables . . ." I trailed off when I saw the despondent look on her face.

"There's no opening, and this path led us even farther away from the spawner. So, we've just wasted a bunch of time."

"It's going to be okay. We'll figure this out," I said.

She looked at me, then she looked over my head to the place my health bar was, except it wasn't there anymore.

"Bianca," she said quietly.

"I know," I said.

I couldn't think of anything to say. The clock was starting to run out on me.

"So what do we do now?" Esme asked.

"We finish the game," I said. "Which means, it's bashing time." And before she could say anything else, I started hacking into the wall, which yielded nothing at first, but as I moved around the room, I eventually found another set of stairs leading up. "Voilà!"

"I was going to be really annoyed if that didn't work," she said, shooting me a grin.

"How would I know?" I answered, gently bumping my shoulder against hers and smiling. "You're annoyed at me ninety-nine percent of the time."

She laughed. "Maybe ninety-six." Then she followed me up the stairs, which led us to the correct level, and onto a balcony that looked down on the middle of the fortress and its network of stairs and passageways that now reminded me of drawings of a nervous system, all leading back to the entrance.

"At least we can get out," I said.

Esme led us straight toward the room with the glowing yellow light. She hesitated at the door and looked in. "There are probably traps."

"After all this?" I asked.

She took out a couple of pieces of rotting meat, and threw them into the room.

Nothing happened.

"Well . . ." I began, and darted around her and into the room.

"Bianca, wait!"

By then I was well inside the room, and facing the black cage of the blaze spawner, with the blaze glowing inside it.

Esme came up behind me. "What if there was a trap?" she asked.

"You already checked," I said. "And look! Blaze spawner! Dead ahead!"

Esme pulled out her sword and held it in one hand, ready to fight. I followed suit, although I wasn't prepared for this enemy. The blaze exited the cage in a howl of fury. I could feel the warmth of it radiating against my skin. As it passed us, I raised my sword to bring down on it, but as soon as I got close enough, the searing heat of the blaze felt like an oven. I missed, coming down hard on the stone floor behind it. Esme, fortunately, managed to make contact, and her Fire Protection armor kept her from injury.

"Why didn't you come with Anton?" I asked, readying for another attack. "Both of you have Fire Protection armor, and I have basically nothing."

"I need to keep my eye on you," Esme said, as she lifted the sword for another pass at the blaze. She hit it again and it howled as it smacked against the wall of the room and turned back on us. The singe mark it left in the wall looked like a screaming face. "I need to make sure you don't disappear again."

This time, instead of letting the blaze get close to me, I threw the sword at it, catching it right in the middle. The weapon stuck for a moment, and the blaze screamed and turned, coming straight at me. *How exactly do you defeat a fire creature again?*

Esme thrust through with her sword. It changed the blaze's trajectory, but it seemed angrier, and more determined to hurt us. The heat in the room was growing more intense by the second. I wished there was some way to cool it down a bit. Suddenly, I was reminded of Lonnie's original plan.

"Snowballs!" I yelled.

"What?"

"My snowballs!"

I opened my inventory, pulled a couple of snowballs for myself, and gave a bunch to Esme as well.

We took turns hurling the snowballs at the blaze, hitting it every time, and distracting its attention. Its colors became dull, and the blaze itself grew quieter, and hung lower in the air between us. Another volley of snowballs got the mob down on the ground, leaving behind a blaze rod, which I swiped quickly, and ran for the door with Esme right behind me.

Just when I thought all was going to be well and that we would escape with no problem, mobs of wither skeletons approached us. There was nowhere to run but down into the room and back out to the network of bridges. Unless . . .

I looked at Esme, then out at the web of thread-thin bridges below us.

"No," she said.

"What are our options?" I asked.

"It's a stupid thing to try," she said.

"No stupider than staying here and trying to fight our way out." I hesitated only a moment to see her face relax from an outright *no* to a slightly softer *maybe*, and then I pulled myself over the railing, aimed for what looked like the closest bridge, and jumped.

You know how when you're playing a game, your depth perception might be a little bit off? What looks near is actually much farther away, and what seems to be a long way off is right in front of your face? That sort of thing? Generally, you need to shift your position a little to get a sense of what's around you and how you're situated inside of a landscape, but it's really hard to shift your position *after* you've done a swan dive off a balcony into the belly of a fortress designed to kill you. So, I don't recommend it.

Anyway, I was falling toward what looked like the closest bridge, which turned out to be a bridge two levels farther down than the actual closest bridge, a fact I only realized about half a second into the jump. *Perspective*, my brain provided, too late to be useful. I reached out with my right arm and bow, hoping to catch the edge of what was actually the closest one, and missed. Then I reached out with my left arm at the next one and banged into it, hanging off the side. With my heart pounding and my arm aching, I scrambled over the railing and onto the bridge, and then took a moment to question the choices that had led me here. That's when I remembered Esme. I looked up.

She was surrounded by wither skeletons, trying to hold them back.

"Jump!" I screamed. "Esme! Jump!"

She looked down at me, her face contorted with fear.

"I'll catch you!" I had a flash of Lonnie's face when he tried to catch me from the monkey bars.

I couldn't tell what the face was that she made, but she climbed up on the railing and dove toward me. But as she did, three wither skeletons thrust their swords at her, each one of them catching her in a different part of her body. I saw her jerk and curl into herself so she was coming down like a rock, and I had no limbs to grab hold of. I stepped up on the railing, realizing that this was probably the stupidest move I'd ever made in my entire life, and held out both of my arms. As Esme came whizzing down, I grabbed and jumped backward in one motion, hoping I had caught her and that I didn't jump so far that I'd fall off the platform.

When I opened my eyes, Esme hung over the side of the bridge. I yanked her up, and she fell in a heap beside me. Both of us panted.

"I wasn't sure that was going to work," I said when I'd caught my breath.

"I was sure that it wasn't," she said. "But thank you."

"You're welcome," I said. Then, "They got you."

She looked down at her body. There were three slashes—one on her torso, one on her arm, and another on her leg. "Yeah. They did."

"One of them got me before, and I'm still doing okay," I said.

"One," she said. "Not three."

The pale face of a wither skeleton appeared in the darkness at the far end of the bridge. I pulled Esme to standing. "We have to get back to the Overworld to heal."

She nodded. I held her against my body and ran toward the entrance as several more skeletons took chase. Then, below us, I heard a series of explosions.

Esme looked confused for a moment, and then her face cleared up. "Anton."

"Let's hope so."

"Maybe he got the nether wart," she said.

Below us, bridges were beginning to collapse from the explosions. Behind us, the wither skeletons were still coming. "We can't worry about that now."

We ran with the nether fortress collapsing around us and mobs on our heels, and made it to the main drawbridge that led out of the fortress. Beneath the drawbridge, the lava bubbled in huge popping bursts as if it was being heated even more than usual. Pieces of the fortress fell in on itself, crushing the wither skeletons as it did, and cracking the drawbridge beneath our feet. I continued pulling Esme along, worried about where Lonnie and Anton might have gotten to, and whether they had made it out of the fortress before it was destroyed.

We stepped off the bridge and onto Nether soil just as the last of the fortress fell into a huge pool of bubbling lava, splashing an arc of it over our heads. I dragged Esme out of the way as it came down and seared the ground right where we had been standing a moment before.

"Do you think they made it?" she asked.

I shook my head. "I don't know." The ground beneath us rumbled. I picked Esme up and moved even farther away, fearing the ground might start falling in soon.

"Hey!" someone screamed from our right.

Anton came from around another part of the fortress that was being obliterated by explosions. The ground cracked and crumbled at his feet as he ran.

"Lonnie!" I called. "Where's Lonnie?"

Anton zigzagged his way through a few pieces of falling rock, and I spotted Lonnie behind him, mimicking his every move. I was about to run toward them, when Esme held me back and shook her head.

"They need our help!"

"We'll only mess them up if we go out there now," she said.

I could feel my heart beating as I stood there watching them get closer to us. In my head, I was chanting, *Come on, come on,* but I didn't dare say it aloud, as if that might jinx us all. Anton's face looked deathly scared, but they seemed to be making it away from the remains of the fortress just fine. I didn't understand why he looked like that until they were closer.

There were ghasts on his tail.

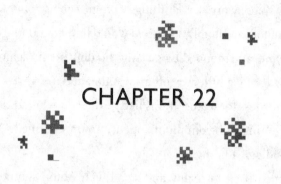

CHAPTER 22

Esme pulled out arrows and lit them, then aimed at the ghasts.

"Don't waste those!" Anton cried out.

She ignored him, executing hits that I couldn't dream of, even though it was clear she was severely weakened. Even as she slumped into the dirt, her last arrow pierced the closest ghast, killing it.

I peeled her up off the ground, and helped her run ahead of the boys. As soon as they fell into step with us, Anton turned and threw a couple of TNT bombs at the ghasts. Two of them fell away, but there were another two coming. They split up and then came at us again from different sides. We ran down a low hill to keep away from them until I realized that they were corralling us into an impossible-to-escape-from location, with a lake of lava at our backs and them coming at us from both sides.

"I can't fight holding on to you," I said.

"This is bad," Esme said.

For the first time, I heard the truly scared twelve-year-old girl in Esme's voice, worried that things were not going to go well. I didn't want to leave her. But I knew I would have to. Lonnie came alongside me, and scooped Esme away, holding her up against his side, and moving a little way off from Anton and me.

I was at a loss for words. It was like he'd read my mind.

"Stop staring with your mouth open!" Anton screamed. "We're in the middle of a firefight!"

I snapped back to reality and stood with Anton shoulder-to-shoulder, firing arrows and throwing TNT bombs. We got rid of one more ghast that way, but the final one was still evading our weapons and pushing us back toward the lava.

I looked around, trying to spot an escape route, but there was no way out. The lava was right behind us and we had nowhere to run.

"Bianca!" Anton called. "You can't just do whatever you want right now!"

Except, it *was* a world where I could do whatever I wanted, if I planned it out right. I turned to Anton and said, "I'm going to try something, okay? If it doesn't work, I'll probably be toast and you'll have to take it down yourself. But I think this can work."

"What are you doing?" Esme called out as I stepped forward to draw the ghast's fireball attack.

"Bianca!" Anton cried.

"This is going to work," I called. "I've got a plan!"

As I watched the fiery projectile racing toward me, I thought about something Lonnie had mentioned during his meticulous planning for our trip to the Nether. He'd said that if you time it just right, you can punch a fireball back at a ghast. "I bet I'll look like a wizard shooting flames out of my hands, you'll see!" he'd exclaimed.

He always had a flair for the dramatic.

I punched my hand out just before the attack would inciner-ate me, hoping against hope that I'd done it correctly. One heart-beat later, I watched as the fireball rebounded and the ghast exploded in flames. I slumped down to the ground, all of my adrenaline gone after facing down the giant mob alone.

Lonnie put a hand on my shoulder and helped me to my feet. I smiled weakly at him. "How did it look? As cool as you were hop-ing?"

"Seriously?" Esme said from behind. "You could've died!"

Anton looked at me silently, his eyes wide in amazement.

I pushed away from Lonnie and walked over to Esme, giving her a hug. She struggled for a second, but then embraced me back. "We're all fine," I said, pulling away. I looked back toward where the nether fortress had once stood.

"Did you blow it up?" I asked Anton.

He just grinned.

"So now what?" Esme asked. "The fortress is gone, and I'm not sure we got everything we need to get to the End."

Anton brought out the nether wart. "We got this."

Esme looked surprised, then glanced at me. I pulled out the blaze rod. The barest hint of a smile played at the side of her mouth.

"I'll get to work on the portal," Anton said. "But while I do that . . ." He pulled up his inventory and took out two enchanted apples, tossing them to Esme and me. "I found them in the fortress. Maybe this will stave off whatever the withers did to you guys."

"That's not how enchanted apples work," Esme said.

"Yeah, but it's all we've got right now, and you two are in bad shape. Or do you want to keep eating rotted flesh?"

"It might waste resources," she said.

"Not if we're under attack again," he pointed out. "Which is probably imminent given the way this game is going. Besides, resources are for moments like this."

Esme held the apple back out to him, but he ignored her and set to work on a portal back to the Overworld. Eating the apple didn't make me feel any better or worse. But Anton was right. You can't just hang on to things forever.

I walked over to Lonnie as Anton worked on the portal and Esme continued to debate the finer points of consuming a rare resource. "Thanks for telling me about punching fireballs. That really saved our bacon back there." He tilted his head, and I laughed. "Well, you didn't tell me right then, obviously, but back when we were planning our initial run to the End." I went quiet for a moment and smiled sadly. "You're always there for me. I just . . . I wanted to tell you—" But of course, I heard the strange, catlike wail of a ghast, and a pair of the giant mobs were coming toward us over the lava river.

Lonnie squeezed my arm and I turned to see a team of ghasts coming at us fast.

"Uh, hey. How are we coming with that portal?" I called over to Anton.

"Are you volunteering to help?" Esme asked.

"No, just noticing that we have some unwelcome company," I said as I pointed to the oncoming mobs.

Esme looked up and made a sound that might have been equal parts frustration, anger, and exhaustion. She pulled out her bow and loaded flaming arrows.

"Eat flame, ghastlies," she whispered. She missed twice, and I realized she was much worse off than she was letting on.

"Why don't you keep working on the portal," I said. "Anton and I can fend off the ghasts."

"Bianca's right," Anton chimed in. "I'm the only one who hasn't been hit by a wither. I have the most health points of any of us, and she probably has the second most."

Esme switched places without argument. I stood next to Anton with my arrows ready. We moved a few feet to the side of Esme, hoping to draw fire away from her so she could finish the portal without being hit.

"What, you don't want to punch them out of the sky with your deflection technique?" Anton asked as I nocked an arrow.

"I'm not confident I'd be able to pull that off again, to be honest, and especially not against multiple ghasts."

"Wait until they get close," Esme said.

"Stop backseat shooting," Anton said. "We can take care of this."

She was only quiet for a minute as the ghasts flew in closer. "Hey!"

"What?" I asked. "We're waiting. Just like you said!"

"Not that. We don't have enough obsidian," she said.

"It's not like we're surrounded by lava or anything," I snapped. "Nowhere to get any obsidian!" I looked back at her. "I thought you were the one who always thought things through. Pull it together!"

She shot me a steely look, but said nothing. I watched as she opened up her inventory and got the snowballs. When I turned back, the ghasts were right on top of us. Anton started shooting and I followed, missing the first time.

"Don't waste arrows, Bianca!" Anton said. "We have a limited supply."

I fired off two more, hitting both the ghasts, and pushing them back a little. "How's that, then?" I asked with a grin. Anton fired off another arrow, which killed one of the ghasts, and smirked back.

"Could be better. How's it going, Esme?" he shouted back to her.

Esme threw the snowballs over the edge of the ridge into the lava. Two obsidian blocks formed that she mined, and then she threw a third and fourth snowball.

"Almost there," she replied, turning to place the obsidian blocks into the almost finished portal. I wasn't sure if we had the flint necessary to light the portal, but I would worry more about that once she was done.

Lonnie jumped to his feet, running just in front of the last ghast.

"Get down!" Anton shouted. "You'll get hit!"

But Lonnie didn't listen. He started to jump, drawing its attention and distracting it from us.

"Lonnie, don't!" I called out. I moved toward him, ready to fire at the mob with my last remaining arrow, but Anton pulled me back.

"He knows what he's doing," Anton said.

"No he doesn't!" I snapped, then froze.

Anton looked me dead in the eye but said nothing.

I watched Lonnie jump again. A fireball narrowly missed him, exploding a few feet away from the portal frame.

"Come on!" Esme shouted. She was mining the last bit of obsidian for the portal, and it was just out of reach.

I took a running jump from the island to the one block of obsidian, then jumped back immediately, mining as I did so I could bring it back with me. I landed right in front of Esme and passed along the final block. For a microsecond, I thought she might be impressed. I mean, I was impressed with myself, to be honest. We shared a momentary glance, but she didn't say anything so I didn't either.

Lonnie jumped directly in front of the portal, and then away as a fireball came streaking toward him. Esme, Anton, and I barely had enough time to dive out of the way before the fireball hit, lighting the portal.

I grabbed Lonnie's hand, not wanting to wait for the ghast to come back around, and flung him toward the portal. Esme dragged him through. Anton was the next closest.

"Go!" I shouted.

He scrambled to his knees and crawled the rest of the way to the portal just as the ghast came up behind him. I let off my final arrow, missing the ghast but hitting the fireball it was about to rain down on us, deflecting the attack. I ran to Anton and bodychecked him through the portal. The ghast flew past, and its attack put the portal fire out, effectively cutting off my escape.

I was alone, with the ghast circling back for another pass. I looked through my inventory. There was one final TNT bomb, but no flint to make a fire.

"If there was ever a time for a wild plan . . ."

The ghast was coming in close. I positioned myself behind the portal, in the line of the oncoming ghast, watching through the open archway as it barreled toward me. As soon as it reached the edge of the island, I ran through the inactive frame and threw the TNT bomb. The ghast exploded, and flecks of fire surrounded me in the air. One of them lit the portal and it flashed purple. At the same time, the blast hit me and threw me back. As I flew backward through the now-active portal, I noticed that the explosion fractured the frame a little. The archway looked splintered and the purple portal light seeped into the cracks.

I closed my eyes as I fell, and hoped for the best.

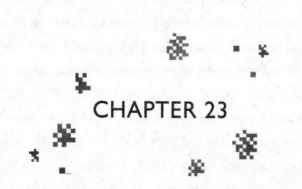

CHAPTER 23

I landed on grass with bright light surrounding me. It took a couple of seconds for my eyes to adjust, but when they did, I noticed things were moving around me. Then I realized that it wasn't the landscape, but me, speeding along the ground. Something had grabbed hold of my upper back and was dragging me. I struggled to turn, or flip, or get a good look at whatever or whoever it was, but nothing I did seemed to help. All I could manage was, "Hey! Hey!" and that didn't work either.

I bumped along the uneven ground, jostling to get free until we got past a few trees and bushes. Then whatever it was let go. I immediately got to my feet and whipped around.

"Lonnie!"

"What are we, chopped liver?" Esme and Anton were a little behind Lonnie and to the right, and they were both grinning at me. Anton gave me a high-five and said, "One step closer to the End!"

He turned to give Esme a high-five, too, but she left him hanging. "One step closer to leaving, you mean," she said.

"What—" I began, when Lonnie grabbed me again and pulled me down to the ground.

"Shhh!" Esme said.

I turned to where they were facing. Beyond the trees, past the portal, an enderman moved through the landscape. Its back was toward us at first and then it turned. It was the same enderman with the scar. I gasped. It turned again, looking directly toward us this time, but it didn't come any closer. Eventually it moved off, and disappeared down the other side of a hill.

"You're kidding me, right?" I said as I turned toward the others.

"I wish," Anton said. He looked exasperated. "Listen, Bianca, there might be an easy way to deal with this mob. You just need to—"

"I'm not causing that," I said curtly. "So, what do we do?" I asked. "It's not like we can go searching for an end portal with that thing roaming around looking for a fight."

"We need a plan to get rid of that particular enderman," Esme said.

"How?" Anton asked. "We've killed that thing twice now. And here it is all over again."

"Third time's the charm," I said. "My grandmother likes to say that."

"There's no charm with that particular enderman," Esme said. "It's out to get us. No matter where we go, it's there."

"What do you suggest?" Anton said.

"We're going to have to lure it into a trap. Something with a lot of explosives," Esme said.

Anton grinned. "I think I have that covered."

"I'll help," she said. "It has to be huge. We should use up anything we won't need in the End."

I bit my lip and looked at Lonnie. He was still sitting near where he had pulled me to safety, staring out between the leaves at where the enderman had been moments before.

"Hey," I whispered in his direction. "Lonnie?"

He turned toward me.

"Do you think this is a good idea?" I asked.

He ignored me and looked out again, as if he was on guard.

"You were always devising traps for the endermen, remember?"

Lonnie shifted, letting the hand I'd rested on his knee fall away. When I turned back to Anton and Esme, Anton was standing, scratching something out in the dirt as Esme looked on. I tried not to let my feelings get hurt.

"We'll have to get the enderman into this spot," Anton said, jabbing at a brown pixel near his foot. "Then we blow it all sky-high."

"Listen," I said softly. Neither of them stopped to look at me, so I said it again, more loudly. "Listen."

"Yes?" Esme asked.

"I'm not sure blowing that thing up is the right idea," I said. "It keeps coming back."

"Which is why we're using all the ammunition we have," Anton said.

I shook my head. "It's a waste of time, and a waste of supplies. We really need to get to the End, and leave this thing here in the Overworld."

"How are we going to do that?" Esme asked. "That thing showed up the moment we got back from the Nether."

"It's not going to be long before it finds us," Anton said. "We need a plan to take it down."

"I think we should distract it, and make a run for the portal," I said.

Esme couldn't hold back her laughter. "Distract and run is your plan?" She laughed again. "You want to run from something that can teleport?"

"There are four of us," I explained. "We can figure out a way to do this without wasting all the supplies."

"I'm with Esme on this one," Anton said. "I don't see the point in running away."

I looked at Lonnie, hoping for support, but there was none. Of course. Lonnie wasn't fully himself yet, especially when Anton and Esme were around. If I got him to the End, maybe he would come all the way back.

"Okay, what if we do both," I suggested.

"How, exactly?" Esme asked.

"We should split up," I said.

"What? No." Anton stood up immediately, shaking his head, and commenced pacing back and forth. "Nope. No. No way."

"We can get more done," I said.

"Uh-uh," Anton said.

"We stick together," Esme said. "That was always the plan."

"And every time we've split up, things have gone totally off the rails," Anton said. "We're not going to do it on purpose."

Lonnie looked at me, then stood and moved closer to Anton.

"You agree with me, buddy?" Anton asked. He raised his hand for a high-five, but Lonnie didn't give him one.

"Okay, fine," I said. "We'll do it your way for now."

Esme looked down, but I could see the smile on her face. And I was kind of glad. I knew that in real life, she probably didn't get her way a lot. Besides, how much could it hurt us to lure the scarred enderman into a trap and blow him to bits?

"We're going to need better protections," Esme said.

"And where are we going to get that?" I asked.

She pulled up her inventory and showed us how much diamond she had collected.

"Wow," Anton said

"It's not enough for all of us," Esme said. "But it will give one of us a really good chance."

Anton smiled. "You mean it will give the one of us who is going to be bait a really good chance."

Esme's face could barely contain her smirk.

"Bait?" I asked. "What do you mean by 'bait'?"

Moments later, I was suited up in diamond armor, walking ahead of the group with my sword up. If this had been real life, I'd expect a little clinking in the joints where diamond rubbed against diamond, but this wasn't real life. I wasn't even sure if all the diamonds in the world would make up one single diamond suit of armor.

I moved slowly and looked around, expecting the enderman to appear right in front of me at any moment. But after I had gotten all the way past the portal and to the edge of the water without anything showing up, I relaxed. A rabbit hopped past me, and I lowered my sword.

"All I see is this attack bunny," I called back to Lonnie, Esme, and Anton.

"That's weird," Anton said.

"Yeah, its ear twitches are particularly threatening," I answered.

"No, I mean," Anton jogged up close to me, still in his iron armor, and sighed. "I meant that the enderman wouldn't stop last time. It was everywhere. And now, *poof*, it's missing in action?"

"He's right," Esme said. "Maybe it's set a trap for us."

"All the more reason to stop trying to lure it out, and just move on with our original plan to go through the portal," I suggested. "If it's really not here, we're wasting time."

Anton and Esme both shook their heads.

"No," she said. "It's going to continue harassing us unless we deal with it. Keep going, just to those boats over there."

We walked cautiously along the shore, huddling close, our backs facing in, so that we could see in all directions. Even though Lonnie wasn't much of a lookout, we gave him a position in the group, between Anton and me.

After what seemed like a few minutes, we approached the

boats that were perched on the shore, nestled between some gray rocks. "Are these the ones we left before?" I asked.

Esme looked at Anton, then said, "No, I don't think so." They moved toward the boats without any further hesitation, and Lonnie followed suit.

"What are you doing?" I asked. "Wasn't the plan to trap him on land?"

"But there are boats," Esme said. "Somebody left them here for us to find."

"And how are you so sure this isn't a trap?" I asked. "You said we needed to stick to the plan, and the plan was to lure the enderman out and blow him up, right there on shore. Why change now?"

"Okay, fine. We didn't tell you the whole plan," Anton said. "We have a working theory. A logical one, not a conspiracy theory," he added after I gave him a hard look.

"Okay," I said cautiously. "What is it?"

"We think the enderman is yours—something from your brain," Anton said, rushing to get through the sentence before I could stop him. "Think about it. We never saw it before you showed up in the game, it keeps coming back every time you're around, and it targets you every time."

"And everyone you're with," Esme added. "We thought that if we could get you somewhere with no distractions, we could get you to start talking."

"Like the middle of a river," I said.

"Yup," Anton said.

I felt awful that they thought they had to trick me for my own good. After all we'd been through together, I felt that I owed them some sliver of the truth.

"I understand," I said, already feeling the weight of the secret lift off my chest. "I think maybe you're right."

Esme looked surprised.

"You agree?" Anton said.

"The enderman has a scar across his face that looks like the guy whose car we collided with," I said. "It's probably just a PTSD thing lingering around in the back of our heads. I'm sure Lonnie has it too, which is why the enderman is so strong."

"What's PTSD?" Esme asked.

"Post-traumatic stress disorder," I said. "It's when you experience something terrible like an accident or an attack, and you have a hard time living your life normally afterwards."

"Huh," Esme pondered this. "What if your entire life is stressful?"

I'd never thought of that before, but it made me wonder about kids like A.J. who never had it easy to begin with.

"Do you still really think Lonnie is still in there?" Anton said.

"Are we really back on that?" I asked.

"That's not what I mean," he said. "Maybe we were wrong. Maybe you're not the one manifesting this enderman."

All three of us looked at Lonnie. But just beyond Lonnie was a much larger boat, a ship, really, in the middle of the water. It was such an elaborate build that I don't know how it could have appeared out of thin air, unless . . .

"Where did that come from?" Esme asked.

As we stared, I got hit from behind. I turned, and the scarred enderman was right on me. Anton took a swing at it as Esme pulled me back and pushed me into one of the boats.

"Move!" Esme roared, jumping into her own watercraft. Anton turned and ran toward us with Lonnie at his side, each of them taking Esme's lead and beating a hasty retreat.

The scarred enderman stared at us from shore as we headed straight for the ship. I could see rows of endermen bustling on board. The enderman with the scar stood on the boat's prow like a captain.

"How?" I asked.

"You were right," Anton said. "It is a trap."

"Are those pirates?" I asked, feeling dread form in the pit of my stomach. I remembered the stories from my dad.

"Someone's mind is really turning this place into their personal nightmare," Anton said, pointedly.

I had to admit that what I was looking at wasn't likely to have been made by anyone else in the game but me. I understood why I'd been chosen as the perfect bait. But it made me wonder what else I was controlling. I took a furtive glance at Lonnie.

"How do I stop them?" I asked, trying not to panic. "Shouldn't I be able to control them then, turn them back somehow?"

"We don't have time to puzzle that one out right now," Anton said. "We have a pirate ship to attack, head-on."

"I don't . . ." I began, then stopped.

"They're not real pirates," Esme said soothingly.

"They're ender pirates," I said. "Worse! How's the plan going to work now?"

Anton shrugged. "Same explosives. Same circle the scarred enderman has to get into. But now we have to use boats for a fast getaway."

"So we're doing this," I said.

"We're doing this," Anton said.

"And I'm going to have to board a pirate ship."

"Correct."

Esme led the way, steering her boat parallel to the ship, then led us on board, scrambling up the side and stopping on the rail just above a group of endermen. They immediately attacked. I clambered aboard and started swinging my sword nervously even before I got up to the rail. Anton was to my left, and Esme to my right. Lonnie was still making his way up.

I jumped onto the deck of the ship, and started slashing my way across. Lonnie took my place between Esme and Anton, wielding a diamond sword that he brought down with enough force to bash holes into the deck. Suddenly I could feel a force from something behind me, and I looked up into the stern where the enderman with the white scar across his face looked down on the fighting. My heart beat wildly as he jumped down onto the deck and made three wide strides, not toward me, but to where Lonnie had just appeared at the side of the ship.

I pushed one of the endermen out of my way and ran across the deck to cut off the one with the white scar. Before I could get there, it extended its hand and knocked me over. I fell on the floor, but I didn't seem to have taken much damage. The fighting continued around and over me for a second before I regained my footing. By then, the one with the scar had reached Lonnie and jumped into the air, coming down hard with both of its arms reaching out. Lonnie was going to be pulverized. I ran again, and jumped up and over Lonnie, turning my chest to the scarred enderman as its long arms came down across me, and despite the diamond armor, I could feel the hard crash of it into my ribs as if I had collided with a car again. For a moment I forgot where I was, and an image of the dashboard pressing against my chest and the other driver's face just inches in front of me came into view.

I screamed.

The driver's face disappeared, replaced by the scarred enderman as it hit me again.

I was back in the moment, back in the game, fending off attacks from this scourge.

I tried to remember the plan. Anton was supposed to be putting down the explosives, and I was supposed to get the enderman into the center. Then we were all supposed to run. But where would we run on a ship?

My brain couldn't work that question out as I was being pummeled. I held an arm out to stop the blows, but I could still feel them against my chest. Lonnie pried the attacker away, taking the next hit.

"No!" I called out, but it was too late.

The enderman stopped trying to eradicate me and turned his attention to Lonnie. I scrambled to my feet. To the right of me,

Anton was making his way around the ship. I knew what that meant. He was doing his part. I had to do mine. On my left, Esme was fighting endermen and gathering the ender pearls they dropped when they were killed.

I shoved Lonnie out of the way and picked up my sword, pointing it at the enderman. I whipped it around, bringing the point into its chest as I stepped forward. Then I turned and whipped the sword around the other way, bringing the full edge of the blade across the enderman's arm.

It staggered back.

Anton whistled, catching my attention and signaling that it was my turn. I stepped toward the enderman again, pushing it farther and farther back as I came at it with my sword. I didn't stop, even when I felt exhausted and like my legs wobbled like Jell-O. We only had this one chance and I wasn't about to blow it.

I got the enderman into position.

Anton jumped onto the deck from the captain's perch and helped Esme with the few remaining endermen and the pearls. Then both of them ran past me at full speed, grabbing Lonnie and pulling him down off the ship.

I only had a couple of seconds.

I made one last pass at the enderman with the scar, a spinning jump that gave more force to the sword I was holding in my hand. But as I came down, the enderman jerked just out of the way, and the sword hit the wood of the deck. Before I could recover, it straightened up and flailed, forcing me into the center of the ship, right where I had been trying to get it to go.

It lurched toward me, its limbs moving jerkily. I wanted to get up, but I was paralyzed. My entire body was frozen there. This was it.

Out of the corner of my eye, I saw the first explosion detonate. The yellow and orange of the bomb was bright against the early morning sky. The enderman turned to see it too. Somehow I summoned up enough energy to get my feet under me and run. More bombs went off in a timed cascade that left only one possible opening at the side of the ship—the opposite side from where we'd left our boat.

I jumped up onto the rail, and dove into the water as the pirate ship blew up behind me.

CHAPTER 24

I was going to drown. Pixels of char and fire floated in the air far above me, then splashed into the water, drifting as I sank. I felt my chest burning for air. This was not the way I wanted to go. I would be locked out of the game. And suddenly I knew why I didn't want to leave. It wasn't just having to finally tell what my part in the accident was. It was the truth I'd been trying to hide from myself. One I could not accept: The reason why no one would tell me anything about Lonnie was because he was no longer capable of being saved. I would never see Lonnie again.

A rising tide of despair seemed to swallow me up from the inside. I pushed back against that thought like I was fighting for my life all over again. I looked around for something that would get me out of there.

Something splashed in the water above me and then sank down near where I was, and then it heaved me up. I hurtled toward a long brown spot on the water. The bottom of a boat, I figured out as I got closer. The bottom of my boat.

Lonnie's face hovered over the side of his boat as I was being hauled up. He and Esme waited as Anton pushed me up. When I was close enough to the surface, Esme reached in and scooped me out, depositing me in my vessel. I lay in the bottom of the boat, coughing.

"Are you okay?" Esme asked.

I nodded, sputtered, and tried to say yes, but coughed instead.

"Well, we did it." Anton climbed into his boat. He looked around and seemed very pleased with himself despite being soaked through. "And you thought it wouldn't work."

"It almost didn't," Esme said. She took a sidelong glance at me.

"But it did," he insisted.

I pushed up to my elbows, spat out more water, and looked around. The pirate ship was gone and there was no sign of the creepy enderman with the scar.

I didn't want to spend time dwelling on the fact that I had created my problems in the game—just like Esme and Anton had told me from the beginning. All I wanted now was to fulfill my promise to Lonnie, especially if this was going to be the last time I did. It was more important than ever.

"We need to move on," I said finally, when I'd caught my breath. "There's nothing stopping us from getting to the End now."

"That thing seems to really hate you," Anton said. "Every time, it goes right for you and him." He jerked his head toward Lonnie. "Why do you think that is?"

"It doesn't matter anymore," I said flatly. "It's gone. It's not coming back."

Esme shook her head. "Maybe not right this minute," she said. "But the things we don't deal with always come back. There's no escape in the game, not really."

"Anton mentioned that," I said. "Can we just get to the End? I'm tired of talking."

Anton shook his head. "No. You're holding something back. That's obvious enough. But what you don't understand is that you're only hurting yourself."

I swear, all that was missing from Anton's little self-help speech was the whole *help me help you* bit. "You have no idea what you're talking about," I said, angry heat rising in my lungs. "You think you know everything there is to know about this game, but you can't even figure out how to deal with your own skeletons—literally! I saw your house, it was going to get annihilated if I didn't do something to ward off the mobs. You're trying to get me to talk when you obviously have your own issues you're not dealing with!"

"You're only trying to mess with me because you're trying to deflect, so you don't have to deal with your own problems. There's nowhere to hide. So what is it, Bianca?"

Esme looked away and said, "Maybe we should just tell her, Anton."

He shrugged.

"Bianca, we just want to help," Esme said. "We already know the truth . . ."

"No, you don't! Whatever you think you know, you don't." I could feel my breath hitching in my chest.

"Then tell us what we don't know," Anton pleaded.

I knew it would help. I knew it. But the words literally would not come out of me. "I . . . I can't," I said softly. I felt the tears welling up in my eyes, but continued on anyway, saying, "We just need to get to the End. Please."

"Okay," Esme said, resting a hand on my shoulder. "Let's go find the end portal." She turned and paddled toward the shore and said nothing else.

I sniffled and wiped my eyes, glancing at Lonnie. He looked at me and smiled gently.

When we hit land, Lonnie and the others walked toward the trees, leaving me in my boat alone.

I watched as Esme and Anton worked on making a new structure to serve as home base. How many bases did we have so far? How many times had we started over? At least we had some of our supplies. Esme had the shulker boxes from A.J.'s house. And each of us had a few supplies in our inventories. No more explosives, though; we literally blew those on the pirates.

Eventually I made my way over to the house. It was one large room. Esme and Anton looked up as I walked in.

"We're going to need health potions," Esme said. "Bianca and me especially, since the whole wither thing."

"We're going up against a dragon, so fire resistance would be handy," I said, happy to be back to planning.

"I can take care of the potions," Esme said. "But we're going to need some food. It's been a while since any of us ate."

She was right. Even without the health and food bars, I could feel how weak I was. Esme, for all her fierce fighting, looked even weaker. I knew it was from the wither skeleton attack, but I also knew she wasn't going to complain about it. Anton was crafting weapons as Esme worked on the potions, so I left to find some neutral mobs that could increase our food and health levels.

I half expected to see the scarred enderman again. But as I walked over the hills and through some forested area, there was nothing but me, some chickens, and a couple of cows. I managed to get some milk, and felt infinitely better after I had some. I got some more for Esme, and returned with a lot of supplies, feeling a bit calmer after some time alone.

By then the enchantments were ready, the weapons were made, and everyone was set to go. This time we suited up Lonnie in the diamond armor, while the rest of us stayed in iron with the enchantments Esme had put on them: Fire and Projectile Protection.

It was time to find the stronghold that would lead us to the End.

Anton walked out ahead and took out an eye of ender, throwing it up into the air, and letting it lead us out of the house. We walked under the spatter of purple that dripped from the eye, and followed it out into the open. We moved beyond the trees with Anton continuing to send up eyes in the air, hoping we would find the stronghold quickly. We moved toward the water, and then back inland again, up and over the same small hill I'd navigated earlier, through mobs of mooshrooms, pigs, and chickens. Anton kept throwing and we kept following, but the eye never went into the ground, no matter where we followed it.

"Maybe there isn't one near here," Esme suggested.

"It has to be somewhere," Anton said. "We've barely started to look." He threw an eye up again, and it came down, breaking apart. I was getting frustrated.

"We're pretty far from the house," I said. "Maybe we should build a mini shelter just in case we don't find it before nightfall."

"That's actually a good idea," Esme said, sounding genuinely impressed.

"Hold on, hold on," Anton said. "I just know it's here some-where. I know it."

Esme and I waited as Anton threw up a fresh eye of ender, and it came down and went straight into the grass just ahead of us. Anton turned back and grinned at us.

"All right," Esme said. "Start digging."

We dug at an angle around where the eye was, so that we weren't going straight down. This was my idea. I'd fallen into holes like that before, and I didn't want to risk it. We moved in something of a spiral, finding a cave a couple of levels down, but no stronghold. Anton threw the eye again, and it went farther down into the stone and dirt. We followed again and broke through onto a set of stone steps.

"You did it," I said to Anton.

He held his hand up for high-fives, which both Esme and I gave. Then I held up Lonnie's hand and slapped him a high-five too.

"All right, all right, can we get through this stronghold now?" Esme said.

Anton snickered. "Come on, Esme. Sometimes being nice isn't the worst thing in the world."

"Don't get used to it," Esme warned, suppressing her smile.

"Noted," said Anton. Then he bowed a little and gestured forward with his hand. "Shall we?"

"Let's," I said, slapping his hand as I walked past.

Esme flipped out the compass. "I'll lead," she said. "You two can hang back and high-five until the mooshrooms come home if you want."

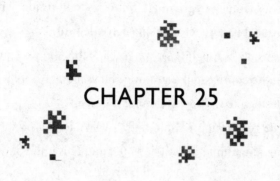

CHAPTER 25

The stronghold was a maze of stone stairs leading to various open rooms. In a couple of them we found chests with loot that we took into our inventories, each of us taking a turn so we could evenly share what we found. There were a couple of swords, apples, bread, and even meat. At first the stronghold seemed to be empty, and then a pair of skeletons passed by. We dodged them by falling back into a small, empty room that looked like a cell, and they went straight past us. After that, we kept the weapons out, just in case.

We went deeper and deeper into the stronghold, checking doors, and taking care not to double back on ourselves. Each of us took a turn leading with the compass, and each of us took a turn making sure Lonnie came along, though we didn't really need to. He was following closely, ducking when we ducked, running when we ran, hiding when we hid.

At the side of what seemed to be the deepest room so far, there was a crawlspace tunnel about midway up one of the walls. The room was just large enough for all four of us to fit inside, with no doors and only two torches, one on each side wall.

"Either we go through it, or we go back the way we came," I said. I held the compass up, squinting at it as if that would tell me more about the crawlspace in front of my face.

"I say we go through," Esme said. "We've done a pretty thorough job looking through each floor already. This is the only path left."

"This is how the monsters typically get you," Anton said. "Cornered in a dark, tiny room."

"Or this is how we get out," I suggested.

"Fine," he agreed. He knelt, providing a boost that I'd need to be able to get into the crawlspace, and I climbed up into it, then clambered through. Lonnie followed right behind me, and then I heard the other two get in.

The tunnel was long, and even though I had a torch in my hand, it was still eerily dark. I couldn't see very far in front of me, which made for a more anxious crawl, not knowing how much farther we had to go. Every few seconds, Anton called out, "Anything yet?"

I kept having to say no, until that got really annoying and I stopped answering, and eventually he stopped calling out.

Then, suddenly, the torchlight showed a wide opening ahead that might have been another room.

"I think we found something," I yelled back to the others.

"Faster, then," Anton said. "I'm suffocating back here."

I moved quickly toward the opening, and dropped immediately into a large room. I fell on my shoulder and rolled, rubbing it to stop the pain.

Lonnie fell down after me, but he got immediately to his feet as if he felt nothing at all. Anton fell through the hole next, and finally Esme's head peeked out of the tunnel. She didn't fall, of course. That would have been very un-Esme-like. She gripped the sides of the tunnel opening and swung her legs and body out, hanging from the wall for just a moment before letting go and landing gracefully on the floor next to the rest of us klutzes.

The room we were in was wide and long, with several door openings all the way around, and evenly spaced torches between the doors that lit up the room. Everything was a dull gray-brown. It also seemed to be an indoor courtyard, of sorts, with two more levels above us, all with doors and balconies facing down onto the floor where we had ended up.

"It's like an auditorium," Esme said.

"Or like an indoor stadium," Anton said. "You know, with the bottom for the main attraction in the center, and several floors up so that people can see the action."

"What action?" I asked.

Anton shrugged. "I'm just saying, it reminds me of a soccer stadium, or the place where Jabba the Hutt dropped creatures that he wanted to see do battle."

"You mean like an arena," I said. "Only what's the main attraction? We're the only ones standing in the middle."

Anton stepped back toward the side of the room. "I'm not sticking around to find out," he said. "Let's start trying some of the doors. Maybe one of them leads someplace useful."

We walked around the perimeter of the room to try each of the doors, but they all seemed to lead to upper floors from which the only openings faced the floor of the arena. The next level up looked like a latticework of iron bars. I thought they were jail cells, but there were passageways between them, so they couldn't have been.

"This can't be it," Esme said, sounding defeated.

"No," I agreed. "It can't."

"Maybe it's a test," Anton suggested.

I began to walk around again, this time running my hands up and down the walls and along the frame of each doorway. Then I found a pressure plate. I barely touched it and it gave way a little. I looked around the room to see what it corresponded to, but nothing had happened. Yet.

"I found something," I said.

Lonnie was the first to come over, then Esme and Anton. I showed them the pressure plate and pressed it again. There was an audible click, but still nothing happened.

"Do you think there are others?" I asked.

Esme immediately started to walk around to see if she could find something similar. She found one a couple of doors down, not in an open archway as I had, but on the wall beneath one of the torches.

Anton found one on the floor toward the other side of the room. He was walking across and felt the ground click beneath his feet, and stepped back instead of putting his full weight on it. "It's weird that there's no pattern to where they were put," he said.

"They're easier to hide that way, and for someone to accidentally trigger," I said. "It's pretty smart."

"Of course you think haphazard is smart," Esme said.

"But it's not haphazard to the person who put them here," I said.

"Is this the last room, though?" Anton asked. "Because if it is, and there's nothing here, we're going to have to find another stronghold to get what we need."

"I think so," Esme said. "There's nothing leading out of this arena. Everything heads back in, to look down on this floor."

"Then maybe this is where we need to look."

"Where? On a bare empty floor?" Esme asked.

"No, I mean maybe it's time to trip the triggers," I said.

"Bianca, we have no idea what that's going to do," she said.

"I know. But what are the options? This is the last room and we haven't found anything yet. Maybe there's something that we can find if we just push all of the buttons at once. Hard."

"That's a bad plan," Esme said, although there was an audible click that said she'd pressed hers.

"But it's a plan," I said, depressing my button.

Anton walked across the floor. As he reached the middle, we all heard the click beneath his feet, but this one sounded more solid. His face registered surprise and fear at the same time. He hesitated a moment as if he wasn't sure what to do, then ran forward toward the rest of us.

Immediately, a part of the floor opened up, and a few silverfish flew out and straight for us.

Esme pulled out her sword and ran out to meet them in the middle of the arena floor.

"No!" I called out, but it was too late. She stepped on another pressure plate and a different part of the floor opened up, with more enemies pouring out.

The silverfish looked vicious, and they came straight toward us with their jaws unhinged, as if they meant to take a bite out of anyone who got close enough.

My sword was already out, so I waited where I was, hoping the fish would come straight to me. But instead, they circled Esme and attacked her. I looked at Anton. We had no choice. We would have to go in. I left Lonnie where he was, leaning against the open doorframe, and ran into the middle of the arena, slashing silverfish with my sword as I went. I triggered a third trapdoor, and more mobs poured out for us to fight. They swarmed around us, unrelenting and hideous, but our armor kept us relatively safe. When we'd gotten through about half of them, I noticed that even more were coming out of the holes we'd made.

"We have to be close to the end portal room," I said. "There are too many of these. They have to be pushing us back for some reason."

"Agreed," Anton said. He dug into two silverfish like a shish kebab with his sword, which by the look of shock on his face I suspected was a lucky shot rather than a deliberate one. Then he tried to do it again and was unsuccessful.

The silverfish corralled us into a tight trio. We stood back to back to back, facing them down.

"We have to find a way to break out of this," I said unhelpfully.

"Unless you have a specific solution in mind," Esme said, "I think all we can do is fight."

"I think we should go down one of the trapdoors that they came out of," I said.

"Are you joking?" Esme said.

"Actually, it makes sense," Anton said. "The silverfish always guard the end portal room, so it stands to reason that if we follow where they came from, we'll find it."

I didn't wait for Esme to get on board. I pushed my way through clouds of silverfish, back to the archway where I had left Lonnie. He wasn't there. Of course he wasn't. I started to run up the stairs to the next level to see if he had wandered that way. From an upper balcony, I could see my friends still fighting off the mob. It was mesmerizing how the silverfish moved like ocean fish—as one organism.

"They're moving in a pattern, you guys. Look carefully."

Anton lowered his sword temporarily and watched the fish swirl around him. Then he began to move in rhythm with their pattern, dipping when they dipped, zigging left and zagging right in perfect synchronous time. Esme watched him, and copied, but was at first a couple of seconds behind him, so not fast enough to stay out of the way. A particularly hungry-looking silverfish caught her in the shoulder, and she screamed and fell to the floor. Anton dove forward and smacked the silverfish away.

I ran through the upper rooms looking for Lonnie, calling out to him, even though I knew he wouldn't respond. I found him finally against a wall, far away from the balcony that looked down over the arena floor. He was curled up with his arms around his knees and his head down, as if he wanted to be as far away from this place as he could get. I understood it. I wished I had time to curl up into a ball myself, but I didn't. I needed to get us out of here. We needed to get to the End.

"Lonnie!" I yelled. I pulled him to his feet. "We have to go!" He followed reluctantly until we got downstairs and I tried to take him into the silverfish mob. Then, he came to a dead stop and resisted when I tried to pull him along. "I know, I know, Lonnie," I said. "But you've got to trust me. This is the only way."

But he wasn't budging.

"This is the End." It was Lonnie's voice floating through my mind.

"Move! You have to move! For me!"

He leaped forward into the stream of silverfish, and down into the hole from the trapdoor. He landed in the next room, and rolled away from the entrance.

"We have to hurry," I said.

"You think?" Anton snarked as he swiped at another silverfish. He jumped in after me, and Esme came in last, grumbling.

We were in another room, the same size as the one above, but only one level deep. Just as in the other one, there were torches lighting up the entire perimeter. Luckily, it looked like all the silverfish were on the floor above us. And at the other end of the room we were in was the end portal.

"Whoa, it looks way cooler than the photos on the Internet," Anton said.

We all stared straight ahead at a large and elaborate end portal, with all twelve eyes of ender fit into the frame. They shifted and blinked like real eyes that were peering at us, which made my stomach curdle. The activated portal was a mesmerizing deep black. I felt it was sucking me in, like a vortex.

"Something's not right," Esme said. "We're supposed to finish building the portal. Only the luckiest of the lucky get an already active portal."

I felt nervous. I looked around the room, expecting to find someone else in there with us. But it was empty. I moved forward cautiously.

"Maybe we should wait?" I said. "It could be a trap and we'll be mobbed by monsters as soon as we step through." I glanced at Lonnie.

"We have to face our monsters no matter where we go," Anton said. He moved up to the portal, and walked all the way around it. "This seems legit, though. We could try the portal and see."

"I don't trust it," I said. Now that we were here, steps away from finishing the goal Lonnie and I had set out to complete so long ago, I felt unsure. I continued to look around, checking the ceiling and behind a pillar. I felt the cold dampness of the brick under my palms.

"We can't stall forever," Anton said. "If we want to progress through the game, we have to go. But it's your choice, Bianca."

"What do you think?" Esme asked me.

I looked at my friends, waiting patiently for me to decide. For my answer, I grabbed Lonnie's right hand and jerked my head toward Anton so he'd hold on to Lonnie's left, and I held out my right hand to Esme. Together, we stepped into the portal that would take us to the End.

CHAPTER 26

I knew something was wrong as soon as I'd stepped through. I tried my best to hang on to Esme and Lonnie as we hurtled through space. But my grip slipped. Suddenly, I was spiraling out of control, whirling through the pitch-black nothing.

In that long silent moment, the truths that I'd been holding at bay reappeared full-force. Nobody knew about Lonnie because he was never checked into the children's ward or the trauma ward.

"He didn't come into the hospital with me," I whispered into the darkness. "He never regained consciousness after the accident." A thin prick of light opened at the limits of my vision. It grew wider, showing a pale green landscape against a starless sky.

Lonnie.

The driver with the scar.

Me holding up the phone to Lonnie's face while he was driving.

It was all me.

It was my fault.

As I pitched forward toward the light, a new shadow took form, blocking out the light I was reaching for. A long-armed enderman came into view, and it had the same thin, diagonal white scar across its face. I screamed. The enderman extended its arms toward me.

I tried to turn and somehow propel my way back to the Over-world. But before I could try, the enderman grabbed me by the hand, pulled me backward, and threw me down on the ground. It kneeled over me, wrapped its hands around my neck, and squeezed.

I choked for air. My legs and arms flailed as I tried to dislodge myself from the enderman's grasp. But there was no escaping it. Its grip was like a vise. No sound came when I tried to call out. I wasn't even sure anyone would hear me anyway.

I changed tactics, reaching up and scraping its face with the tips of my fingers, and kept trying to grasp it. Finally I found an edge that my finger fit into and I scratched at it hard. The ender-man didn't let up. I tried again. This time, I caught it at the bot-tom edge of the raggedy white scar that went across its face. My finger went in, too far. It was like I had found the crack in an empty bottle. There was nothing behind it. No flesh. No bone. No person. I dug my fingers in farther and pulled as hard as I could. The enderman's face cracked open like the mouth of a beast, but it let go. The struggle sent me wheeling on my way toward the End.

There was a long pause when I couldn't hear or feel anything. All around me was the same swirling blackness, and then everything went white. It was like being sent to oblivion.

The game rendered again and I found myself somewhere off to the side of the central island on a long obsidian platform. Esme was at the other end of it, crouching in her armor with a sword gripped in her hand. Lonnie was already standing behind her, while Anton was a little way farther on, closer to the circle of obsidian pillars where the dragon kept its egg. I ran to Esme's side, and armed myself with a bow.

"That took a while," Anton said, walking back over to us. "You okay?"

Before I could respond, Anton's eyes went wide with fear. I looked back at the portal. The scarred enderman was emerging. The wound I had pulled at had opened farther. There was nothing behind it. Nothing at all. But one eye remained open, and it was looking straight at Lonnie. I lunged forward and placed myself between the enderman and Lonnie, with Anton taking up a position at my side.

Esme's gasp from behind us was loud enough to pull the enderman's focus, but only for a moment.

It stood before us like a ghostly watchman, but it didn't attack. There was nowhere for us to go. We wouldn't move away and leave Lonnie vulnerable to attack, and on the long platform there was only one other direction we could go. We were stuck. The enderman looked at me with its one eye. Its empty face sent shivers down my spine. Then it leaned forward, its gaze shifting to Lonnie.

"No," I said. "No." I moved closer to my best friend.

The enderman reached a long arm toward us. I squeezed away, avoiding its grasp.

"No," I said, this time more forcefully. "You can't take him!"

The enderman lunged, but I ducked down and scrambled past it, dragging Lonnie with me. The enderman struck him as we passed, but as it pulled its arm back again, I turned and delivered a flying kick that sent the scarred enderman through the portal again, its battered form dissolving into nothingness.

"I told you it would come back," Esme said, with a sidelong glance at me.

"I'm working on it," I said quietly. "Dealing with the things that I have to deal with, I mean." I looked at Lonnie, who was standing ahead of us as if nothing at all was happening around him. "I just need to finish this game."

Esme frowned for a moment, then said, "If you're sure that's what's going to help you." Then she turned toward the pillars, focused on the task at hand.

"Why hasn't it shown up yet?" Anton asked.

We all looked around. The dragon should have been here by now.

"It's awfully quiet," I said.

We moved to the end of the platform and stepped out onto the firm, green-tinged earth of the End dimension, taking up a position in a straight line with Anton to the right and me to the left. Then we began to walk in a triangle formation, with Esme at point and Anton and me forming the bottom points. Lonnie we kept in the middle as we crept toward the circle of pillars.

There was the sound of something large, and the feel of wind blowing down at us. Anton was the first to look up. I followed his eyes to the ender dragon. It was larger than I would have imagined, and black as the hollow we'd braved to make it through the end portal.

"It's huge," Esme said. The dragon circled overhead, and then came around again, aiming down, but still giving us a wide berth.

"That's weird, right?" Anton asked. "It hasn't tried to attack us."

We continued to move toward the obsidian pillars until the end crystals came into better view. Of the ten pillars, four of them were very tall, and two shorter, while the other four were of varying middle heights. As the dragon wove and dipped in the air, it stayed always close to one of the crystals, so that when necessary it would be healed without a moment lost.

The creature's large purple eyes blinked once, and I felt it was looking straight at me. Lonnie's face surged to the forefront of my mind.

"Hey, what are you doing here?" Lonnie sat on the edge of the park bench that faced the playground. His hair in his eyes and his tablet in his lap, he was trying to play Minecraft with one hand. A bright red cast wrapped around his right wrist like a hard-shelled glove.

"Hi," I mumbled, digging my toe into the wood chips of the playground. I wore my purple overalls that day, the ones I tried to wear way past the time they'd actually fit. "My mom drove me here to apologize to you."

"It's okay," Lonnie replied, shrugging. "I was trying to be a hero. It didn't work out."

"It was a good try, though," I said, hopefully. I looked to see if there was any trace of anger in his gray eyes. But there was only focus and determination as he tapped furiously at the screen.

I peered over to see Lonnie's avatar shooting arrows at a mob of creepers inside a cave.

"Do you still want to teach me Mineraft?"

"Mine*craft*," Lonnie said. "And I don't know, do you still want to learn?"

"Yes." I nodded enthusiastically. "I do."

"Bianca?" My mom appeared behind me, placing her hands on my shoulders. "I didn't hear you apologize."

"Oh, right!" I said. That was why we were there in the first place. "I'm sorry, Elon."

"Call me Lonnie," he said, extending his free hand out to shake. I smiled as I felt the warmth of his hand in mine.

"I'm sorry, Lonnie."

"I'm so sorry, Lonnie," I repeated, closing my eyes, and feeling those four words stab like a sword through my own heart. "I'm so, so sorry."

I could feel the dragon's energy surging toward me. It was me it was waiting for. The whole game—everything in it, and everything that had happened—was what I'd created, my problems brought to digital life. Minecraft was a world you made, wasn't it? And I'd made one heck of a world.

I knew what I needed to do.

I broke formation and ran toward the dragon with my bow pulled tightly against my shoulder. The dragon snaked around again, folding nearly in half as it circled back. I didn't hesitate. I continued running, straight at it.

"You can't kill the dragon without getting rid of the end crystals!" Anton called out.

"Maybe you guys should start on that!" I shouted back. "I'm going to be the bait. Only this time, it's my choice."

The *thwack* of bowstrings resounded and I saw a volley of arrows go shooting into the air as I barreled toward the dragon. It whipped its head around so that its eye leveled at me, the size of my entire head. I skidded to a stop and gasped. Now that I could see it directly, it was hard to ignore the long scar that cut across its face from its left eye down through its nose and snout, ending at the bottom right of its tooth-filled mouth. I took a deep breath and let my arrow fly off, straight into its iris. It blinked just in time and the projectile bounced off its eyelid. But at the same moment, several other arrows hit their marks, clinking against end crystals all around the dragon.

The dragon's eyes narrowed and it turned, whipping its tail around and hitting me. It sent me flying to one side of the central island, and I rolled all the way toward the very edge. I tried to get my hands to secure a grip on something, but the earth there was too slippery and the edge of the island was getting closer, fast. I raised my bow above my head and brought it straight down into the earth in front of me. One end of the bow stuck in the ground, and I held on desperately to it, while my legs dangled off the side into nothingness.

I pulled myself up and swung my legs back onto the island. Esme and Anton were in the middle of the obsidian pillars, firing arrows as the ender dragon circled them, shooting fireballs. Lonnie was off to one side, between two of the taller pillars, when the dragon came around again and careered toward the ground. The whistle of air that went past the dragon's wings was audible, even from where I was standing on the edge of the island.

The dragon had taken a few hits, but it wound its way up to the nearest pillar and was already being healed. I ran to a column on my right and aimed an arrow at the end crystal two pillars away. It was a short one. I had a pretty good shot. I let the arrow go and it struck, the *ping* on the crystal echoing throughout the island. The dragon looked toward it, then around to see where the attack had come from. I squeezed myself behind one of the pillars, out of the dragon's line of sight.

Esme used the distraction to shoot off another two arrows at the same spot. She was more successful, and the end crystal shattered in a sprinkle of pinkish-purple shards.

I let my head dip out to see where she was, and she nodded once in my direction.

The dragon roared as Esme ran to find cover. The beast turned on her as Anton targeted another crystal, and I followed up with two more shots of my own.

Without discussing it, we had settled into a neat pattern: one person would be bait, while the other two tried to take out crystals. It was a good plan, and it was working.

Anton and I managed to destroy yet another end crystal. The dragon howled again, and Esme got off a couple more shots into its skin. It looped upward toward one of the high crystals to be healed. Next, I ran into the center of the circle, taking aim at the dragon and the crystal it was using to fix its injury. I got solid hits on both of them, and then ran back to hide behind one of the pillars.

Esme and Anton took out two more of the crystals. There were only six to go. As the dragon came down, strafing us, I ran out, zigzagging to avoid being hit, and fired off one last arrow toward a crystal on a high pillar. It shattered, but not before one of the blasts from an ender charge sent me flying straight into an obsidian column. I felt it rock with the force of the blow.

Anton took his turn in the middle as bait while Esme and I continued to shoot. We taunted and teased the dragon, luring it and shooting until there was only one crystal left—the highest one. It was impossible to get an angle to shoot it from inside the circle. Someone was going to have to go out far from the center and take the best shot they possibly could, maybe from the edge of the island, where it was the least safe. There was nowhere to hide there. The pattern we'd fallen into to get rid of the rest of the crystals wouldn't work now.

Anton, Esme, and I blinked at each other from our positions behind cover. No one made the first move.

The dragon rose to the tallest pillar, hugging the end crystal with its huge, black wings and sending down ender charges for good measure, in case one of us got the wrong idea that this was a crystal we should try to mess with.

Anton shot off a few arrows, and the dragon roared, but did nothing to expose the crystal. We were at an impasse.

Then Lonnie sauntered into the center of the obsidian pillars.

I froze. I couldn't think of what to do or say.

The dragon spotted him and roared, then sent down two ender charges. I felt the blast of them, but neither of them seemed to harm Lonnie at all. He opened his mouth and roared back at the beast. The dragon flapped its wings, lifting itself up and off the final crystal, and then made a dive-bomb toward Lonnie again.

Somehow I managed to move, diving toward Lonnie and knocking him out of the way as the dragon came in low and scraped its belly against the ground. The sound rang out like metal scraping against metal. I threw my hands over my ears to blot it out, but it went on and on, and I felt paralyzed. The dragon reached the opposite side of the circle, and miraculously neither Lonnie nor I had been harmed. And now the monstrous creature was far from the one pillar that held its salvation. Maybe it wasn't worried. It was an impossible get, after all. The mob perched on one of the middle-height pillars and waited for our next maneuver. But it didn't have to wait long.

I pulled Lonnie up to stand, and the dragon stared at us. I waved my hands at the dragon as we walked away from where Anton and Esme were hiding, but it didn't move from its perch. When that didn't work, I shot off one arrow in its direction. The monster perked up. It shook its massive head, then leaped into the air, banked right, and dipped straight for us. I moved Lonnie and myself into position and waited. Lonnie stood tall next to me as if he was waiting too, as if he knew what was coming. But I knew he didn't. He had no idea what was coming. Not now. And not before.

I turned to face the dragon, knowing I was facing it alone. I could finally feel tears on my cheeks.

Its eyes blazed as it charged straight toward us. I could feel the heated air radiating from its flapping wings. Just before the monster hit us, I tackled Lonnie, knocking us out of the dragon's path. Its wing *whooshed* over our heads and the beast barely missed us, flying too fast out of the circle to easily turn back around. Its final crystal was now unguarded.

I looked across to where Esme and Anton stood. Always quick on the draw, Esme was already walking backward to get the right angle. She pulled her bow tight as she found the perfect spot, sighting the crystal. Esme's arrow flew. It arced over the circle of pillars and straight at the target. There was another arrow, and then another. Anton had caught on. At five, the crystal shattered, and there was a burst of purply-pink crystal pixels. The dragon had finally wheeled around and was now hovering in the sky above us, flapping, furious, but finally vulnerable.

It was time to take this thing down.

It was time to end the game.

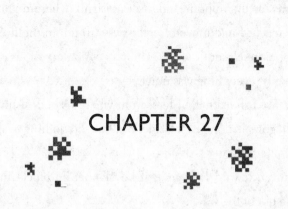

CHAPTER 27

The dragon circled and strafed as Esme, Anton, and I crisscrossed each other between the obsidian pillars, making sure it never had a steady target. It screamed and howled, blew fire at us and dropped ender charges. The world was a cacophony of sound and blurred movement as we fought with everything we had in the hope that sheer force of will would get us to the end of the game.

It wasn't working.

The dragon twisted, turned, dipped, and dove out of the way of our entire assault. Few hits landed, even from Esme who was easily the best shot of the three of us. The dragon rose again, so high into the air above us that it was little more than a black splotch. It came down once more, roaring, then turned and flew away from the pillars, circling the outer rim of the island. It was teasing us. There was nothing we could do but wait. Finally it curved inward, flying straight for us. It was a few seconds before I realized that it had targeted Lonnie.

He was on the opposite side of the island, where my arrows couldn't reach. I had moved too far away from him. Both Anton and Esme were closer.

Suddenly, everything was quiet.

Esme fired shots that, at least from where I stood, seemed to hit the dragon all along its left side. But that did nothing to slow it down, or alter its course.

Anton ran toward Lonnie as if he planned to block him, or push him out of the way.

The dragon dropped its wing and clipped Anton on his back. He lurched forward, landing at Lonnie's feet and staring up at the sky. Anton didn't move.

Esme's mouth opened into a scream as Anton's body dissolved into a mass of black and gold pixels, and then disappeared. She took off running, leaving the relative safety of the pillars, shooting as she went, catching the dragon in the belly before it twisted like a corkscrew and doubled back on itself. Esme was near the middle, shooting straight at the dragon's head. There was nowhere to hide. No pillar was close enough for her to run behind it and fake the dragon out. As it leveled its purple eyes at her, Esme dropped her bow and stood tall as the dragon charged her, sending her flying. Black and gold pixels filled my vision as she disappeared. The dragon turned to me. The white scar slashed across its snout was blindingly bright. Cold realization flooded my stomach.

This thing was always my monster, and my monster alone. The only one who could face it was me.

Feeling flooded back into my body. I moved slowly around the island as the dragon resettled itself on one of the mid-height pillars. It started preening, perhaps trying to heal, while keeping a watch on me with one purple eye.

I looked at Lonnie, standing like a scarecrow propped against a pillar. I pressed forward and scooped him up, hauling him away from the battle. I placed him in a sheltered part of the ground that had a little bit of an overhang. He fell on the ground just ahead of me, flopping over like a rag doll. The spark that I had seen in him before—that, I realized now, I had *made* in him with my thoughts and hopes—was gone. This villager was never the Lonnie that I knew, no matter how hard I pretended.

"Lonnie, I . . ." I began to speak but my words tangled in my throat. There was nothing I could do or say in the game or in real life that would ever make up for the pain I'd caused. There was too much of it, like a tsunami that would drown me where I stood. I swallowed my sorrow back. I gently placed my hand on the villager's face, the one that looked so much like my best friend, Lonnie. I closed the avatar's empty eyes.

"Power through, power through, power through," I said, repeating the last part of Lonnie's advice to me.

I took off my armor. I dropped my bow, since I was out of arrows anyway, rendering it useless. All I had left was the single diamond sword. As I moved toward the center of the pillars, I could feel the ground beneath my feet. It was hard, but had some give. I could see the dragon's belly heave as it breathed, and the huge scales that covered it glistened in the dim light of the End.

The dragon stopped grooming and looked down at me before

leaping from the pillar and landing on the ground in front of me in a cloud of dust. I strode toward it without hesitating. For just a second, its purple eyes looked almost piteous. Memories of my friends swirled in my mind. I saw Anton chattering away happily while looking over A.J.'s traps. There was Esme giving me a small nod of acknowledgment. And finally I thought of Lonnie, laughing and gesticulating wildly as he explained the next perfectly planned-out adventure we were going on, his gray eyes full and happy.

"Well?" I asked the dragon. "Isn't this what you've been waiting for?"

The dragon tilted its head and peered at me as I spread my arms wide.

Maybe the dragon was so sure that I was easy prey that it simply stopped trying. Hubris, that's what it's called. I got all the way up to its body, positioning myself before it as if a willing offering. The dragon lowered its head, the better to look at me, or sniff me, or slowly swallow me, I wasn't certain. I'd never had to face down a dragon of my own making before. The diagonal white scar across its face gleamed a garish green tint in the light of the end world. It seemed deep and, like the scar on the enderman, there wasn't anything behind it.

I knew what it meant, that nothingness. It was inside me. It was how I felt, my guilt and anger manifested.

I took a few more steps until I was close enough to touch the dragon. It didn't try to kill me, or even move away from me. It was waiting. It was waiting for me to choose.

My sword gleamed in the light. I shook my head, then thrust

up with my entire body. The sword slipped into the dragon's belly with little resistance. I left the sword embedded there and staggered away from it, waiting to see whatever was going to happen next.

The dragon's purple eyes dulled, and it let out a single roar before it slumped to its side in a heap. A lump formed in my throat as I watched the monster draw a final breath. I felt the shuddering weight of it, simultaneously heavy and insubstantial, and I stifled a sob when it finally exhaled. The dragon burst into beams of purple light, blinding me for a moment. When I was able to see again, the dragon had gone. In its place, an exit portal appeared. It loomed in front of me, beckoning, and I didn't hesitate.

It was time to go through. Lonnie may not have made it, but I had. Everything he'd taught me and everything we had done together was going to be lost if I didn't go through that portal and live my life out in the real world, where I belonged.

As I moved toward the exit, another memory of Lonnie flashed into my mind. I heard the playground swings in motion, the screws at the top squeaking as the two of us pumped hard and fast trying to get the feeling that we were flying. Lonnie turned to me and smiled. I reached my hand out to catch his fingers.

I squared my shoulders and stepped through the portal, ready to face reality.

The screen of the VR goggles retracted from around my face. The lights were exceptionally bright. I couldn't see anything at first through that glare. It was like waking up after a very long sleep. I squeezed my eyes shut. Sounds rushed around me, barely distinguishable, but it all sounded vaguely like talking and beeping. I could, however, smell antiseptic. And beneath me, I could feel the crisp thinness of a sheet. Something was moving. Maybe it was me. I tried to lift my hand, to feel where I was, and I came up against the hard, plastic rail of a hospital bed.

"She's up. Isn't she? She's up!" a voice said that I didn't recognize.

I squinted and the moving stopped. I heard someone say, "On three," then two voices counting in unison, and then I moved again, up and over, and onto another set of crisp sheets and a slightly more cushioned surface.

There was the feeling of someone fussing over me, gently pulling and tugging my sheets, but I could feel the heat of them as they worked, and then the coldness that rushed in as soon as they moved away.

Then the colors came, still blurred, but slowly forming into recognizable shapes. There were three bodies standing at the foot of my bed. I blinked, trying to get them into focus, trying to figure out who they were. The one in the middle was exceptionally tall. The other two were shorter. I kept blinking and slowly they all came into view, still blurry, but clear enough for me to tell one from the other. One long, thin boy with dark, sunken eyes stared back at me between two others: a small bald girl with a round face in a purple bathrobe with flowers on it, and the sweet, curious face of A.J., my hospital neighbor.

"She's alive," the girl said. Then she reached down and patted my foot. "Looks like you stuck to the plan."

"Esme?" I asked.

"Yeah, who did you think?"

"Anton," I said to the tall boy. He produced a thumbs-up.

I smiled at both of them. Then I looked at A.J.

"Boy, do I have some questions for you," I began. "Starting with, why did you think this was a good idea to throw me into a game like this?"

"Because it helped me." He shrugged, his answer just that simple. "How do you think I survived living in this hospital all this time? Besides, I like making friends and building things in the game."

"You'll have to show me how to get some of those redstone circuits right," Anton said admiringly. "Your fortress is amazing."

"Thanks," A.J. said sheepishly.

"Wait, but what about all those mobs and monsters that my brain conjured up?" I asked. "Didn't you know I'd make those? I wasn't ready for them."

"You weren't ready for what was out here," A.J. said. He leaned in a little. "When you asked me about your friend, I already knew what had happened. I'd heard your mom and dad talking. They knew they were going to have to tell you, but they also knew you weren't going to handle the news too well. So, I just figured . . ." He trailed off.

"That you'd help out by giving me a little more time?" I suggested.

"Well, that, and I thought Minecraft would help you process," he said finally.

"For a little kid, you're really very smart," I said. I turned my attention to Esme and Anton. "Do you all know this?"

Esme chimed in, "The mobs always come up, even when we think we're doing better. Figuring your emotions out is kind of an ongoing thing."

"But luckily for us, A.J. has coded lots of mods to keep everything manageable so we're not always getting locked out," Anton said, slapping the younger kid on the back. A.J. beamed a little.

"Though, I have to admit, that scarred ender dragon was tough," Esme added.

"Seriously!" Anton said. "I'm sorry it took us out before it was over. I know we promised that we would stick with you until the very end."

I smiled a little. "It's okay. I knew it was my mob to face. And besides, you're both here now."

Anton and Esme looked at each other. "Yeah, we had to scramble to get to your room to see what was going to happen next," Anton said. "We still weren't sure you were going to get out."

"You all are quite the little support group," Dr. Nay said as she poked her head in. My mother came in behind the doctor and moved to my side, gently taking my hand.

"How are you feeling?" my mother asked.

"I know about Lonnie," I said, my voice real quiet. Hearing the words come out of my mouth felt strange. I had done so much work to come to grips with this fact. But it was still so hard to say out loud.

My mother bowed her head and her eyes got watery. Dr. Nay said quietly, "Come on, kids, let's give them some space."

"No, I—I want them to stay."

Dr. Nay gave a small nod and backed out of the room. Esme moved around to my other side, and Anton rested a hand on the foot of my bed.

Salty tears cascaded from the corners of my eyes, streaming into my braids. I opened my mouth to ask more questions, but only racking sobs came out. I wanted to cover my face, but I couldn't move. I could only look at the blurring ceiling and weep.

My mother tried to dab at my tears but I'd already soaked through the tissue. Anton moved to her side, handing her more.

"I miss him," I cried, my body shaking.

"There will be questions that have to be answered," my mother said gently. "Not right now. When you're ready."

I nodded. "I know."

Esme grabbed my hand and gave it a gentle, reassuring squeeze. The warmth of her palm felt solid and real. It was like when we stood on the edge of the end portal, willing ourselves to go through it together as a team, only better because this was real.

I looked at the new friends crowded around my bed. They'd never replace Lonnie, but they had helped me fight off a relentless enderman, narrowly escape the Nether, and slay a dragon. Our friendship was built by going through a trial by digital fire. I knew there was no plan, no amount of prep work, and no processing mess that they'd back away from. Whatever happened next, they would help me power through.

Despite everything else, that was the best feeling of all.

TRACEY BAPTISTE is the author of several works of fiction and nonfiction for children, including the Jumbies series and *The Totally Gross History of Ancient Egypt*. Baptiste volunteers with We Need Diverse Books, The Brown Bookshelf, and I, Too Arts Collective. She teaches in Lesley University's creative writing MFA program and runs the editorial company Fairy Godauthor.

traceybaptiste.com
Facebook.com/traceybaptistewrites
Twitter: @TraceyBaptiste
Instagram: @traceybaptistewrites

JOURNEY INTO THE WORLD OF

MINECRAFT™

—BOOKS FOR EVERY READING LEVEL—

OFFICIAL NOVELS:

FOR YOUNGER READERS:

OFFICIAL GUIDES:

DISCOVER MORE AT READMINECRAFT.COM